Punished

The Crescent City Creatures Series:

Punished
Hunted
Enspelled

Punished

A Crescent City Creatures Novel

Samantha Stone

Dedication

For my mom, RJ, who showed me the importance of reading. What a gift.

Acknowledgements

A *huge* thank you to:
Ansley, for taking a chance on me.
Victoria, for being such a wonderful editor.
Charles, for encouraging me every step of the way.
All of the LSB team—you're so incredibly encouraging.
And finally, Johnny. You know why.

Chapter 1

"You're going to be executed." Raphael's oldest friend, Heath, got in his face, a hairsbreadth away from pressing their noses together. "Do you understand that?"

Raphael knew he was a screwup, had known for hundreds of years. Lately, he'd gone too far.

He didn't care.

Raphael shrugged before he turned his back on his friend. Heath slammed into him from behind, his fist swinging toward Raphael's face. Raphael's punch landed first, knocking Heath back, his four rings drawing thin lines of blood.

"What the hell are you doing?" Alexandre approached them, surprise apparent in his voice.

Raphael let himself be dragged back only because he knew his friends wouldn't let this go until he told them what they wanted to hear.

"I won't do it again," he lied, feeling absolutely no remorse.

"Do what?" Alex asked.

"He's been killing mortals."

Raphael didn't cringe at his friends' shock and disgust. "They deserved to die," he growled.

"You can't be the judge of that," Heath said seriously. "When we abuse our strength, we die."

"I *stopped* abuse," Raphael said. He was cold, emotionless. No, not completely emotionless. He felt rage, and let it guide him. A small part of him remembered he shouldn't hurt his friends. Another part of him wanted to hurt them for defending those who merited no defense. Those who didn't only deserve to die, but deserved to be mindless in their pain, begging for death before it was mercifully bestowed upon them.

Three weeks ago, he'd seen the condition those women were in. They'd tried to tear past him on Canal Street, barefoot with tangled hair. It had taken Raphael three hours to convince them to speak with him, and another two hours for them to understand that he wanted to help. Women should never be so rightfully terrified.

They hadn't yet been touched, or Raphael may have burned downtown New Orleans to the ground. But they had been drugged, kidnapped and tied together in a run-down house on Esplanade Avenue.

Heath was right. If Raphael were caught breaking the rules, he would be killed. He, like Alexandre, Heath and the rest of his friends, were werewolves. More importantly, they were in a *clan prohibitum,* meaning they weren't allowed to simply live their lives. They were exiled criminals bound to New Orleans and monitored by Jeremiah, their *lupus dux,* and forced to adhere to specific rules. They couldn't kill humans, and could only harm immortals in self-defense.

The rules had been created to better control the uncontrollable, to protect weaker humans, and lower the body count caused by criminal werewolves. If the exiled refused to comply, there was a simple solution, a threat that hung over Raphael's head each day: death.

Raphael had chosen this life, known that his very existence hinged on how well he could follow orders. Others, like Heath, were forced to join the clan as punishment for a crime.

The irony. Raphael would now die for allegedly breaking laws he so wholeheartedly agreed with.

And die I will. He clenched his fists. *It's better me than them.*

Should he tell the rest his pack what he'd found, all five of them would be dead men walking.

He would end this operation alone.

"You know what? Let's shelf this discussion for tomorrow." Alexandre thumped Raphael and Heath on their shoulders, turning them toward the door of the old firehouse they lived in. "It'll make great hangover talk because it's about time for me to head out, and I've decided you two will be my wingmen." Had he not known Alexandre so well, Raphael wouldn't have realized his grin was strained.

Raphael cut a look at Heath, who rolled his green eyes.

"Hey! We're going out; are you assholes coming?" Alex yelled from the pole just before the door.

"No," shouted Cael, a shut-in who was barely seen by any but the clan.

"I guess Sebastian isn't home," Alex said. "Typical."

They stepped out onto South St. Peters, turning toward the Quarter. "I won't forget," Heath murmured, his eyes narrowed.

Raphael ignored him. He didn't plan to stay with Heath and Alex long. He'd incapacitated all of the underlings involved in kidnapping the girls, but he knew he hadn't yet cut the head from the snake. He also had to make sure there weren't more kidnapped women. He had much to do, and now that Jeremiah had found out about the dead humans, he had a strict timeline in which do it.

* * * *

An unwelcome hand grazed Mary Newman's back, lowering until she finished pouring sherry into the unfamiliar man's turtle soup. Her humiliation was tangible; she wanted to crawl under the table and shield herself with white linen until all the guests went home.

Did she have *easy* written across her forehead? *Why do they keep doing that?*

She moved around the ornate Mackenzie-Childs table, careful not to accidentally kick a hand-painted leg. Ten drink orders and eight soups later, she excused herself to pour their drinks. Safe at the butler's pantry, she gripped the cool granite counter tightly, the blood receding from her fingers.

I need this job, she repeated to herself, over and over again. *We need it.* The thing was, serving wasn't her job. She was a nanny for the Van Otterloo family. Their four-year-old daughter, Molly, had originally been her only charge.

She much preferred the delightful child—who'd only tried to set heinously expensive curtains aflame twice—to the men Richard Van Otterloo constantly invited over. It was the third time this week Mary had been felt up; she simply didn't understand it, didn't know what she could do differently to prevent them from touching her.

There was nothing overtly sexual about her appearance. She wore loose black slacks and a white button-down, which she'd done up to her neck. It was the uniform the Van Otterloos requested for instances when she helped serve dinner parties and after-dinner drinks.

"We may ask you to every month or so," Richard's wife, Natasha, had said eleven months ago, right before they hired Mary. At first, Natasha's words were truthful. After a few months, they asked her to serve their guests at an increasing rate. Now she donned her uniform almost every day.

Over the course of the next three hours, she served the main course of grilled flounder filets and a delicious-smelling dessert she couldn't pronounce if she tried, followed by after-dinner drinks. Finally, she was able to pull off her stained apron, which hadn't protected her shirt, and dragged herself over to the small house her sister and she shared. She'd asked for this night off, hoping to see her sister's biggest dance performance of the semester.

"We feed and house you," Richard had said. *"You have the best gig any uneducated twenty-five-year-old can hope for. You aren't too good to serve a little dinner party, are you?"*

"No," was all Mary could say, her pride stinging. *"I'm not."*

The mention of her education still hurt. Three years ago, long before she kept Molly, Mary had been two months from graduating

Summa Cum Laude from LSU. She'd been accepted into every graduate program she applied to, and planned to relocate to a top school in Rhode Island.

Then her parents were murdered.

Her sister was a senior in high school, four months from turning eighteen.

Mary had done what she had to do—take care of Leila. For two years, she'd worked two jobs and tutored on the side, only to barely make a dent in the mountain of debt they now had to bear, all the while living in a part of town where she'd been afraid to come home after her night shifts.

Richard was right—she couldn't hope for better. Now she made three times as much as she used to. Leila and she lived rent-free in a carriage house behind a mansion on St. Charles Avenue. She was given what to wear and told what to eat. She made herself dye her hair.

Now she served dinner parties and men's cocktails.

Fingering a dry piece of chocolate-colored hair, Mary realized she hadn't had a day off in eight months. She knocked before entering her sister's room, where Leila was taking pins out of her hair.

A blue orchid lay on the table beside her vanity, the sight causing Mary's apology to die on her lips.

"Who's that from?" Mary asked, hoping it was from supportive friends.

Richard, Leila signed. Mary's stomach sank. *Aren't they beautiful?*

Mary sighed. Leila adored Richard, who had helped her receive a scholarship at Tulane for dance. When that financial burden had lifted, Mary was thrilled. She'd mistakenly thought Richard must be the most generous man alive.

"She deserves it," he'd said, waving off her thanks. *"How often do you see a dancer who is both talented and deaf? She's earned every penny."*

He was right—Leila worked harder than any of the other dancers in her program. She'd earned the money and praise not because she was deaf, but because she was *that* good. The scholarship committee Richard introduced Leila to agreed.

Even so, Mary feared for her after next year's graduation. Every day it became clearer that kind gestures came at a price. She didn't want her life for Leila, who'd already lost so much. Nothing should stand in the way of her sister's dreams.

Leila looked at her expectantly.

"How'd it go?" Mary asked.

I nailed it, Leila signed, smiling proudly. Yet, she didn't appear happy.

"Then what's wrong?"

After it was over, everyone went to the Spotted Cat. No one asked me to come, again.

None of the dancers in her program knew the manual code for English, the signs Leila used. They complained about her translator, finding her rapid hand movements distracting during rehearsals. Mary knew every complaint and dirty look was a blow to Leila. She was sure the pettiness stemmed from jealousy—she herself had heard the dancers sputter, disgust marring their normally beautiful faces.

"How can she be that good? It's just not fair. She can't even hear the music," they would snarl. Leila didn't need a translator to understand every cruel word they said. She had a cochlear implant that allowed her to hear, and she could talk if she wanted to. Only speech took effort and therapy neither of them could afford. Leila hadn't said a word since the night of their parents' deaths.

Mary couldn't blame her. Leila had been there when they were killed. She wouldn't speak or sign about it—not to Mary or the police.

"Want to go out with me?" Mary asked, hoping to cheer Leila up. "We'll have a better time than those divas."

Where do you want to go?

"How about Thump?"

Thump was a new club on Bourbon Street, replacing some bar even a television show couldn't fix. Mary had heard about it for weeks, and had secretly wanted to go. The word was that men who looked like Greek gods could be found there.

And she'd had enough of forty-year-old men in stuffy suits.

In that case, we both need to change, Leila signed. She smiled, the action lighting up her face.

Freeing her hair of its ponytail, Mary looked in the mirror above her chest of drawers. In an effort to make herself look unappealing, she never dared to wear a speck of makeup. There was nothing to cover the subtle bruises under her eyes, causing them look a more piercing green. Straight dark hair hung to her waist, the blonde already peeking through at her crown and in strands around her face. *I need to buy more dye.*

She changed into a tank top and low-slung jeans that used to be snug but now inched their way down her hips, making her pull on a belt. Mary didn't enjoy baring her skin anymore. She wished it wasn't too hot outside for a sweater.

You look frumpy, Leila signed. She had on a glittering blue micro-mini with a halter top to match, the blue only a shade darker than her eyes. The hours she danced every day showed, slim muscles covering her lithe frame. The white-blonde hair hanging over her shoulders made Mary want to weep.

I want my hair back, but sometimes what you want doesn't matter. "Good," Mary said.

* * * *

Hardcore rap played so loud that the floor vibrated. Thump, apparently, referred to the bass Mary could feel in her bones. Leila seemed to have forgotten about her disappointment; she danced with a different man every song, looking every bit like a woman who danced every day of her life. *Utter joy* radiated from her, just like it did every time she danced.

A pang of guilt hit Mary. *I should have been there today.* She wished she'd stood up to Richard and gone to Leila's recital.

Mary smiled as Leila made her way over to her place at the bar.

Why aren't you dancing? Leila signed.

It was so loud Mary didn't attempt to speak aloud. *I'm just tired. I'll come out when I finish my drink.*

Leila finished it for her, raising her eyebrows over the rim of the cup. *Let's go, after you buy me one of those.*

Unease settled over Mary like a cloak. Now that she was in vicinity of the dance floor, men eyed her like she was a Bloody Mary they had a craving for. She was so sick of that look, she could spit. It was why she never wore makeup—between Richard and his friends, she was under constant scrutiny. Lip gloss and even skinny jeans were an invitation for straying hands. It wasn't their fault, she had *invited it* by the way her hair swung above her ass as she walked. She shouldn't walk that way, taunting innocent men with the movement of her hips.

She'd learned. She learned more every time she brought the men cocktails.

She knew she stood as stiff as a board. Her upper lip had certainly thinned in the way her mother used to, not unkindly, say was unattractive. When she thought she felt a hand nearing her, she lurched away, causing her to almost fall into the crowd of dancers, drinks sloshing and curses following behind her.

Then she saw him. He stood almost a head taller than all the other men in the club, but he wasn't thin. He had a massive chest that tapered to lean hips and muscular thighs, all encased in matte black. His hair matched his clothes and she couldn't make out his eyes, even when the strobe lights flashed, but she was sure they were as dark as his hair. Unlike the other men in the room, he looked like it was just as hard for him to be there as it was for her. He didn't appear bored, but as if there was somewhere else he had to be, and it was not here. His grimace was feral; she thought she saw a fleeting slash of bared white teeth.

He frowned at the two men on either side of him. All three seemed to spend the majority of their time at the gym. The man on the right was slightly unhappy, but less angry than his friend. He was leaner than the other two, with sandy brown hair and slitted eyes. Tattoos sleeved one of his arms. The man on the right reminded Mary of Thor, with blond hair curling to his shoulders, his blue eyes sparkling as he ignored his friends' ire. How he was so cheerful in the midst of the Angst Brothers' tempers, she didn't know. She couldn't help but notice Thor still seemed dangerous, despite his smile. *He's just the friendliest of the three.* She decided not to cross any of them.

Suddenly the dark man turned his head, meeting her gaze. She'd been caught staring. She felt a blush creep up from her chest as she quickly dragged her eyes away. *Going to avoid that corner of the room.*

Leila finally stopped, satisfied with her new place on the dance floor. Mary stood there, anxious about what to do. She hadn't thought she would be expected to dance. Panic rose. The music was too loud, there were too many people, too many hands around her, reaching toward her...

A hand waved in front of her face. Leila.

You're going to dance with me, she signed. *Eat your hearts out, men of NOLA!*

Leila grabbed Mary's hands and lifted her arms up, moving her hips to the heavy bass. Her gaze implored Mary to copy her. She complied, shoving thoughts of handsy old men to the back of her mind. Mary *would* have fun tonight. She deserved some good in her life.

Her movements became more natural; she stopped thinking about how to dance and let her arms and hips move on their own, knowing she was doing something right from Leila's approving smile.

Soon Leila was dancing with a strange man, but Mary didn't care. She kept dancing, kept enjoying the rare moment where worry didn't weigh heavily on her heart and spirit. Now, she could be sexy, could finally feel good about herself and let others see—

A hand grabbed the back of her shirt and pulled her back, causing her to stumble. Layers of dancers gyrated between her and Leila, whose eyes were on the redheaded man she swayed with. Good. Mary didn't want her to worry.

She turned to face whoever had grabbed her.

It was the dark man. She'd been right—his eyes were as black as the starless sky outside.

Mary didn't care that her head didn't quite reach his shoulder, or how he was almost twice as wide as her. She shoved him back, hard. She was done being manhandled. No man would ever touch her again without her permission. He actually stumbled, and he *smiled*. It was a real smile, with dimples that could barely be seen from behind his stubble.

"Don't—"

You won't be able to hear me, he signed. He could sign?

You and your sister need to leave.

She sent him her most intimidating glare. *Why?*

That man put something in her drink.

Her stomach lurched. She looked over to her sister. Her moves, normally so graceful, had turned sloppy. Her eyelids drooped. The redhead leered.

Mary grabbed Dark Man's hand, intending to lead the way to Leila. When the dancers didn't move, Dark Man shouldered his way through, clearing them a path. He didn't let go of Mary's hand, his calloused fingers swallowing hers.

When they reached Leila, she was swaying on her feet. Mary wrapped an arm around her, struggling to support her sister's slight weight. She internally chastised herself for never attempting to lift weights.

Then the weight was lifted. Thor had cradled Leila in his arms as if she were a guarded treasure. *Good.* The man's gaze on Leila was tender. *That is the type of man she should go for.* Mary approved.

Dark Man had the redheaded dancer by the neck, was forcing another path to the door of the club. Mary followed, Thor and Leila beside her. The last man trailed behind their group, his gaze hot on Mary's back.

When they stepped out the door, Mary felt like she'd just left a bubble of chaos. Relief sagged her shoulders, quickly replaced by indignation as she looked at her sister, now sleeping in Thor's arms.

"You asshole!" she shouted, marching over to the redheaded man and kneeing him right between the legs. "I've had it with men like you. Do you hear me? This city is not big enough for people like you. *Stop being a dick or leave.*"

I have some serious pent-up anger. She surprised herself.

Dark Man, who still had a hold on the man, smiled at her. The lean man looked at Dark Man strangely with eyes the color of pine needles. Thor laughed, his big body causing Leila to shake. She didn't stir.

"I'm Alex," Thor said, adjusting to hold Leila with one hand as he held the other out to Mary. She shook it, smiling sheepishly.

"That's Heath." Alex gestured to the green-eyed man. "And Raphael."

Raphael. The name seemed so fitting, Mary felt like she'd already known it. "I'm Mary, and that's my sister Leila."

"I'll see you two home," Alex replied. "My car isn't too far from here."

Even when she'd been in college, Mary never allowed men she met in bars to come home with her. But she couldn't carry Leila home herself, and the way Alex held Leila told her everything she needed to know about the man. There was no faking that level of gentleness, not from a man who could obviously snap them both in two without breaking a sweat.

Mary wished Raphael would join his friend, but his focus was on the slumped-over redheaded man. Raphael had been angry in Thump; now he was furious.

"I'm going to take care of this bastard." A muscle flexed at his jaw as Raphael spoke.

"I'll help," Heath said, his voice quiet.

"No." Raphael didn't spare him a glance. "I won't let you—fine," he gritted out. His eyes were on Mary.

Knowing they were about to part, she rushed forward and placed a kiss on his cheek. He was rough and warm and smelled clean, like soap and spices. "Thank you for helping us." Immediately, she knew why she whispered. She wanted the closest thing she could have to a moment alone with him.

There was a connection between them, so close to being tangible she could almost see it in the damp heat of the night.

Raphael seemed speechless, but his gaze was hungry. Finally, he nodded.

Mary forced herself turned her heel on Raphael and Heath, following Alex over the cracked streets as he led her and Leila home.

* * * *

The name the man gave Raphael was Phil, although Raphael didn't bank on it being his real name. He suspected this man was Leon, a name that had come up more than once when he asked thugs for the identity of their boss.

Men wouldn't give the name of someone who truly scared them, like someone high up in this syndicate, and this man had been attempting to find these women off the streets. Guaranteed, Leon's boss did not touch the girls while they were still out in the open.

Raphael watched the man with distaste. He whimpered like a baby, one of his eyes swelling shut.

"Tell me your real name, or I'll take that eye out."

"No, he won't," Heath said from beside him, just loud enough for Raphael to hear.

Raphael fought the urge to bodily toss his friend from the small, windowless room that used to be a large pantry for the firemen.

The man moaned. Raphael punched him in the other eye.

Tears ran down his cheeks. "Leon," he cried. "I'm Leon."

Progress. Raphael smiled without humor. "Leon, tell us about what you do with the girls once they're drugged."

He shook bodily, his tears now forming streams down his face. "I don't know, man," he sobbed. "I only take them where I'm told to, tie them up, and then leave. I don't see them again."

"You've been drugging girls and leaving them helpless for how long?" Heath said, his voice quiet but lethal. He turned to Raphael. "This is why you were killing humans?"

Raphael shrugged.

"You should have told us."

Raphael pointed to Leon. "We need to deal with him now. We can talk about the rules later." He looked at the now-whimpering man. "Tell us what you know."

An hour later, Raphael knew Leon was a go-between who received instructions followed by payments from his boss, instructions meant for Leon's own men, all of whom were dead.

Leon had to find a woman in a certain age bracket, based on a certain description, and deposit her where he was told. Rarely did he have the same type of woman to find, or the same address to take her to.

The address where Leon had intended to leave Leila was in Raphael's hand.

Heath took a wicked-looking dagger from a hole in his jeans as he walked swiftly toward Leon.

The man cringed, waiting for his deathblow.

Raphael held out a hand, putting himself in the path of Heath's knife. "We can't kill him."

"You killed the others!" Heath shouted indignantly. "You were right, they deserved it. *You deserve death*," he said to Leon, menace lacing every word. He raised his knife again.

"I didn't kill them."

The knife dropped. "What?"

"I followed the rules," Raphael said truthfully. "I hurt each one of them, badly, but it wasn't I who dealt the killing blows."

He'd never dreamed of killing a human, a creature so beneath his level of raw power that the death would be akin to squashing a bug. More importantly, once he'd finished with Leon's men there was no reason to kill them. Had they lived, they would have been far too scared to so much as accidentally bump into a woman, much less kidnap another.

Heath crouched low, rubbing a hand down his face. "Whoever it was, they have to know who we are, the rules we follow."

Raphael nodded. "They're trying to get me killed."

Chapter 2

As Mary made eggs-in-baskets, Leila put on coffee and tea. Their first houseguest, Alexandre Henri Villeneuve, talked and signed at them animatedly as he ignored the Saturday morning cartoons he'd insisted they put on. He paid special attention to Leila, who seemed both embarrassed and thrilled.

"Thank you again for letting me crash on your couch," he said.

It was so nice of you to look after us, Leila signed. *It's nice to have a guy around.*

Alex had insisted on staying over, just in case someone else came for Leila. Mary had wanted to protest, but Leila had been in enough danger in her life. If Alex, an almost total stranger, helped her feel safe, he could come over whenever he wanted. Besides, Mary knew she could trust him. No one who looked like Alex could be anything but kind. He had the anti-bitch face. He looked and acted like Thor's carefree surfer brother.

"For me?"

At Mary's nod, Alex released a high-pitched *"Yay!"* and settled himself at Mary and Leila's small bar. Mary stacked three pieces of toast, each with an egg cooked in the middle, on his plate. The other two she gave to Leila.

Aren't you eating anything? Leila signed, frowning.

"I'm not hungry," Mary lied. She was starving, but Richard's cold words rang through her head. *"I don't pay fat people because they don't need to eat."*

She put a bit of honey in her tea to cut the bitter taste. As she sipped, she watched Alex and Leila. They both kept their eyes on each other, smiling when their eyes would meet. When Alex, his plate now cleared, reached for a piece of Leila's breakfast, she stopped him with a fork to the hand. *I'll eat your arm off,* she signed, smiling wickedly.

Alex held up his hands in defeat, grinning.

Her sister deserved more joy in her life. She loved her classes, and would be hired to dance once she was out of school, but she struggled socially. Now, a gorgeous man who knew how to sign was paying attention to her. *As he should.* What a win for her sister!

Despite her happiness, she released a sigh. Never had someone looked at her as Alex currently looked at Leila.

Mary hadn't dated since her parents died. Because of the jobs she'd kept, there simply was no time. Maybe, when Leila was out of school and they were out of the Van Otterloo's house, she would find someone nice. Someone she would always want to be around, someone who could make her smile even when she didn't want to.

Someone like Raphael, she couldn't stop herself from thinking.

Before any of that could happen, she had to get to work. She needed to take care of Molly until this afternoon, and then wait on the men before and after dinner. "I have to get going," she told Leila and Alex. "Please feel free to stay as long as you like," she added, smiling at him.

We'll see you out, Leila signed, following her to the door. *I want Alex to glimpse inside the McMansion.*

Leila loved to sit on the bench outside the carriage house and wave until Mary made it inside. Mary knew she also liked to see the glamor that was the inside of the home; she was sure they didn't own a single knickknack worth less than ten thousand dollars, a notion that caused her to take great care when she worked.

When Mary took the short path to main house, she was

surprised to see Richard waiting for her at the door.

"You had a man stay the night," he said. His normally handsome face was mottled with red. She could have sworn his eyes turned from brown to black, his normally straight white teeth forming sharp, yellowed points.

"Yes." She wouldn't apologize. She wouldn't let this man scare her anymore.

"That is not allowed," he spat, inventing the asinine rule on the spot. *"You belong to me."*

She stepped toward him, angling her chin up. "No, I *work* for you. You don't own me."

A hard slap cut across her face. Lights blinked in front of her eyes; the pain dazed her. She felt blood drip from beneath her left eye.

Never in her life had she been hit. *I will not cry.* After everything Richard had said and done, she should have expected this. *I will not cry.*

Only one more year of this. I will not cry.

She looked out the window at Alex and Leila. Had they seen? She was so ashamed; she desperately hoped the tall shrubbery blocked their view.

Leila seemed untroubled, signing to Alex excitedly. For a split second Alex's eyes met Mary's, his gaze uncharacteristically hard. He shook his head slightly.

Leila hadn't seen, and he wouldn't tell her.

Thanking God for small favors, she tried to brush past Richard for the pajama stairs that led to Molly's room.

Richard grabbed her wrist in a punishing hold. "You're going to regret crossing me," he promised. He smiled, his teeth still appearing impossibly sharp as he let her go.

* * * *

A few hours later, Mary's cheek still stung. When she first walked into Molly's playroom, the four-year-old reached out a small hand and touched her face, asking, "What dis, May Wee?"

Mary told her to always be careful when playing catch. Richard's action made her scared and ill, washing away any trace of rebellion like a tidal wave. When she saw Molly, her anger came back. *What will Richard expose this child to?* She'd rarely seen him and the child in the same room together.

In this city, children were generally involved in their parents' social scenes. The Van Otterloos were an exception—they kept people like Mary, and backups like Mary's friend Thérèse, who was on staff as a maid, to ensure they had minimal contact with their child when she wasn't in her preschool program.

It wouldn't last. What would happen to Molly when she was older and no longer needed a nanny? Would Richard hit her when she mouthed off to him, as most teenagers would?

It's not my place to save her. She should be safe for now, anyhow.

Mary knew she wouldn't continue to work for this family in ten years. She had a feeling she would, however, find a way to check up on the child who was currently trying to draw a Jazz Fest poster, her brown ringlets swinging around her cherubic face.

Large, rich brown eyes looked up at her. "Do you like my picture?" she asked.

"I love it," Mary said honestly. She knew the girl would be an artist someday, or something else wonderful. Molly could do no wrong.

As Molly moved from drawing to playing with Barbies, their smiling heads rolling, Mary's thoughts turned to Raphael. The strangely handsome man looked like no one she'd ever seen before. He was pure male; he wore no jewelry except for wicked black rings on each finger of his right hand, and he had a deep tan that obviously wasn't courtesy of a bed or a bottle. His long black hair had been tied into a ponytail.

That ponytail made Mary want to change her stance on the man-bun debate. His body was large and honed in a rugged way, as if he did manual labor on a daily basis. Did he work on an oilrig?

"Why did Midge's head come off?" Molly asked, interrupting Mary's daydreams. She picked up the decapitated plastic head by her red hair, studying Midge closely.

"Because she didn't drink enough milk," Mary answered.

"Do I drink enough milk?"

"Yes." Mary smiled. Molly loved nothing more than to ask endless streams of questions.

Mary wanted to ask Raphael a few herself. How did he know to watch over her and Leila? What had he and Heath done with the man who'd tried to drug her?

Why hadn't Raphael left that man with his friends, and escorted Mary and Leila home himself? Alexandre was nice—and more importantly, seemingly trustworthy—but he didn't command Mary's attention like Raphael. Alex made her want to give him a hug, not leap into his arms and beg for a kiss she'd never be able to forget.

I really *need to go on a date.*

From Richard's reaction to Alex, dating wouldn't be in the cards for a long time. *As if I'll ever see Raphael again anyway.* She sighed. She would probably have to ask Alex not to come back.

Leila would be furious, and Mary wouldn't blame her.

Again, her anger had left her, leaving her feeling helpless. She couldn't do anything about Richard. This was too great of a job to leave, despite its drawbacks.

She had a safe home, *which Richard had the key to.* She earned what most people with Master's degrees earned per year for watching a child. The loans for her sister's tuition were being slowly, steadily paid off. At this rate, Leila would begin her working life debt-free.

It would be selfish to leave only because she was unhappy— because her boss had hit her, and would again—or because Mary had no control over her life.

She could put up with *anything* for Leila, and for only another year, when she would hopefully have sixty more to enjoy? She would stay. *One more year.* Her stomach clenched, and she gagged. Her body physically rejected the idea. *Tough shit, Newman. Life is hard, but it'll only make you stronger.*

"Does Mom drink enough milk?" Molly asked.

"I'm sure she does."

"Daddy said she gots no head no more. She needs milk?"

Cold, stark fear lanced through Mary. "Your mom has a head, silly," she said, smiling tightly. "It's up on her shoulders just like yours."

"I don't think so, but milk will fix her." Molly nodded decisively.

Mary wished it would. *Natasha can't be dead. Richard wouldn't kill anyone, would he?*

She remembered his teeth, and the way his ringless hand had cut deeply into her cheek.

Had her boss killed his wife, and then bragged to his daughter? Mary had seen Natasha two nights ago, but she'd been absent from last night's dinner. Had Natasha been dead this whole time?

Deep down, she knew Richard was a monster.

She found it hard to breathe, dark spots clouding her vision. She raised her knees, resting her forehead against them, her long hair forming a curtain around her. A small hand patted her shoulder.

This child's mother is dead.

* * * *

Raphael jabbed the screen on the treadmill with so much force it cracked. Sweat snaked to his neck and chest as he stepped off the incline, stopping in front of the weight bench. He lifted five hundred pounds up, brought it back.

Like with the others, he hadn't enjoyed letting Leon go. The wait, however, ate at him like acid. He glanced at the screen of his cell phone. It was still black.

Quickening his pace, his breath came out in pained grunts.

He didn't know if Leon had been killed like the others. If he were, the blame would be heaped on his shoulders, and now Heath's. Both of them would die for crimes they hadn't committed.

That's not true.

They would die for the crimes they committed years ago.

Again, he looked at his phone as he lifted. Nothing. The man was to let Heath and him know where he'd been told to take a woman this night, supposing he was still alive.

He probably wasn't.

Raphael had been so green and stupid, so easily led. In old

Estonia, many people had been accused of being werewolves or witches, sometimes even both. It was as common as Twitter wars today, only macabre and corrupt. When a man's sheep would die, suddenly a malicious witch had preyed upon him. When a woman was raped, a werewolf had lost control and taken her.

They were both killed, just to be safe.

Now Raphael could see that under the torture he'd inflicted, a poor goat farmer would admit to having the appendages of three men and a woman in order to stop the pain, to simply *end* his short life devoid of the light of mercy.

Half a century ago, Raphael killed two innocent men. He didn't understand why he'd been allowed to live, why his small village embraced him as a protector and hadn't shunned him for bringing lies and shame upon them all.

He'd been ignorantly following orders. The man who decided the fates of those people, who could turn a werewolf trial into a witch trial, or determine that, while innocent, someone should be killed for keeping information to themselves, was a werewolf himself. Hans Ivar was the father that orphaned Raphael never had. The members of Ivar's church looked up to him, and were the only family Raphael had known. They trusted the good priest's judgments without question.

Ivar held the trials to mislead the villagers. He was protecting his reckless pack, none of whom had ever faced repercussions for their actions.

"You have too much potential for me to let you pass your peak," he'd said to Raphael on the night he finally learned the truth. He'd just lived to be a score and a half. *"You were meant to be one of us, a* vârcolac *like my father and the man who came before him.* Now *you are truly my son."* He'd bitten Raphael, and instead of claiming the family who'd fed him lies his entire life, Raphael asked to be punished for the innocent lives he'd taken, the innocent people he terrorized. *And for what?*

For nothing. He swung the barbell up. He'd ruined so many lives for absolutely nothing.

He hadn't killed since, embracing the regulations of the *clan prohibitum.* It was his penance. Without it, he didn't deserve to live, *should* be extinguished.

Alexandre swung into the room, interrupting Raphael's thoughts. He put the weight down.

"Guess who shared a bed with a beautiful woman last night." Alex hopped onto the treadmill jauntily.

"Heh," Raphael said absently.

"Hey, did Cael break the treadmill again? I told him, anger is for punching bags and cockblocks, *not* treadmills or women."

What Alex first said registered. Raphael leapt over the treadmill, his hand gripping Alexandre's throat, slamming him against the wall. Plaster fell over them, dusting Alexandre's shocked visage.

"You slept with Mary?" Raphael growled. He'd been so distracted by Leon that he hadn't given the woman much thought until now.

The notion of someone touching her gave him base, violent urges.

Her expression had caught his attention the night before. She'd been apprehensive but overcame it; joy washing over her as she'd danced. Her beauty kept his attention. She had full lips that stretched into a wide, giving smile. Her up-tilted eyes kept a twinkle, her long, dark hair a stark contrast to her creamy skin. Suddenly, he wanted that hair to slip through his fingers like water.

After less than half an hour in her presence, he wanted her writhing underneath him, calling his name as he made her his.

If he'd made different decisions, decisions that hadn't damned him to an existence of deserved exile, he would have thought this woman was his mate, the one woman whose love he was meant to cherish for the entirety of his life.

But he would never deserve such a gift. Finding a mate was so rare, most weres never found their other halves in their immortal lifetimes.

Even so, Alexandre couldn't have her.

"Okay, I stayed on her couch. And you're thinking of the wrong sister, bro." Alex was eyeing him warily, but Raphael could see a touch of amusement. "Mary's cute, but she pales in comparison to Leila's absolute hotness."

Raphael punched him.

"Not the face!" Alex shouted admonishingly. "How am I supposed to ask Leila out with a black eye?" His expression darkened, becoming serious for the first time since he'd entered the workout room. "So you want Mary, right?"

Raphael gave him a short nod.

A muscle twitched in Alex's jaw. "I'm glad to hear that, man," he said. "Because I saw a guy hit her today, and you're just the man to take him out."

Rage clouded Raphael's vision. Had that been what she was scared of at Thump? He would make sure no man ever hurt her again. The alternative was wholly unacceptable. "Consider it done."

"I'll help, of course. I like her, and it would've upset Leila, had she seen." Alex said *Leila* with the reverence generally reserved for a deity.

"Heath said you have the address for where that asshole was supposed to take Leila?" Raphael could see the fury in Alex's expression, his eyes changing from blue to yellow.

Raphael pulled it from the pocket of his gym shorts and handed it over.

Alex's yellow eyes became gold before his claws made an appearance, shredding the paper.

"The man was to take Leila to where she already lives." Alex's voice sunk octaves, its gravel making him hard to understand. Raphael felt his own rage blossoming again, blood dripping from his clenched fists as they, too, released razor-sharp claws.

"Mary's boss tried to kidnap Leila," Alex shouted, his fist tearing through the treadmill's plastic front. Alex lifted the machine over his head and tossed it at the wall.

Raphael let the waves of anger lap over him. He was unworthy to avenge these women, he knew. Yet he would still take this man who tried to kidnap an innocent woman, this man who marred the beauty of Mary's face, into death with him.

The screen of his cell phone lit up, Leon's number popping on the screen. The same address he'd given the night before, the address Alex had just torn was the first part of the message, followed by: HE'LL KILL ME IF I DON'T BRING HIM SOMEONE TONIGHT.

* * * *

Mary tried not to shake as she tied a black apron around her waist. She'd already taken too long buttoning her crisp white shirt to her neck due to trembling hands. A glance in the mirror showed three angry red stripes across her cheek, but there was nothing she could do about that.

Mary had desperately hoped she wouldn't have to serve Richard and his business associates tonight. Now, although she dreaded it, she wasn't afraid of their hands, or even being hit again by Richard. She feared for her life. *The worst thing I can do is let on that I know.* If she seemed ignorant of what he'd done to his wife, he might let her go. She would leave—she had no death wish. *The longer they keep me here, the lower my chance of survival.*

Albeit terrified, she'd come to terms with the danger she was in. She already texted Leila, telling her to pack their things. Mary also told her to leave, without her, as soon as she could.

There was no argument—Leila sent a simple response. *Done. Let me know when you're safe.*

"Mary," Richard called, his voice jovial, excited. "You're needed."

She shook her hands once, twice, trying to get rid of the tremors. She pasted on her most bland smile and walked down the hall to the men's half of the double parlor. She allowed herself one breath before she opened the pocket door.

"Would ya'll like anything from the kitchen?" she asked the room. Three men Mary had seen a few times before sat on the leather sofa, smoking. Richard opted for the large armchair across from them. All wore impeccable suits and the unmistakable air of wealth. None of them had drinks in their hands, a strike against Mary.

"No, Mary dear, but we would like our drinks now. You've made us wait," Richard chided. His voice was gentle, but the expression on his face was unmistakably peeved.

With perfectly parted thick brown hair and few lines on his tanned face, Richard looked like the type of man to donate to shelters for battered women, not a man who would kill his own wife. His smile was so charming that Mary hadn't found fault with him until months into her employment. *Stupid, stupid.*

"Of course," she answered. "What would you like?"

With four drinks in mind, she moved to the wet bar at the far end of the room as the men began talking. Surely they couldn't hurt her here. The intricate rug at their feet was worth thousands. A huge Blue Dog painting hung on the wall, standing out from darker pieces depicting rivers. Blood would spoil the room, she decided. Expensive vases would break, and the detailed molding would be stained. She was safe, for now. Besides, surely the other men were run-of-the-mill Garden District well-to-dos. Richard would do nothing untoward in front of them.

Slightly more secure in her safety, she brought them their drinks and asked if they would like anything else.

"Actually, yes. Mr. Gaspar has requested that you sit in his lap. It seems a female's touch would be the perfect cure for his headache," Richard said, gesturing to a dark-haired man on the left side of the couch. The man smiled at her, revealing perfect teeth and dull brown eyes.

"Sir, if you'd rather, I'd love to go fetch you some aspirin," she implored.

"No." Gaspar reached out a hand. She tried not to recoil. "You'll do just fine."

The misery that had been slowly drowning Mary for months swept her under. She could have sworn the men in the room could feel it too, *enjoyed* her reaction, as all of their eyes brightened, their smiles widening.

She'd been wrong. She wasn't safe here.

So she did the only thing she could do—she took Gaspar's hand and let him pull her against him.

His breath against her neck made her cringe, but it was his erection that made her want to reach back and twist his head in a full circle. She knew she couldn't, and focused instead on keeping her face blank.

"You like this, yes?" the man next to Gaspar asked her.

"I just hope his headache eases," she managed, avoiding his gaze.

Fingers lifted her chin. Richard's face was inches away from hers. "You will like it and hate yourself for it," he told her. His eyes had turned black again. With his words, Mary felt odd, as if there was something *so close* to touching her, but couldn't quite reach.

She tried not to gape at her boss, who was obviously touched in the head. She wanted to be sitting *anywhere* but where she was.

"She doesn't feel pleasure." Gaspar's breath tickled her ear. "How strange."

These men were *all* absent from reality, it seemed. "Would you like your drinks refreshed?" Mary asked, keeping her voice as neutral as possible.

The men ignored her. "Perhaps I could—" Gaspar began.

"Do it," Richard said, too eagerly. "After her outburst earlier, she deserves to be punished. Besides," he continued, grabbing a hunk of her hair, "I'm sick of this color. When you have her under control, you will have her wash this shit out." He let go of her hair as if it disgusted him.

She'd dyed her hair because she knew he preferred her natural color. *At least I did something right.* She didn't know what Richard meant by *under control,* but her gut told her that simply wouldn't happen for them. They could hurt her, she was sure, but they couldn't control her.

Gaspar's arm tightened to a vice around her. Now she struggled. "What—"

His hand covered her mouth, his other hand catching the corner of her vision.

He held a knife. "You're going to do as I tell you, or I'll cut you."

She panicked. She bit his hand, drawing blood. "No!" she shouted as he withdrew from her face. Frantic, she tried to rise, only to feel the sting of the blade run deeply up her thigh. She stilled; he was inches from her femoral artery.

"You will eat this." Gaspar shoved something bitter into her mouth. "And *listen to me.*" He brought his rum and coke to her lips and tilted it back, forcing her to wash it down.

He brought the knife back to her leg. "Look at me," he said. She obeyed, watching blood pour from her leg in her peripheral vision.

She was losing too much blood, she realized, feeling faint. *This could kill me.*

"Once we have her, can we get her sister?" the man on the far end of the couch asked hopefully.

No.

Red filled Mary's vision, from the blood or her anger, she didn't know.

"You will like this." Gaspar moved his hand up her arm.

"No!" Mary shoved at him, and this time, he let her go. She heard the knife *thud* against the carpet. "We should have her by now," a man, she could no longer decipher their voices, murmured. "She can't resist us," another said. "She will want us."

"No!" she shouted. *"I will not!"*

Hands reached for her. The knife was picked up. Richard, she realized, watched with interest from the opposite end of the room.

Everything is red. These men are bad; everything *is bad.*

Someone took hold of her, the knife biting into one of her shoulder blades.

They wanted her, and they wanted Leila. *They are evil. They can't live.*

The red became opaque, until it was all Mary could see. It made her feel powerful. It whispered to her, telling her it was *their* blood, just waiting to be shed.

Scream, it told her.

She did, releasing all of her hatred and disgust. She could feel the force of her screams shaking the room, cracking the walls. Blood, *not yours,* coated her hands, drenching her.

Mary kept screaming, wanting more.

Chapter 3

Wish watched this house every night, desperate to gain entrance and always refused. The damned blue paint on the mansion's shutters and above its wraparound porch kept him from entering. Haint Blue, purposefully used on homes all over the South in order to keep his kind out.

Unfortunately, it worked.

He knew no one would ever paint over it, yet he came for as long as he could each night, always reaching as far as he could.

His daughter and her mother lived there with the man who killed him.

Natasha didn't know he was dead. Molly didn't know he existed.

He hovered around the perimeter, trying to see what he could through the closed blinds.

Wish hoped Natasha was well, and that Molly was the happiest child in New Orleans. He hoped there was more of her mother in Molly than him, despite Natasha's false promises to leave Richard and run away with him. She was a good woman, so she must have become a wonderful mother.

What if she isn't? What if Molly is being mistreated, and you've done nothing about it?

All he knew for certain was the child lived in the lap of luxury. That didn't mean she was happy, or received everything a child was due. *I hope she plays. She deserves fun, to have no notion of inhibitions.*

He thought about Molly and Natasha every night, wishing he could be closer to them. If Molly looked out her window, straight at him, she may not be able to see him for all the dense trees surrounding the house.

Wish kept a tight grip on his fragile thread of hope. Someday, his daughter would know him. If he could publish scholarly articles for a major university, he could find a way to have a relationship with Molly.

A scream rang from the house. It was an *unnatural* scream.

Wish quickly moved to hover near one of the front parlors, away from the bedrooms.

The screams continued, increasing impossibly in volume.

Banshee.

Wish felt himself go even colder than normal, but he didn't panic. Blood wasn't freely flowing from his ears, and it would have been had the banshee's ire been aimed at him. They were reasonable creatures that way.

Someone had disturbed her. He heard a catch in her scream; whoever it was, they'd hurt her too. That someone was either in excruciating pain or dead.

Still, worry gnawed at him. Something awful had happened in that house, and his Molly had better not have been a part of it.

He bounced off the invisible force field as he tried, for the millionth time, to get in.

The screams died, replaced by booted footsteps.

Three fierce-looking men were walking quickly down the broken sidewalk. Unnatural lumps in their pants indicated dozens of weapons were strapped to them. They looked like they could take out most men barehanded.

They were headed toward the house. Those men, men who looked like they ate four-year-old children for breakfast, were going to Molly's house.

Oh, hell no.

Wish smiled darkly. Before his death, he was the youngest scholar to ever receive a PhD in Southern fiction and folklore. He was a nerd, and would have rightfully cowered before such men.

Now he was a haint, and there was a reason people painted their homes to keep his ilk away. Now Wish would unleash it on The Rock, John Cena and Vin Diesel.

Those men weren't going near that house.

*

Raphael, Alexandre and Heath heard the screams over a mile away. They were Mary's screams, Raphael was sure.

After their conversation at the firehouse, Raphael and Alex rounded up Heath, who'd been prowling down Pirate's Alley. After they caught him up on what they'd learned, he wanted to go with them to confront Richard, Mary's boss. All three agreed not to tell Sebastian or Cael in case their involvement warranted a death sentence.

It may not. Alex was convinced Richard wasn't human; he said the man smelled like a water shapeshifter. Raphael thought their fate depended on what kind of creature he was, and whether the *lupus dux* felt especially merciful. If Raphael had the position in Jeremiah's stead, he would have very little mercy. After all, lack of mercy had been what put them all in the *clan prohibitum* in the first place. An eye for an eye, he figured.

As they neared the house, the screams stopped. It was Mary—he couldn't have forgotten her voice if he wanted to. *She's in pain.* Her screams may have been abnormal for a human, but they were laced with agony.

He had to help her.

A force pushed him back, as if two hands had beaten at his chest.

Raphael swung blindly, but could make no impact. Closer to the house he saw Alex struggling. He heard Heath's grunts behind him. The tang of blood rent through the air, but Raphael smelled no mortality; whoever was hurt wasn't human. Alex may have been right about Richard. *What does that make Mary?*

He took a deep breath. She was bleeding, and he couldn't get to her. He roared before punching, kicking, and slicing with his claws. Bruises formed on his chest, but he gained no ground. He didn't care. He kept fighting, blistering frustration blurring his thoughts.

"If you're protecting that house, stop."

Heath.

Raphael glanced over his shoulder; Heath stopped struggling, but was breathing hard. "We're trying to help someone inside, the woman who was screaming. Her name is Mary, and she's a nanny to a little girl—"

Like that, all of them were free. A tall, thin man floated in front of them. Raphael swore his hand trembled as he straightened his wire glasses. He was a haint, a ghost who could wreak havoc. Haints had tempers that rivaled a werewolf.

"Save the girl and the child," he said. His expression darkened. "Watch out for the owner of the house."

For a second time, they couldn't move. "Promise me you'll bring me the child," he continued. He paused for a moment but shook his head, as if chasing off an unwanted thought.

"No," Raphael growled. He wasn't going to give a child to a ghost.

"Why?" Alexandre asked.

The man drew a long-fingered hand through his dark hair. "I'm her father, and the man who lives here killed me before she was born."

Raphael sucked in a breath. Surprising himself, he said, "Follow us when we leave, and we'll talk. You have my word." *Right now we need to focus on Mary.*

The ghost nodded, and they were free.

Raphael tore across the lawn to the door. Locked. He didn't bother to wrap his hand before he brought his fist through the glass and turned the lock.

Shaking the blood off his hand, he turned to the parlor off the foyer, shouting for Heath and Alex to search the house. He heard Alex curse behind him before stomping away. Mary was sprawled, bleeding, on the carpet. An unmistakably dead man stared at the opposite wall from his place on the couch behind her, a blood-covered knife lying beside him. Bloody shoe prints hurried from the room. Three other men had been here, had escaped through a back or side door.

Alex or Heath could worry about them, he reasoned.

He sank to his knees beside Mary. She had shallow cuts on her right shoulder blade and cheek, but there was a much longer, deeper cut running up her thigh on the same side. A glance under her shirt confirmed bruises on her sides matching those on her arms. She was unconscious from blood loss, not shock. If she didn't receive help soon, she wouldn't survive this night.

That thought didn't sit well with him.

Pale, bleeding, hair in tangles over her shoulders, she was the most beautiful woman Raphael had ever seen. *She's mine.*

He didn't bother to contradict himself. She *would* be his, and her current condition was intolerable. Everyone who touched her would feel ten times the pain they inflicted upon her. He would ensure it.

Seeing her hurt, helpless, wrenched something deep inside him. He gently covered her ears and released an anguished roar. Her ears had suffered enough today. Blood came away when he pulled his hands back.

He took out his phone and dialed Cael, who answered on the fourth ring. "I need Aiyanna," he said shortly. Cael growled. "A woman's badly hurt."

Cael sighed. "Where are you?"

Raphael told him the address. In response, Cael hung up.

He'd agreed not to involve Cael or Sebastian, but they wouldn't thank him for sacrificing this woman for them, and for whatever reason, Aiyanna only listened to Cael.

Raphael ripped strips of fabric from his shirt and tightly wrapped Mary's thigh. It slowed the blood, but not enough. Soon the fabric was soaked through.

He moved to put her head on his thighs, spreading her hair out behind her. Finger-combing through the tangles, he did the only thing he could think of. He sang to her.

Tule, tule, unekene,tule, uni, uksest sisse,
astu sisse akenasta,
kuku sisse korstenasta.
Kuku lapse kulmu peale,
lase lapse lau peale,
jäe seisma silma peale.

Raphael had always wanted to sing to someone he loved, always wished to touch someone gently and be touched tenderly in return. He'd grown up hearing mothers, fathers and siblings sing the lullaby, but never was it sung to him. His voice caught on a line; how he hated the circumstances they were in. As he gingerly smoothed the last tangle from her long hair, he told himself they would have those moments, beautiful moments. "Someday, I'll brush your hair, if you'll let me," he promised her. "I'll try to bring you enough joy you'll forget about this night."

He continued to sing, ignoring Heath's entrance to the parlor. Heath pulled out a plastic cellphone wedged in the couch cushions before he sat beside the dead man silently, picking up the knife as he scrolled through the phone.

Alex came tearing into the room. A pretty, dark-haired young woman in a housekeeper's uniform carried a sleeping child, following close on Alex's heels. Upon entering the parlor the woman held the child closer, covered her eyes, and murmured in a strange dialect of French.

"This is Molly—Mary's her nanny," Akex rasped. "I couldn't find Leila; she's gone."

Heath held up the phone. "Mary told her to leave." He tossed the phone—Mary's—to Alex. "Call her, make sure she's okay." Alex nodded and left.

Raphael watched the others, but continued singing to Mary softly. Heath approached the woman with the child.

"Will you watch her in the room across the hall?" Heath asked. "We don't want Molly completely out of our sight, but there's no reason for her to see this."

Nodding, still muttering under her breath, she held Molly close and left for the other parlor.

"There were other men; they escaped," Heath said.

"I know," Raphael murmured. The mere thought of them made him want to rage.

"I can't tell what they are—this one's not human."

Raphael didn't answer. He didn't know either.

The front door opened. Aiyanna hurried to Mary, concern darkening her expression. Cael followed her, taking in every detail of the lavish surroundings. He made toward the maid and Molly, speaking to the woman in her preferred language and lifting the child from her arms.

Holding Molly, a grin broke across his face. Raphael was certain it was the first time he'd ever seen Cael smile.

Aiyanna saw it too, warmth lighting up her eyes.

It fizzled when she turned back to Mary. "What happened to her?"

"I think that man stabbed her." Raphael looked to the dead man. "But others hurt her as well."

Aiyanna nodded, her black hair falling over Mary. She pressed a coffee-colored hand on Mary's heart. "You hurt the other men, didn't you?" she said soothingly. "She has no idea she's a banshee, bless her heart."

So her *screams* killed the man.

"You have the power to hurt them right back, you know," Aiyanna continued, taking the makeshift bandage off Mary's leg.

Could she hear her?

"They can never control you," Aiyanna continued. "I'm sure they tried, that's what botos do."

As she spoke, most of Mary's bruises disappeared, the cut on her back healing completely. The gash on her leg knitted together partially, then stopped.

"I'm out of energy now, honey," she told Mary. "I got into some things earlier today, so I wasn't completely charged. You'll heal the rest of the way just fine."

Aiyanna's voice had grown weaker, trembling at the end. Cael put Molly down and came into the parlor. "You okay?" he asked Aiyanna gruffly.

"If I said no, would you kiss me?" Her voice was barely audible, even to were ears.

"No," Cael answered.

Aiyanna sighed. "Figures," Raphael thought he heard her whisper before she closed her eyes and lay back on the carpet next to Mary.

Cael's frown deepened.

"Let her sleep it off," Heath said. "Both of them."

"But not here," Cael said. "The ones who escaped may come back for Mary, thinking she'll be weakened or dead."

Raphael's phone vibrated in his pocket. "They're not coming here, but I know where they'll be. Leon has a woman for them; they changed their minds, told him to bring her somewhere else."

"When?"

"Now," Raphael said gravely. "Our first priority should be getting Mary and Aiyanna somewhere safe. Then we'll go after those men."

"Botos," Cael murmured, his attention rapt on Aiyanna. "Sebastian should be here any minute." He turned to Raphael. He should have known Cael would fill Sebastian in. "You and Heath should go after those men."

"We will. Where's Alex?" Heath asked.

"He left to find Leila," Raphael answered. The man had bolted as soon as he received Mary's phone.

Heath paced the room. Cael kept his eyes on the woman he rejected on a near-daily basis.

Raphael didn't want to move, unless it was to settle Mary in his arms and bring her back to the firehouse. The thought of Cael or Sebastian carrying her made his claws sharpen.

I need to concentrate on something else.

Sebastian swept into the house, his dark auburn hair sticking up in spikes around his head. "I love being the last person invited to the party, guys. Really, I feel so appreciated, being your last resort and all."

Raphael ignored him and rose, gently lifting Mary in his arms. Cael did the same with Aiyanna.

"Careful—her leg." Raphael handed her over to Sebastian. The man didn't say anything as he took her, his eyes hardening at the sight of the wound.

It's still too deep. It will scar, badly.

"Take her to my room at the house," he said. At Sebastian's nod, he found the sleeping child and her maid. "Come," he told her. The still-perturbed woman lifted Molly and followed, relaxing slightly when Cael fell into step beside her.

Outside, the haint lowered from a hover at the sight of them, settling on his feet. There were ghostly tears in his eyes.

It was Cael who approached him. "Can you hold her?"

The man nodded, his mouth working but producing nothing. Cael frowned at him. "You may hold her, but you will stay with us. If you take that child away, I will find someone to end your undeath within the hour. Do you understand?"

"Yes." He reached pale arms out out for the girl.

The maid hesitated. "*Non! Mon Dieu, il est un fantôme,*" she exclaimed.

The ghost smiled at her. "*Oui, cher*" he said, "*mais je suis son père, et je s'aime.*" *Yes, but I'm her father and I love her.*

"I'm Aloysius Sutherland," the haint said, "but most people call me Wish. You should probably leave this place and never come back." He looked at the men. "You too."

"*Je m'appelle Thérèse,*" she told him, still keeping Molly out of reach. "I want to check up on the child." The strange woman spoke English with no accent, despite her preference for French. "I trust I'll like what I find?" There was a threat in her voice, and in that moment, she was twice as intimidating as Cael had been.

Wish only smiled. "Of course."

Thérèse cast an untrusting look at the men, but gave Molly to her father. If Raphael had any doubts of his sincerity, seeing the man hold his child for the first time washed them away. The ecstatic, anguished expression on his face revealed all. He gripped her like she was a priceless treasure.

"Wait." Again, Wish seemed to be engaged in an internal debate. "Did you see another woman inside? Her name is Natasha; she's Molly's mother."

"*Elle est mort.*" *She is dead.* With one last confused scowl at

Wish, who'd become impossibly paler, Thérèse turned on her heel and sprinted away.

"She's weird, but really hot," Sebastian offered. "Makes me wish I spoke Cheese-Eating Surrender Monkey."

Heath and Cael rolled their eyes. They all knew French, and most other languages. As immortal criminals, it was one of the few benefits of being a werewolf they were allowed to keep.

"If we need backup we'll let you know," Raphael said to Sebastian and Cael. "Otherwise, keep them safe." They would follow up with Thérèse regarding the dead woman, but that task could be done at a later time.

The need to kill the men who'd hurt Mary was taking over his body. His muscles were tensed, ready. His teeth sharpened, eager to rip through muscle and bone.

As their group broke apart, the women and child headed for a much safer place, Raphael's heart warmed, taking the edge off his fury. Mary would be okay, and he was sure Alex would find her sister safe too. No harm would come to little Molly.

He pulled out the machete he'd strapped to his thigh. No matter how long it took, he would take out those men, the botos, as Aiyanna called them. He would get to the bottom of their operation and eliminate it.

Then he'd give Mary their heads.

Chapter 4

Spring 2012

Mary had had a fantastic day. She'd been accepted into her dream graduate program to receive her Master of Fine Arts in painting from the Rhode Island School of Design. She'd sent along her portfolio on a lark, thinking that at the very least, she would have a letter from her dream school. She'd thought she would be framing a politely worded rejection letter, not a thick envelope filled with congratulations and dreams come true.

At this point, she'd convinced herself that envelope emitted glitter and rainbows. Incidentally, those were two of her favorite things.

She'd done it. All the haters who'd thought her art major was the same thing as "hopeful MRS degree" could suck it. She was getting her MFA, thank you very much. She spread more than a few bangles on her wrist, checking her shining nail polish, and straightened her pink minidress.

She could be dedicated to her art *and* keep her vanity. After all, she had a date with Bradley, a Delta Kappa Epsilon she'd flirted with at their last couple of parties. Mary ran a brush through the long, white-blonde hair she shared with her mother and sister.

At the thought of her sister, she texted a picture of herself making a kissy face to Leila. *You're gonna love college, sis,* she wrote.

Immediately, she received a message back: *As long as I'm not living here. Home's got REAL weird lately.*

Mary didn't reply—she'd deal with that weirdness tomorrow. Tonight was all about positivity. After one last check in the mirror, she grabbed her purse and left her room in the sorority house, graciously receiving so many heartfelt congratulations on her art program from her sisters, she made poor Bradley wait ten minutes longer than she'd planned.

After leaving the restaurant—nice by Baton Rouge standards, but terrible compared to typical New Orleans fare—Bradley took her to the DKE house. She gracefully declined retreating to his room, betting she could beat him and his friends in a game of pool.

With only the eight ball left for her to worry about and four stripes left for Bradley, he would soon owe her five dollars and his favorite DKE T-shirt. The only thing disrupting her fun was her phone. It was ringing, over and over again. She didn't recognize the number, but it had a New Orleans area code. Finally, after the ringing sabotaged what could have been an incredible shot, Mary answered. "I think you have the wrong number."

"This is Brett, from the New Orleans police department. Are you Mary Newman?"

The man's firm voice made Mary gulp. Had she done something wrong? Sure, she'd helped spray paint the pair of lions in front of a certain fraternity house pink, and she'd been skinny-dipping without considering the repercussions more than a couple of times, but she'd never *hurt* anyone.

Why did the police have to become involved, especially the New Orleans police, and not the officers working for the university?

"Yes." She held up a finger to the guys and walked through the house to the backyard. "This is she."

Brett's voice softened. "Mary, I'm so sorry to tell you this, but your parents have died."

Mary sank to the ground. "Wh-what?"

"We believe there was foul play involved, but we can't tell you much more until we complete our investigation."

She couldn't feel the tears streaming down her face, but she could feel the air leave her lungs and refuse to return. She couldn't breathe. She would never breathe again. *Mom and Dad are dead.* "Leila?" she asked.

"Your sister is fine," the officer said. "She, uh, she doesn't speak, does she?"

"She does speak," Mary snapped. She reined herself in. "You probably scared her," she said more gently. *Of course she's scared.*

"Maybe when you get here you can help her talk to us. It's imperative for the investigation that we speak to her. We have a sign language interpreter here, but she won't talk to her either."

When I get there. Mary hadn't been planning on going home. *Mom and Dad are dead.* She kept forgetting; it just sounded so strange, so unlikely. *Leila is at home, all alone.* That thought pierced her deeper than any other, tearing out her heart in small pieces.

We're alone. Alonealonealonealonealone.

She hung up on the officer and cried. She cried and cried for years, until a lullaby in a strange language roused her. *What a beautiful song.*

* * * *

Raphael dug a claw into the armrest of the already beaten-up Land Rover, peeling away vinyl. Back in the early 1900s, when they'd first started buying cars, he'd been so excited by the invention he'd endeavored to take care of his T-bucket. He lovingly washed it and kept it serviced more than it required. It didn't take him long to understand that having a nice car in New Orleans was akin to never seeing a flying cockroach—it simply wasn't going to happen. Now, almost all of his pack's vehicles were as beaten up as they could be. *And the roads are worse than ever.* He inwardly cursed as the SUV lurched, trembling, over another pothole.

They were driving through an upscale neighborhood on Lake Ponchartrain, the homes shouting their infancy. The area had been ruined during Hurricane Katrina, and then painstakingly rebuilt. New buildings were not typical in this city, something Raphael let himself enjoy. It helped him feel less out of place, knowing New Orleans, too, was an immortal creature herself.

He parked a few doors down from the strangely modern home that was their destination.

"That it?" Heath asked.

Raphael nodded. He didn't see, hear or smell anything strange. He didn't hear *enough*. There was sawdust in the air from construction about a mile away. A couple of cats and dogs prowled the yards. "I can't smell any botos from here." He used the term Aiyanna called the man who'd stabbed Mary.

"What is a boto?" Heath asked, his mouth thinning.

"I don't know," Raphael said. "But we'll find out."

They entered the house through an unlocked side door. "Something's wrong," Heath murmured. "If they're housing kidnapped women here, there's no way they would leave a door unlocked."

"It smells like the river, and something else—"

"Death," Heath said. "Someone here is dead."

The house was empty. As they walked through a bare kitchen and living room, he checked the floor. It was dry. There was no water in the house, but he was certain river creatures lived there, probably shapeshifters as Alex suspected.

Upstairs, each bedroom had a made-up, untouched bed and a set of shackles. The third bedroom was different. A blonde, lithe woman lay on the bed, bruises creating a necklace around her throat. Leon was crumpled on the floor, his head bent at an odd angle. Both humans were dead.

The wrongness of killing creatures so much weaker, whose lives were already so short, sent waves of fury through Raphael. Leon had been *pathetic* for aiding the kidnapping of women, but he hadn't wanted this for the mortal.

The death of the woman sickened him. Her only sin was being in the wrong place at the wrong time, and it had cost her her life.

Heath's phone rang. He tilted it to Raphael, showing him Jeremiah's number. "What?" Heath snapped impatiently.

"That house on St. Charles, get back here *now*," Jeremiah said.

Raphael heard as if the call had been for him. He nodded.

"I'll be there," Heath growled, hanging up.

Ten minutes later, they were back at the house that still reeked of blood. Beneath it, he could barely detect the botos' river water stench. Jeremiah stood at the doorway, shattered glass at his feet. His mouth was curled into a snarl.

"Explain this to me," he said as they followed him inside.

A woman was sitting where the dead boto had been earlier, her head placed on a cushion beside her. Precise script flowed above her body, the color of dried blood. It read: YOU KILLED NATASHA. WE'LL KILL YOURS.

It was a threat toward Mary.

Raphael had never seen the dead woman before, but this had to be the woman Wish had asked about earlier, who Thérèse said to be dead.

He would be blamed, again, for a death he hadn't caused. This time he hadn't so much as touched the human before her death. He felt the same about this woman as the one he'd seen, strangled, mere minutes earlier: *Ill.* Another senseless death at the hands of men who were always one step in front of him and the rest of his pack. These men knew what the consequences of killing a human would be for them.

So how could Raphael not know a thing about the botos?

Part of him wanted to rebel and fight for his life. He'd followed the rules, *always*. He hadn't killed a human in over five hundred years. *But I deserve to die.* However they chose to kill him, for whatever reason they decided to, he would deserve it.

He wished every innocent he'd ever harmed could watch him suffer, should it bring them peace. Each day he saw the faces of the children whose fathers he'd killed, the hatred of the men's wives and siblings. He heard the sobs of the parents, frail with age, as they realized they wouldn't outlive their child.

He wasn't good enough to be allowed to live, and hadn't been for centuries.

"I believe she's dead," he told Jeremiah, who had a short dagger at Raphael's throat before he could blink.

"You're not denying," Jeremiah growled, pressing until blood drew, "*beheading* an innocent woman?"

Raphael said nothing. He wouldn't lie, but he didn't deserve to defend himself.

"He killed no one," Heath said.

Jeremiah frowned, scrutinizing both of them. His eyes were like slivers of ice, utterly cold and unfeeling. "You understand that you *may* have gotten away with killing the other humans. I looked into it, and they might have deserved their fate, not that it was yours to give. Neither of you have rights. You're not human, and you are not truly were."

Heath flinched at Jeremiah's last words.

Their *lupus dux* lifted his hands. Streams of water rushed into the room, turning into pencil-thin blades of ice. They flew at Raphael and Heath, catching their clothes and the edges of their bodies, pinning them to the wall.

As he had gone immediately into exile after Hans forced the Wolf upon him, Raphael never received his full powers. While werewolves only became wolves on nights of the full moon, they could each command an element all the time. Rarely, someone could command more than just one element. That gift had been taken away from his pack, weakening them so they could be more easily controlled.

"Do not try to move, or I will execute you both, Elders' permission be damned," Jeremiah continued. "Have you killed a human?" he asked Raphael.

"Yes," he answered honestly.

Jeremiah narrowed his eyes, shook his head. "Have you killed a human within the past ten days?"

Raphael met his gaze unwaveringly. He showed no pain, despite the ice starting to *burn* in the dozens of places it touched him. "I will take whatever punishment that's dealt with no complaint. I expect no mercy."

"He's killed no humans! *None*," Heath shouted, jerking in his bonds. Raphael could see his blood streaming down the cream-colored wall.

Jeremiah raised an eyebrow. "Are you willing to stake your life on it?"

"Don't do it." Raphael met his friend's eyes. "*Don't.*"

"I am." Heath turned to Jeremiah.

"So be it." Jeremiah spread his hands. "I'll bring this to the Elders, and if Raphael is found guilty of murdering humans, *any* humans, you will receive the same punishment as him."

Heath raised his chin. "I'd rather die defending a friend, an *innocent* friend, than live by stepping on the downtrodden. We've done our time. I know it's because of you that we haven't been freed yet."

Raphael looked at Heath sharply. There was an end to their exile?

A blade of ice shot between Heath and Raphael, cutting deep into Heath's cheek. "There is nothing innocent about either of you," Jeremiah spat.

"That may be true," Raphael said, "but we've been trying to stop harm toward true innocents. We require help." When Jeremiah said nothing, his expression blank, Raphael pressed on. "Botos have been kidnapping females from around here and it needs to stop. We've been trying to help the problem, but the five of us may not be enough."

A supposed leader in justice for werewolves, Jeremiah laughed. "Of course they're kidnapping women." He smiled terribly. "That's what encantados, botos as you call them, do. They feed from misery and pleasure, but especially both at once."

"You see nothing wrong with what they're doing to human women?" Heath asked incredulously.

"Have they touched a woman who is were?"

"Not that I know of," Raphael answered.

"Then we have no problem. The packs can't become involved," Jeremiah said. "The way they treat humans is not our concern. What *you* do to them is, which is why you will both die."

The ice fell to the floor. Blood trickled freely from Raphael and Heath.

"Do you know why they came here?" Jeremiah asked, the ice in his gaze sharpening.

Raphael shook his head.

"They know the strongest group of immortals, the weres, can't do a damn thing to them here."

* * * *

Leila was sitting on a fat chaise in the dressing room of a closed store where she couldn't afford a single piece of clothing, including the small scraps of lace they marketed as bras. Not that she would ever wear such a thing. *Are they supposed to go over bras?*

She'd been there for hours. The boredom was obviously getting to her, as was her curiosity. After everything Mary had done for her, she trusted that when her sister said to pack her things and get out, there was an explanation. She wondered if maybe Mary and Richard were having an affair, à la *Mystic Pizza.* The thing was, that wasn't Mary's style, never had been. *So what happened?*

Before, well—*not going to think about that*—before Leila started college, Mary had been almost a completely different person. She hadn't been selfish per se, but she'd never had to worry about anything, either. Neither of them had.

Even when Leila contracted meningitis in the eighth grade and lost her hearing, she'd immediately received two cochlear implants and help from the best audiologists and speech-language pathologists in the southeast. What could have been a travesty brought their family closer together, each supporting one another in learning Signed Exact English, a sign language different from American Sign Language in that it was a code for English, not an entirely different language.

With the help of her family, Leila could hear, speak and sign. She had done well in her private high school, had plenty of friends, and took as many dance classes as she could. She'd wanted for nothing, just as Mary had wanted for nothing, even when she'd been at LSU. They were *happy.*

Now Mary was worried all the time. She had hollow cheeks and her clothes hung on her. She dyed the hair she always swore she would never touch. Worst of all, she emanated utter misery. Leila knew Mary had been worried during her first two years of college—

money was tight, and Mary wouldn't let her get a job so she could focus on her schoolwork. So Leila threw herself into it, never receiving less than an A in a class, making sure she practiced enough to always earn the parts she wanted in ballets and recitals.

It had been hard, letting Mary take care of her, seeing the look of embarrassment on her face every time they entered their seedy old apartment. Leila hadn't minded. They kept it clean and padlocked, so there were no problems. And if someone tried to hurt them, Leila could just—*don't think about it.*

Leila shook the thought from her head, holding the transmitters and processors attached to her as she did. She *hadn't* been thrilled about moving to the Van Otterloos' carriage house. She thought they were doing just fine under the circumstances. But her sister was so proud, so excited to be living somewhere similar to what they were used to—not that they'd been wealthy, by any means—Leila went, smiling, along with the plan.

Almost immediately, she'd seen a change in Mary. No longer was she just tired from work, but upset and angry. *Humiliated.* Leila knew something was wrong in that house, and she knew trying to get Mary to discuss it wouldn't work.

Mary was so stubborn, she could probably make any politician back down from their own cause. She was set on the house and the money, and that was that.

Leila would rather have struggled with money like before and seen her sister happy than have fancy endowed scholarships and extra spending money like they did now. *Well, we had extra spending money.*

She caved and tried on the dress she'd been eyeing. Truthfully, she was glad to have any reason to leave. Another few months working for that crazy ass family may have killed Mary.

Someone knocked on the door. It had to be Alexandre, the sexy Nordic-looking man who crashed at their house last night after apparently escorting her very drunk self home. She'd been so relieved when he called to tell her Mary was safe and she'd asked him to come get her.

She hurried to change back into her clothes before she went to the door, her right hand fluttering to her chest to sign an apology for having it locked.

"Don't be sorry," he said. His voice was ridiculously deep, his smile grim. That morning, he'd been downright *jolly.*

What happened? she signed, worry dawning.

"Mary was hurt," he said. "But she'll be fine, I promise you."

In her panic, her *anger,* red bloomed in her vision.

How badly was she hurt?

"If we hadn't found her, she would have died." Alex's gaze was soft, comforting. Leila had just enough self-control to shove him through the door, out of the store before she slammed it shut.

She did something she hadn't let herself do since her parents' death. She opened her mouth and screamed.

The store rumbled and shattered around her.

* * * *

Mary woke to a dull, throbbing pain in her throat that was quickly overshadowed by the sharp sting in her leg. She lay in a sparsely furnished room with beige walls, a black dresser and the bed she was currently tucked into. Pulling the sheets around her, she smelled soap with just a hint of spice. Was this Raphael's bedroom? *Impossible.*

Yet the male in question strode into the room with an impatient air, as if he'd been waiting for her to stir from sleep.

Raphael surprised her—he perched at the very end corner of the bed, as far from her as possible, tense as can be.

"Do you know where Leila is?" she asked. Her voice was hoarse, rough.

"She's here, sleeping," he said. Relief rushed over Mary, a balm to all her other concerns. The list of what she should be worried about was endless, beginning with the fact that they were homeless, *again.*

She shut her eyes, took a deep breath, and then looked up at Raphael. "So you saved me, huh?" she asked, trying not to cringe. She *hated* the thought of having to be saved, but she'd needed it. *I was so in over my head.*

Raphael looked surprised. "You saved yourself. We only came in and made sure you were healed."

The screaming, *her* screaming. "Did I kill them?" She hoped she had, and it came through in her voice. People had to stop messing with her and her family. They'd been through *enough*.

Raphael's full lips twisted into a slight smile. "You killed the man who stabbed you, but you only hurt the others."

"Gaspar's dead." She sighed, nodded. "That's something." At his raised eyebrows, she added, "Trust me, you wouldn't blame me if you knew him."

"May I move closer to you?" he asked, his tentative voice at odds with his intimidating presence. The question soothed her frayed nerves, assuring her he wouldn't touch her unless invited to. Her lack of anxiety was so foreign to her, she felt weightless.

At her nod, he slid down the bed to sit next to her. She scooted over to give the massive man more room. He settled beside her. His long legs were dusted with dark hair, extending a foot past where hers ended. She breathed in his clean scent.

For a moment, they were silent as they sat so close. She looked over, and he was watching her intently, almost curiously. "Mary, what did they do to you?" he asked softly.

As previous night's events rolled through her memory, she decided to go with the truth. Raphael's honesty had saved Leila untold horror; the least she could do was answer his question.

"I was hit, stabbed, fed a strange herb, and they attempted to do some sort of mind control voodoo that did not work in the slightest," she said in a rush. The veins in his neck and arms stood out, and he released a menacing growl.

Absently, she took his hand and palmed it between hers. It was the second time she'd reached out to hold it, and she *liked* it. The way he almost instantly relaxed at her touch made her want to pump a fist in the air. "I'm not after revenge," she told him in a whisper. "I have too many problems to add those pervs to the list." She meant it. She couldn't afford to focus on men like Richard and Gaspar.

"What problems do you have?"

At her silence, he squeezed her hand, his expression imploring.

"I'm homeless now," she said, embarrassment heating her cheeks. "I also have no form of income. One of the men who hurt me was my boss—he used to let my sister and I stay in his little guest cottage."

Raphael raised a hand to her face, and gently traced the cheekbone Richard hit. She felt her shoulders sag; she must look like a complete mess.

"You're beautiful," Raphael said. "What was done to you was—" He paused, shaking his head angrily. "You have to know that nothing has taken away your spirit, from the way you fought back against those men. I've seen hardened soldiers taken down by less than what was done to you. "You will stay here," he announced. "Over half of the rooms here are empty, so there is no reason for you or your sister to leave."

Sensing her protest, he shook his head. "Besides, we have a haint here who is—*unknowledgeable*—about children, and it would be nice for someone to help him with Molly from time to time."

What the hell? Trying to keep calm, Mary said, "What is a haint, and why does he have Molly?"

Raphael picked up the ends of her hair from her waist. "A haint is a ghost who was so furious about being killed, he has remained in our world as a powerful spirit who can touch, feel and be hurt. Wish, the haint, is Molly's father."

"Richard is her father."

"No, but I think Richard killed Wish," Raphael said drolly.

Mary considered for a moment, but knew there was no real choice. *Raphael* knows *he's given me no choice,* she thought. She couldn't leave Molly.

"Fine," she said. "I will live here because I can't leave Molly with a moron, and I have no place to go anyway. But," she added, "I want a real job. Wish needs to raise his own daughter; I'm not here to be a nanny."

"Done," Raphael said, rising to stand before her. He held out a hand. "Are you ready to see your new home?" he asked. His smile was all dimples and gleaming teeth. *He's truly happy I'm staying.* She felt herself smiling back, warmth tugging at her chest.

Mary took his hand, pain lancing through her leg as she swung it over the side of the bed. Raphael's smile vanished, quickly replaced with a furious expression. Determined, she stood, proud that she hardly swayed at all. She still wore her uniform from last night. It was caked in dried blood.

"Thoughtless," Raphael murmured. "Of course you'll want to shower first."

She nodded eagerly. She'd *kill* for a shower.

Like that, Raphael had her in his arms, was charging toward a darkened door on the side of the room. When he flicked on the lights, Mary saw the bathroom of her dreams.

The shower itself was larger than the carriage house's kitchen, the walls and floor were white marble pierced by at least a dozen gleaming showerheads. Raphael swung open the shower door and gently placed Mary on the wide bench. To her right was a button for a steam function. *It's a steam room too!*

"I'll be just outside the door. Call if you need me," Raphael said gruffly.

As he turned to leave, Mary caught his arm.

"Thank you," she said. "For everything." He nodded, his eyes burning into hers. Then Mary was alone with heavenly-scented soaps in the world's largest shower.

She would have to try the steam out. After all, she had a new job and a place to live. She wasn't dead, and her sister was safe. She smiled to herself as she started turning every knob she could get her hands on.

*

Leaving Mary alone in his bathroom was one of the most difficult things Raphael had ever done. She looked so fragile and trusting, her thin frame curled up on the bench, her eyes wide as she'd thanked him so sincerely. Her last words made him want to puff out his chest and act as a personal shield for the small female.

At the moment, it meant shielding her from himself. He'd wanted to tip her head back and kiss her, forcing her to forget all but him. He hardly kept himself from taking off both their clothes and bathing every inch of her. He wouldn't have neglected a single inch.

I'll do those things, but only if she wishes. He would leap off the tallest building he could find before harming a single hair on Mary's head.

She was beauty and salvation incarnate. She made him forget the things he'd done, the shame and the bitter regret that contaminated everything he did temporarily wiped away.

What circumstances caused her to be dependent upon the boto for her well-being? Had she no one to care for her? *She takes care of her sister and Molly, but there is no one for her.*

That would change. Soon he would die, but he would see her cared for before his death. He wanted to feel the flare of her hips, see her cheeks rounded in her smile. He wanted the marks under her eyes replaced with light and crinkles at their corners.

Most of all, he wanted to see her without worry. He wished he could take away all of her concerns, and as he vanquished the botos, he would eliminate her burdens as well. It was only fair, he reasoned.

A mere smile from her took away his greatest pain.

Her scream interrupted his thoughts. He didn't consider her privacy as he stormed into the bathroom, past the pile of her stained clothes, and wrenched open the shower door. She'd protectively brought one leg against her chest; the other was straight in front of her, the partially healed cut deeper than he remembered, trickling blood that turned the water pink around her.

Water that was absolutely *scalding,* he realized.

Quickly, he turned the knobs to a temperature that wouldn't burn her. He lifted her into his arms, ignoring her nudity as best he could, and tilted her chin to look at him. "May I bathe you?" he asked.

She nodded. He was confident some of the wetness around her eyes came from tears, not just the spray. "It hurts," she said, looking at the six-inch gash. "I thought to wash it out with that thing." She lifted up a handheld showerhead, pushed the button to turn it on. "But it hurt too much with the water pressure."

She was right. He'd had it set to hard, thin lines of water that couldn't have helped her wound. *My fault.* "I'm sorry," he said miserably. "I didn't think to—"

She actually laughed. "Don't be sorry, I'm the one being a big baby." She wiped her eyes. "Would you do me a favor?"

Her hair was clinging in ribbons to her lithe body, her face pink from the heat. Red, full lips were turned up in a wry smile. Looking into her bright green gaze, he thought, *How could I deny this woman anything?* "You can ask anything of me," he said honestly.

Her smile widened. After everything that had been done to her, how could she smile like this? Rather than seeing the evil in the men who'd hurt her, she focused on the good in him. It humbled him.

"Will you sit with me in the steam before you help me bathe? I'd give my eye teeth for a few minutes in just ... *warmth.*" He wished the longing in her voice were for him, not a feature of his shower. Instead of attempting to change the direction of her desires and scaring her, he simply sat in the bench, settled her in his lap, and turned on the steam.

She sighed, curling her arms around him and placing her head in the crook of his neck. He knew she could feel the growing erection through his soaked gym shorts when she stiffened, frowning. He was about lift her from him when she looked up into his face, her upper lip thinning and a crease forming at her brow, but she suddenly relaxed. Obviously, she hadn't deemed him a threat.

She gifted him with a brilliant smile, and he couldn't help but grin back.

"Those dimples." She reached up to touch outside the corners of his mouth. What was she talking about? "You have dimples that girls would kill for you to let them take shots out of."

He had no idea what she meant, but she was touching him happily, and he could ask for nothing more. Her soft touch was a contradiction to the roughness of his body, and he wanted *all* of her softness wrapped around him. *There will be time for that.* Even his body willed him to *take.*

She'd been through too much in too short of an amount of time. He would wait until she was healed, physically and mentally, before touching her.

Though he certainly never wanted to move her from her place on his lap, his time was limited. He had much to do this day, and the sooner it was accomplished, the sooner he could come back to Mary. He forced a serious expression. "I'm going to clean you now," he said.

As gently as he could, he shampooed her hair, frowning as some of its darkness seemed to rinse out with the soap swirling down the drain. "I dyed it," Mary said, her eyes closed. "Richard once said he much preferred blondes; I hoped he'd find the change unattractive."

Raphael gritted his teeth as he lathered up a rag. "That's not what you should have done."

Mary cast him an irritated look. "Then what should I have done?"

"You should have quit," he said quietly, running the rag up her smooth back. It was truly without flaw, beginning with dainty shoulders and ending with two dimples that stood in stark relief against her creamy skin. He wanted to kiss just where it dipped, and he would. *Soon.*

Mary turned her head as if to say something angry, looked at him from the corner of her eye, and let out a long, slow breath. "I know," she murmured. "I put myself at risk, and by extension Leila, too. And *that* I can't do again."

He finished washing her, careful not to leave as much as a speck of blood or dirt anywhere on her body. Feigning helping her to stand, he wrapped an arm around her back, only to flip her around, tugging her chest against his. "You will not put *yourself* in danger again either," he growled angrily. "Promise me."

"Why do you care?"

Because you're mine. He wouldn't dishonor her by voicing it aloud. There was too much blood on his hands for a woman like Mary to ever claim him. If she knew the truth about his past, she would be horrified, and rightfully so. He would make sure she never found out. He would never embarrass her by publicly declaring her as his, despite his every instinct screaming that he do so. The were in him wanted to lean down and bite her neck so it left a mark, a sign for others to keep away from her.

Raphael would find another way to make sure she would be untouched.

"You're here with me now, and that is my rule." He tightened his grip on her, splaying both hands flat against her back. Warm water poured on both of them, making it difficult for Mary to look up at him, pressing against Raphael's sodden clothes. Mary reached around him and turned the water off.

She wrung out her hair and pressed two soft palms against his chest. "Are there any other rules I should be aware of?" she asked, her voice happy, teasing, as if she'd liked his response.

"That's my only rule," he said, again trying his best not to look at her exquisite body. *This is not the time.*

He handed Mary a towel and went back into his room, rivulets of water pouring to the floor as he walked. His steps were stiff, mimicking a particular part of his anatomy. *He* wanted to pat her dry, wanted to make her wet all on his own. Instead, he began to peel his clothes off, throwing them to the floor.

"You have clothes in the first drawer," he said. "Leila brought them for you; she said everything you'll want is in there. This is the room you'll stay in—I'll sleep elsewhere." Placing her here was a clear message to the rest of the clan: she was his and his alone. Mary would never know.

"I have things I need to do, and there's someone you must talk to before you see Wish and Molly." He pulled off his shorts. Now *he* was the one completely naked.

Her bright eyes huge, she handed him her towel with a murmured, "Here."

Mary's cheeks were pink. Raphael felt her gaze on him as he quickly toweled off and pulled on another black shirt and pair of shorts. At the scent of her arousal, he couldn't help but grin. If she wanted him, nothing would stop him from having her. He would leave this earth knowing the beauty that was Mary, inside and out.

"Who do you want me to talk to?" she asked, her voice even more hoarse than before. She cleared her throat, her hand fluttering up to her chest.

"Her name is Aiyanna, and everything she will tell you is true," he said seriously. "Listen to her."

Mary nodded. Raphael led her from his room, down a hallway and a flight of stairs to the firehouse's living room. Alex and Leila were playing a racecar video game projected onto a screen that covered the far wall. Cael sat in one of the lounge chairs, likely watching Aiyanna, who Raphael couldn't see.

When he turned the dimmed lights up Alex groaned, and Leila turned around curiously, the expression on her face turning panicked when she saw Mary.

Mary, honey, why don't we get you something to eat from the kitchen? They have your favorite flavor moon pie, she signed, her expression imploring.

As Mary shook her head, Raphael saw she was shaking all over.

Alex, you said she wouldn't see her like this! Leila signed, her motions jerky, frustrated.

Raphael turned to see what Leila was talking about. Aiyanna, a shapeshifter, was curled up on the seat opposite Cael in panther form. She winked a yellow eye at Mary.

He barely caught her as she fell into a dead faint.

I told you she was scared of wompus cats. You said you'd warn Raphael, Leila signed, exasperated. She turned to Aiyanna. *I know you can understand me, kitty. You didn't have to shock her like that.*

Raphael swore he heard Aiyanna chuckle.

He set Mary down on the couch next to Leila and pulled Alexandre up by his shirt. "If you so much as let her be scared by a *spider* again, I'll kick your teeth in," he growled.

Alex pulled away, now fully laughing. "I'm sorry, man, it won't happen again ... they called Aiyanna *wompus.*" He gripped his sides and bent over, his laughter failing to subside.

Leila frowned at him, then looked at Raphael. *Normally I'd mention something about how violence is bad, but he deserves it,* she signed. *And she is a wompus cat.* She made a huffing sound.

Said cat was *definitely* laughing now, but before Raphael could turn his ire on her, Cael was in front of him. "No," was all he said, his face blank, before he returned to his perch.

Raphael sighed, ran a hand across his face. If Mary fainted at the sight of a panther, what would she do when she found out he was a werewolf?

Leila was lightly slapping Mary's face, trying to wake her up. What would she do when she learned she wasn't *human*?

Chapter 5

Someone was lightly slapping Mary's face. "Leila says she'll sic the wompus cat on you if you don't wake up," an obnoxiously cheerful voice said. Mary guessed it was Alexandre, who sounded like he was at least ten feet away.

She reached up and covered her eyes. There was definitely *not* a giant cat sitting near her, and it definitely *hadn't* winked at her. She'd been afraid of the beasts ever since she was a child. Her mother had told her and Leila stories about creatures all their lives, but the ones that stood out the most were the sack man and the wompus cat—those two were said to drag bad little girls from their beds and eat them.

Mary groaned and uncovered her eyes. She *really* didn't want to be eaten ... unless Raphael was involved. In that case, she wanted to be devoured. Although initially shocked by his entrance to the shower—she hadn't realized she yelled *that* loudly—shock turned to being touched, literally and figuratively.

She saw the way he tried not to look at her, not to embarrass her, but he'd also been strained, stress lining his mouth, the hardest part of him pressing against her. He fought himself for her, just to make her feel more comfortable. Hell, it would have been enough that he'd helped wash her when he was *fully clothed,* which had to have been miserable. He hadn't seemed to notice.

He was too busy taking care of her, something no one had done for her in what felt like a lifetime.

Mary didn't think she'd ever recover from seeing him naked. The mere sight of him ruined her for all men, as he made them seem like another species altogether. A deep tan covered his body, where muscle stretched across more muscle. Black hair spread across his defined pecs down in a line to reveal just how well-endowed he was, and *large* was an understatement. Given, she'd only seen one other naked man before, but she had no doubt Raphael made the vast majority of the male population seem puny in comparison.

Apparently Greek gods do go to Thump.

As she'd gazed, most likely drooling, at Raphael, she couldn't help but think *this man would protect me.* This man could be the end for all the horrors Mary and Leila had gone through. How could he not? He looked utterly *invincible,* and even though he probably didn't know it, he simply emanated power. Everything about him was dangerous for his enemies, and Mary knew with a scary level of certainty that he would never hurt her.

So as not to set back the Feminist Movement thirty years, she would protect him too. She didn't know how, exactly, but she'd find a way. Who looked after him, anyway? Who told Raphael not to place himself in danger?

From now on, both Leila and he had a protector in Mary, and she'd make damn sure she did a good job.

To her right the cat flashed, startling Mary, into a beautiful human woman who looked to be about her age. She shook back shiny black hair that matched the cat's coat. "Not a cat person, huh?" she said on a tinkling laugh.

"You've got some effed up gris-gris," Mary said darkly. She *really* didn't like big cats.

"Girl, you have *no* idea." The woman's smile widened.

"That's Aiyanna," Raphael said helpfully. He sat in a soft-looking, well-used chair next to an unfamiliar man who looked like he belonged on a runway. His face was expertly chiseled, surely an intimidating example of what true aristocracy looked like. Chin-length black hair was pushed back from his eyes, his blue gaze resting on Aiyanna.

"Who're you?" Mary asked him. Raphael growled. The man just looked at her, his bored expression saying, *"You are nothing."* Mary decided he was the type of handsome that made him completely unapproachable. *Or maybe that's just him*, she thought.

"He's Cael," Aiyanna said. "And he wants me." She blew him a kiss. Leila and Mary exchanged an impressed glance. Maybe the wompus cat wasn't *so* bad.

Cael narrowed his eyes, disgusted, and stormed from the room. Aiyanna only shrugged, but Mary could see she was upset. The light in her yellow eyes left with the irritated man.

"It's nice see you're a local," Aiyanna said. "These dogs wouldn't know gris-gris from a Mardi Gras doubloon." She hooked a manicured thumb at Leila. "Your upbringing helped her accept who she was—and who we are—a lot easier than most."

Mary felt her breath catch as the new information clicked into place.

The stories their mother had told them were real. Stories of witches and voodoo priestesses, men who turned to wolves during the full moon, ghosts, vampires, the beautiful and deadly Fae. Kelpies who lured teenagers into the lake, and women whose wails brought death.

Wails. Her screams, Gaspar—"Am I a banshee?"

"Helped her accept who she was," Aiyanna had said.

Mary looked over at Leila. "Are you?"

Leila brought her fist forward, signing, *Yes. We both are, I think.*

Understanding dawned on Mary. Leila hadn't spoken since the night their parents died. Had she found out by accidentally hurting those who'd killed their parents? Was it why she didn't speak? Did she know who killed them?

By now the case had gone cold. If Leila would finally tell what she knew of the killers, maybe something could be done. At the very least, it would bring closure to a festering wound. It wasn't easy facing every day knowing the people who'd broken into their home and killed their parents walked free, could be next in line at the supermarket.

"You've known," Mary said, receiving another *Yes.*

Mom told me, before, Leila signed.

"So that's why—"

We'll discuss it later.

Meaning, she wouldn't discuss it at all. Disappointment filled Mary, overshadowing any shock that so-called mythical creatures exist. She'd never thought they were an impossibility, anyway; her mother had seen to that, and now she knew why. More than anything, she was hurt Leila wouldn't confide in her. She'd tried so hard to be everything she could be for her sister—a friend, a provider, a guardian.

She knew what we were, and never told me. How could Leila keep something like that from her for three years?

"Do you really call yourself a wompus cat?" Mary asked Aiyanna. She couldn't focus on Leila, *wouldn't.* She had to focus on what she could control. Besides, Raphael said this woman could be trusted. She could be a vault of information.

"I'm a shapeshifting voodoo sex goddess," Aiyanna said. "The feline part is courtesy of my Choctaw half, the voodoo my Haitian half. You watch, one of these days Cael will back me up on my goddess status."

Mary couldn't help but smile.

"She partially healed you," Raphael told her.

"That comes in handy more than you would think." Aiyanna nodded. "Sorry I couldn't finish that place on your leg—once my energy replenishes, I can try again."

Mary couldn't believe it—she was going to be friends with a shapeshifter. As she looked at Raphael, she realized she was okay with that, so long as Aiyanna's wicked panther jaws steered clear. "So what are you?" she asked Raphael.

He visibly cringed. "A werewolf."

Mary nodded, as if she knew anything at all about werewolves. *But maybe I do.*

"Some creatures," her mother had said seriously, perched on

the side of Mary's bed, *"are not at all what they seem to be."* It had been before Leila's hearing was taken away; Mary remembered Leila chattering excitedly beside her, asking if the story had a Fae prince. It didn't; it was about a priest ... and a werewolf.

"One day a priest was traveling and came upon a forest. A great beast came from within. He had the body of a large wolf, yet he walked on two legs and could speak. He asked the priest if he was afraid, and the priest said he had the protection of God, so he was not. The wolf-man told the priest his wife and he had been cursed, causing them to be forced to live in the bodies of wolves at times. His wife was shot for her pelt, and was close to death. He begged the priest to go with him deep into the woods to hear her confession and give her absolution. The priest bravely did so, barely making it to the she-wolf before her death. The newly widowed wolf-man took the priest back to where the forest ended and left him there. For years the priest tried, but he could never find him again.

"You must always remember," her mother had said, careful to look both of them in the eye, *"what something looks like on the outside does not mean it looks that way on the inside."*

Mary felt Leila's gaze. She could tell by Leila's expression that she was thinking of that same old Irish story.

Across the room Raphael watched her, his mouth set into a thin line. His eyes belied his stern expression. *He seems hopeful.* It warmed her—never, not even in college, had someone seemed to care what her opinion was. She wasn't a math genius or a prodigy in *anything.* She wasn't the most beautiful, or the most athletic, and she certainly wasn't as physically strong as Raphael. Yet there he was, waiting as if her reaction over what he was actually meant something to him.

So she stood and walked over to him, her eyes never leaving his, and sat herself in his lap, careful of her thigh. Features stern, she got right in his face, her finger lightly tapping his nose.

"If you don't make period jokes about me, I won't make moon jokes about you," she told him, smiling.

He laughed, his dimples coming out in full force. He wrapped both of his arms around her and squeezed. "But you'll still make moon jokes about them, right?" he whispered in her ear.

Alex feigned a hurt expression. Apparently werewolves had fantastic hearing. "Of course," Mary said, wishing she would never have to move. The man was hard all over, but *seriously* warm and comfortable. Besides, she could tell he liked where she was from the hardness pressed against her back.

"Well," Alex huffed dramatically.

"On that note," Aiyanna said, unfolding her long legs and standing, "we're going to go help the haint with that devil child. Loft on the fourth floor." Leila followed her from the room, her eyebrows high.

"We still on for—" Alex started.

"Yes," Raphael said shortly, cutting him off. "I'll meet you out front in a few."

With a nod, Alex left, leaving Raphael and Mary alone again. She relaxed against him, her head against his chest, far too content to move. "You really don't mind what I am?" he asked.

Truthfully, she shook her head no. She wouldn't judge him to be a monster just because he could outwardly turn into one. "Do you care that I'm a banshee? I'm pretty sure a walking death symbol is more of a bummer than a werewolf."

The stories she'd been told always had a beautiful blonde woman who would wail, her cries heard by the family who would lose someone to death within the week. In contrast, some stories depicted crones who furiously tried to wash bloodstains from the clothes of those who were fated to die. She didn't think those women were banshees, though. At the very least, they weren't Irish in origin like Mary's parents were.

Mary wondered, once again, if Leila had screamed the night of their parents' deaths.

Raphael seemed to contemplate her question, humming a familiar tune under his breath as he ran his fingers through her now considerably lightened hair. "I think you're more of a sign of peril," he said. "Perhaps those who heed your warnings—without fixating on them—could change their fate and survive."

She had no answer for that, but she liked the idea. Maybe she could turn a curse into a gift. Either way, being a banshee had pretty decent defensive features. She'd have to learn exactly how she hurt Richard and his friends, both to help her if she found herself in similar situation again, and so she could prevent herself from accidentally hurting someone.

Strong hands lifted her to her feet. Beside her, Raphael stood. "I have to go, but I'll be back in a few hours."

His onyx eyes were hard, as if he loathed leaving her.

She faked a smile, ashamed that what she *really* wanted to do was wrap her arms around him and beg him to stay. "See you," she said as casually as she could. *Damn.* There was definitely a tremor in her voice.

Raphael craned his head. He was close enough to kiss her. Instead, his lips were at her ear. "Next time, we will both be naked, and you will *not* be in pain."

Mary could only gape at him as he walked away. As she made her way to the loft where Molly and her "father" were staying, she had to consciously wipe the silly smile from her face. She wanted to be with Raphael the Werewolf, but first she had to learn about him and his kind, as well as her *own* kind.

She entered a room walled almost completely in ornately draped windows, bright light filling the space. An abnormally tall man was floating a foot in the air, four open books hovering around him at eye level. One of them was titled, *How to Raise an Intellectual,* another *Over 138 Tips to Not Screw Up Your Kid's Childhood.* The man had the same dark hair and cleft chin as Molly—if he wasn't her father, he was another close relation. *This must be Wish. The haint.*

"May wee!"

Molly ran forward to give Mary a hug, leaving Leila and Aiyanna behind her. The two were surrounded by toys.

"Finally, someone who *knows* her," Wish said, bookmarks floating into the books before they neatly stacked themselves on a table. Wish drifted to the floor. "I'm Aloysius, but everyone calls me Wish." He held out a hand. Mary shook it, surprised at how *normal* he felt, considering he was a vengeful spirit.

She took a second to marvel at how strange that particular thought was.

He didn't seem like Raphael, or now that she considered it, Alexandre, Heath and Cael either. She would paint them with bright red underpaintings, the first layer before more details and color would be painted on top. She would use a soft blue for Wish, the color of his veins under his pale skin.

"Would you tell me everything you know about Molly?" he asked earnestly. "Or better yet, write it out for me?"

He reached out to touch her shoulder, his hand falling as if he'd thought better of it, and wrung his hands. "I so badly want to be a good father to her," he said raggedly. "I physically haven't been able to be a part of her life until now, and I want to do it right. I will pay you *anything* for your help. You know her. Please do this for us."

Hair standing on end, his glasses askew, Wish looked at her as if she held the secret to world peace. As he flicked a glance to Molly, whose little hand gripped Mary's T-shirt, she saw a glimpse of both absolute devotion and steel. *No one* would take this child away from him again, that much was clear. Mary held out her hand, and immediately Wish floated a pen and legal pad to her.

"I don't want payment," she said, smothering a grin at Aiyanna's disapproving look.

"*Always accept payment,*" she stage-whispered.

Leila signed, *Ignore her.*

"Hey, I know your fancy English signs," Aiyanna said before signing, *Kiss my ass, screamer.*

Leila rolled her eyes. *You never take what the wolves offer you.*

Aiyanna flipped her hair, raising her chin, but nodded.

Mary realized the two must have spoken more than she thought while she slept.

"When Big Ears here isn't around, I'm curious about how you became separated from her," Mary said to Wish. She had a terrible feeling Richard had something to do with it. Was Natasha her mother? She'd rarely seen the woman and expected Molly had seen her even less. "And I want to know about the werewolves," she told Aiyanna. She liked that she wouldn't have to ask Raphael for details.

What about banshees? Leila signed.

"I don't know much about that," Aiyanna said. "You're pretty rare."

Wish put a hand on Molly's head and tapped Mary's legal pad. "I know a few things about banshees," he said with a smile. "Maybe we can help each other."

As Wish pulled Molly away to show her a book about cats, Aiyanna grinning proudly as she looked on, Mary settled into a chair with the pad on her lap. Leila absently did a twirl that probably had a French name, a sign that she was relaxed. *This isn't so bad.* So she clicked the pen and wrote, scouring her mind for any detail that could help Wish connect with his daughter.

* * * *

For the second time in two days, Raphael crashed his fist through a window. He shook out his hand, feeling the skin stitch itself back together. Alex reached through and unlatched it. Lifting the pane, he said, "Subtle, Raphe. Real subtle, buddy."

Raphael ignored him. He wanted this *done.* Not only was the existence of a place such as this an insult, but for the first time in his life he had a woman at his home, waiting for him. He was terrified that when he went back, she'd be gone.

Alex handed him a jug of *incendie sûr.* "Be careful where you put this," he said. "If we run out, it's going to be your ass who has to ask the Fae for another two jugs." He shivered. "They're weird, and not in a fun way."

The Fae ran *le marché noir,* the black market in New Orleans, and from what Raphael knew, most black markets around the world. In terms of business, they were fair to a fault ... if the buyer knew how to *make* them be fair. Otherwise, for instance, a human might find himself enslaved to them forever simply because he amused them. Raphael had once seen a human woman buy a love potion from *le marché noir,* a potion she had no way of knowing would make her lover become forever entranced by the beauty of cacti.

He avoided the Fae whenever possible.

They would have to make do with the *incendie sûr* they had. Each bottle held a couple gallons of a sort of kerosene. When lit, one drop of the liquid would engulf everything in a three-foot radius. No more, no less. With correct placement of the *incendie sûr*, Alex and Raphael should be able to burn this house to the ground without harming any of the surrounding homes.

Raphael couldn't let this house that smelled like river water, a house where there were only beds and chains, continue to stand.

When he tried the door this time, it had been locked. Now that they'd broken in, they needed do a sweep of the place to make sure no innocents were caught in the flames. "I'll do the upstairs," he said. Some of the bedrooms were untouched. Others smelled of human, with beds covered in rumpled sheets and marks scoring the walls from their fragile nails. Raphael tore through a mattress and box springs, down to the metal frame, which he ripped in half. He did the same to the headboard and yanked the chains from the walls.

He noticed Alex watching him. "This place needs to *burn*," Alex murmured. His hands, too, were cut and bleeding; he'd done some destruction of his own. They picked up their *incendie sûr* and went to work.

An hour later when the sun set, they stood a half block away from the house, watching what looked like an innocent single-family home light up and burn, no flames reaching for any of the neighboring structures.

A young human couple from a nearby house sat on their front porch and watched. "What a shame," the woman said. The man scratched his head, making a face.

"Who lived there, anyway?" he asked. "I bet they're those people who keep knocking on our door at night. Don't talk to them, Coco," he finished sternly.

The woman shrugged. "I've only seen someone there once, anyway. Probably a rich man who lives in Baton Rouge and keeps a house here."

"We should get a beach house," the man mused.

"Ha! In ten years, when we can afford it," his wife said.

"Try twenty," he corrected.

Alex nudged Raphael, distracting him from the intriguing couple. "We need to leave before the police get here."

Raphael nodded.

Their car was safely parked blocks away, toward the river. Strangely, from the opposite direction he caught the scent of the river on the wind. "Botos," he said, stopping.

Alex followed as he stalked in their direction—and they were nearby, close enough to know their house of horror was burned to the ground.

As the scent grew stronger, Raphael heard music becoming louder. They walked between houses, coming out onto a street that ended in a cul-de-sac filled with humans and botos. A mansion had speakers and a DJ set up in its yard. Alcohol flowed from open bars—the creatures were having a party out in the open. Tonight, many *looked* like creatures. At least half a dozen botos were in what Raphael assumed was their natural form: Wide mouths filled with long, sharp teeth, pointed fins jutting from their backs and elbows. Their skin was a sickly blue, with black eyes devoid of any white.

The strangest part was the water flowing around those creatures, wrapping close to their bodies in a spiral. A human woman licked the water, following close to a boto with a loving expression. There were as many women as there were monsters, and none struggled or tried to run. Human men prowled the perimeter of the party, semiautomatic guns strapped over their shoulders.

While Mary slept, Aiyanna had told them what she knew of botos. She said they used live together in a utopian community in Brazil, near the Amazon River. They were the epitome of peace, and never wanted for anything.

Naturally, one boto became bored with his easy life and left their community to discover humans, who he found to be weaker creatures he could control. He learned that the stronger the humans' emotions were, the more powerful he, the boto, became.

Eventually many botos followed, leaving their utopia and using their powers to evoke strong emotions from humans. They began to feed from the humans' feelings, causing enough misery to enrage the god Bochica, who cursed them to never again produce female offspring.

Molly could have never been Richard's blood daughter.

These creatures were feeding from the women they'd taken and possibly the humans guarding them too.

At that moment, what bothered Raphael the most was the spiraling water. Aiyanna had mentioned nothing about abilities to control the element—but he knew someone who could, someone who'd known what the botos were doing to humans.

Raphael assumed Jeremiah simply didn't want to get involved, but clearly he'd been wrong. Jeremiah was *helping* them.

"Do you see him?" he asked Alexandre.

Alex didn't ask who he meant. "No," he said, anger permeating his voice, "but we know he's here."

Raphael tried to take another step toward the cul-de-sac, but Alex's arm was thrown in his path. "We're outnumbered, man," he said. "Besides, we can't harm the humans, and they're using them as a shield."

He was right. Raphael and Alex would have to make it past armed humans to get to any botos, and apparently, Jeremiah. Even with their full powers, it would have been a risk. Without them, they would have no chance against all the lines of defense.

It was a moot point. Raphael didn't know what his full powers were. He'd joined the *clan prohibitum* so quickly that he'd never used his elemental abilities. *I probably didn't have any to start with.* A feeling of helplessness consumed him. It wasn't the first time over the centuries when the powers he'd never known could have helped another, an innocent.

No matter what choices he made, those choices hurt people. Had he not punished himself, there would be no justice for the many he'd wronged, for their families. Yet there he was, kicking himself for his uselessness. *That* was the word he'd been looking for. *Useless.* How could he do anyone, especially Mary, any good the way he was?

"There," Alex said.

Raphael looked up, storing his dark thoughts and focusing. There Jeremiah was, right in front of them. He held a glass filled with an amber liquid; a giggling woman sucked a curling stream of champagne from the air beside him, delighted with Jeremiah's trick. Another clung to his right arm, running a hand through his curly hair. Raphael's claws sharpened. Any respect he had for that man, one who'd overseen their clan for longer than Raphael had been in it, was gone, along with his respect for their punitive system.

"He deserves punishment."

"I agree, but, dude, we cannot do anything now. It would be suicidal," Alex said insistently.

Raphael blinked. He hadn't meant to say that aloud. Reluctantly, he acquiesced. They dragged themselves from the terrible scene, both men shaking with anger. Someone had to stop Jeremiah and the botos. The alternative was unthinkable.

"We need to meet with Heath, Cael and Sebastian," Raphael said. "All of us need to lay out everything we know, everything we can do, so we can find a way to stop this."

Alex was already dialing his phone. "Done," he said.

* * * *

Wish is not a moron. In terms of Molly, he was as clueless as any new parent, but regarding everything else Mary, Leila, and Aiyanna had spoken to him about, he was a wealth of knowledge. A professor of Southern literature at Tulane, he knew all about both mortal and immortal beings—and whether they existed or not.

Apparently the sack man was just a sadistic human who'd been dead for over a century.

Mary and Leila grilled the poor haint for over an hour, with Aiyanna chiming in occasionally. Mary learned banshees were all women, and although fairly powerful, Leila and Mary were mortal, unlike werewolves and shapeshifters.

"The closer you are to someone or some family, the harder it will be for you to sense any upcoming deaths," Wish had said.

Leila had paled at the news, wiping away any ideas Mary held about her sister predicting their parents' murder.

She was determined to turn over a new leaf in her life. There would be no more humiliation, no more feeling unsafe, and especially no more deaths in their little family. Mary wanted to have fun again. She wanted to paint, to feel beautiful simply for the sake of feeling good about herself.

The only wrenches in her plan were the delinquent werewolves she now lived with. Or so she thought, until Aiyanna added her two cents. Wish had explained how werewolves only turn into their wolf forms on nights of the full moon, which was in less than a week. Unmated weres, meaning every man aside from Wish who lived in the old firehouse, would be completely uncontrollable on those nights,

"They only know two things," Wish said, *"mating and killing."*

At Mary's alarmed gasp, Aiyanna quickly chimed in, shooting Wish an annoyed look. *"These men contain themselves with chains enchanted to subdue werewolves with full powers."*

Powers these men didn't have. So long as Leila and she stayed away from where they were chained, they would be safe.

The thought of crazed wolves still made Mary's knees weaken. If it weren't for Aiyanna and Wish's earnest reassurances about the men, coupled with their lacking abilities most werewolves had, Mary might have run from the firehouse, dragging Leila along with her.

Something wonderful—fragile, but worth cultivating—was forming between her and Raphael, but giant, relentlessly angry wolves were up there with large cats in her book.

She learned the loss of their powers was another punishment for their crimes. No one could tell Mary what the weres, namely Raphael, had done to deserve this.

"They're all good men," Aiyanna had assured her. *"Whatever they've done, they've been punished enough for it. I promise you, there is no safer place than here."*

Then why don't you live here? Leila had signed, earning a growl from the shapeshifter.

"Cael won't let me," she said.

"If I'd seen or heard evidence that they were dangerous, Molly would not be here," Wish said. More than anything, that appeased Mary's worries. Wish wouldn't risk any harm coming to his daughter.

It was a relief; it felt like a luxury to have certainty about Leila and her safety.

Even before hearing Wish and Aiyanna's defense for the werewolves, Mary hadn't doubted Raphael. She'd feared the other four, especially the one she had yet to meet, Sebastian. She couldn't, *wouldn't* be convinced Raphael had a cruel bone in his body. Even now, as she absently folded the clothes Leila haphazardly threw into his dresser, she wished Raphael were there. He not only made her feel secure, but as if she *mattered.* Not to mention how his touch melted her, left all her hard-earned reservations about men forgotten.

With him, she might be able to let all of it go.

Loud, angry footsteps sounded in the hall seconds before the man she'd been fantasizing about slammed into his bedroom. She jumped, turning to face him. *What happened?* Gone was the man who'd held her so tenderly earlier that afternoon. His long hair was free of its ponytail and tendons revealed themselves in his neck. His eyes were a dark navy blue, not their usual dark brown. Raphael was furious, and Mary had no idea why.

"Are you okay?" she asked, reaching for him.

He flinched away. "You have no reason to speak to me." Raphael's bared teeth were sharper than usual. "I can't bring any good to your life. Trust me, you'll be glad when you no longer have to see me."

Hurt, anger and worry replaced all the hope she'd had mere minutes ago. "You're kicking Leila and me out?"

"Of course not," he snapped, surprising her.

"Then what do you mean by me no longer having to see you? Are you going to be freed soon?" That had to be it. How else would he be allowed to leave? She should be happy for him. She wasn't.

"Something like that." His back was to her as he stuffed weapons into a duffel bag with a few pieces of clothing. She gaped at the covered knives, different sets of brass knuckles and single gun. Apparently finished packing, he hoisted the bag over one shoulder.

"Please," she implored, grabbing his shoulder. "What happened?" Even if he was being released, *something* had made him this way. He'd helped her so much; she wanted to do the same for him.

Raphael dropped the bag, swung around and pinned her to the wall, caging her with his body. She met his eyes defiantly. She'd seen the kindness he was capable of; he didn't scare her. When she didn't cow, he cursed darkly, slamming his hands into the wall beside her head. She refused to flinch. From the *thud* and wood chips sprinkling the floor, he must have hit—and annihilated—a stud.

"*I am no good*," he growled, his breath tickling her ear.

"Why do you reek of smoke?" she asked. Had he burned something? Was he hurt?

"I burned down a house," he said.

Great, I can begin his list of crimes with arson.

"Why?" she asked. "I don't think you, the philanthropic man who's housing two women in need, would go burn down a house for shits and gigs." She pushed at his chest. "No, I *know* you didn't."

"You know nothing!" he roared. He slammed another fist into the stud, causing wood to rain again. Each of his fingers was tipped with a razor-sharp claw. "You almost got yourself killed yesterday, and today you've rashly decided to try your hand with criminal werewolves. You're either stupid or suicidal. You don't know us; you have *no reason* to trust us with your life, or the life of your sister."

She shoved him away, surprisingly easily, as Cael and Aiyanna burst into the room. "What the hell are you doing, Raphael?" Cael snarled.

"Sweet cheeks, it's obvious he's being a royal dickwad," Aiyanna said in a saccharine-sweet tone. Cael rolled his eyes.

Mary felt lost, and for the first time in her life, completely alone. Her sister was keeping God-knows-what from her, her parents were still dead, and the man who'd given her hope, who she'd thought found her *worthy*, was throwing her away as if she were trash.

Maybe she hadn't been prudent. Maybe she'd made rash decisions by working for Richard and trusting the werewolves. *I'm doing the best I can, but I'm not stupid or suicidal.*

With that in mind, she shoved out of Raphael's room, angrily flinging the tears from her eyes. Unfortunately, she couldn't as easily fling away the hollowness in her chest. *I can't have one day. Not one single decent day.* What had she done to deserve this? She didn't just ask for trouble, as Raphael thought.

For years she'd tried her hardest for Leila. She'd failed on all counts, miserably. Hell, because of her, Leila would probably lose her scholarship. No wonder Leila felt she couldn't confide in her.

Thankfully, no one followed as she found the huge, circular hole in the floor. She grabbed the pole, ignoring the burning in her hands as she slid to the first story. She was out the door in seconds with one thought clinging to her: *I have no one.*

Chapter 6

"Raphael, you stupid man," Aiyanna said, her voice low, dangerous. "What did she do to deserve that? What could she have *possibly* done to you, huh?"

Nothing. He shouldn't have yelled at Mary, and she had done nothing to merit him, someone she'd trusted, scaring her. And what did he do? Pushed her into a wall and yelled at her, calling her the most hurtful names he could think of. But moving in with his pack *was* reckless.

Trusting Raphael was downright dangerous.

He didn't deserve to be trusted. *He* hadn't earned that sweet smile she'd given him when he first came into the room. As if she'd been happy to see him, may have been waiting for him.

In that moment she'd been everything he wanted, everything that had never been within his reach.

Of course, he'd immediately ruined it all. That was what he did—he was physically incapable of making someone happy. *It's better this way. Now I won't hurt her later.* His words guaranteed her distance from him. *Better for her.* Then why did it feel utterly wrong? He wanted to follow her, to beg for her forgiveness. Every instinct he possessed wanted to rebuke each word he'd said. He wanted to apologize for all the tears he'd caused. Seeing her that way made him feel like the worst of creatures.

He didn't want to leave her, but he had no choice in that. After seeing Jeremiah with the botos, he had no doubt that the man would soon execute him. *And Heath.* For that reason alone, it would be kinder to keep distance between Mary and him.

Every cell in his body disagreed. He was restless with the need to follow her. Had she left the firehouse?

Could she be his mate? It would explain the wrenching pain her sadness brought him, his absolute need to console her. *No.* A mate was never in the cards for him, but he could love her. Of that he was certain.

"I made a terrible mistake," Raphael admitted.

"That's a step in the right direction," Aiyanna said wryly. Cael nodded his agreement.

"I'm going to find her," he said, determined. She was the personification of kindness and selflessness. She may forgive him. If not, he wouldn't blame her. Either way, he would make her as happy as he could for the days he had left. Never again would he treat her like this.

At the front door, she'd taken a left, her lilac scent lingering where she turned toward the French Quarter. Guilt stabbed Raphael. It was after dark in the Warehouse District. While it wasn't the worst area of New Orleans, it was by no means safe for anyone on foot who was unarmed and untrained in self-defense. If he hadn't hurt her, she would be secured, perhaps in his arms, at this very moment.

Raphael growled, quickening his pace to a sprint. Her scent suddenly became stronger. He stopped by a coffee shop so small he wouldn't have noticed it if he hadn't been looking for Mary. Inside, it was dimlylit by patrons' laptop screens and a few light bulbs on their last breaths of life. Mary sat alone on a worn couch, a chocolate concoction topped with towering whipped cream in one hand. The other held a tissue, wet from her tears.

When Mary saw him enter, she stood to leave. "I've come to apologize." Raphael held up his hands. "Please, allow me to."

Mary wiped her eyes one last time and set her drink down. "I'm not crying because of you, you know," she said with a sniff.

"Everything just ... hit me, I think."

He hoped it had. She'd adjusted to the knowledge of strange, new creatures so well he'd assumed she went into shock.

Raphael nodded solemnly, easing onto the cushion beside her. He looked into her eyes, now bright with sadness. "In ten days or less, I'm being set free." It wasn't a *complete* lie. "You will never see me again. Something angered me earlier, fueling what I said to you, but I truly thought it would be kindest if I made sure we were sufficiently separated while I'm still here."

Mary tried to speak, but Raphael held up a hand. "It was a mistake. I still have duties before I leave, but when I'm not occupied by them, I'd like to be with you." Mary inhaled sharply. Raphael pressed on. "You see the world for its beauty, and that's something I've never been able to do. If for the coming days you share your beauty with me, I swear I will rip my own heart out before I betray your trust again."

As he fell silent, Mary said nothing. She wrapped two thin arms around herself as she thought, frowning slightly. How Raphael wished he knew what she was thinking. Light hit the planes of her face, highlighting the circles under her eyes. *The first step toward making her happy is helping her get some sleep.*

Mary glared at him. "You think I'm either stupid or suicidal one moment, and the next you decide I'm some wonderful optimist. I don't understand."

"What I said was wrong," Raphael stated simply. "I'm so sorry I hurt you, scared you."

Mary laughed and picked up her drink. "You think you scared me?"

Raphael nodded. How could he *not* have? He'd gotten in her face, yelled, and torn apart the wall behind her.

She shook her head. "You may not be able to control your words, but you control your body very well. I knew you wouldn't touch me."

Raphael smiled. No one ever had such faith in him. Even when he'd been unkind to her, she still believed in him. "May I touch you now?"

"No." She clutched her drink like a weapon.

"Do you like chocolate?" Raphael asked.

Mary stared at him. "I'm female. Yes, I like chocolate," she said dryly.

"Is there coffee in that?"

She looked at him like he'd lost his mind. "Yes."

Raphael plucked the cup from her hand and threw it into the trash, her softly uttered curse following him. At the counter, he said, "I want two hot chocolates, one with extra whipped cream." He tipped the heavily tattooed man who took his order and resumed his seat.

Mary scowled at him. "Why did you do that? I liked what I had before."

"You need to rest, and hot chocolate has less caffeine."

She exhaled for a long moment, her lips forming the most perfect *O* he'd ever seen. "I hate that you're right," she grumbled. "Thank you." She clasped and then unclasped her hands.

"Do you know a lullaby that goes like this?" She hummed the first notes of what he sang to her when she was hurt. He finished the song, singing the Estonian words. She allowed him a small, wary smile. "You sang to me," she murmured. "Do you know it brought me out of a nightmare? I was reliving the night my parents were murdered."

That's why she cares for Leila. He had assumed she had no parents—he'd never had any, and could recognize the loss in others.

He'd had no idea they were murdered. He shut his eyes, more shame falling upon him. *She's been through too much in her short life.* He grieved for her. His voice cracking from emotion, Raphael asked, "May I touch you now?"

She barely inclined her head. Taking that as encouragement, he gingerly took her hand, like she'd done with him before. "I'll sing to you whenever you ask," he told her. He would do anything she wanted him to.

Mary shivered as their drinks were placed in front of them. "I'll give you one more chance," she said after she took a sip. As she licked the cream from her lips, Raphael instantly felt his body stir. "But it's only because you sang to me and know how I like my hot chocolate."

Raphael laughed, put her drink on the table, and then pulled her into his lap. "You won't regret this, *ülikena*." He pushed her soft hair from her ear and kissed it. "For the next ten days, you're *mine*."

Mary chuckled; this time her smile took over her face, lighting her up. "Only if you're mine in return."

Raphael gave her a light squeeze. "I believe we have our terms."

* * * *

Back at the firehouse, Heath waited for them by the front door. "Sebastian just got here—now we're waiting for you," he said.

Mary gave his hand a squeeze. "I'll wait up," she said with a smile.

At her words, Raphael felt hope bloom in his chest. She'd waited for him earlier, and she would do it again despite his harsh words. *What an extraordinary woman.* He ran his thumb across her cheek. "Thank you," he told her. Oh, how he *meant* it.

When Mary left, Raphael watching her hips swing to the same rhythm as her waist-length hair, Heath walked in the opposite direction, toward the garage that used to house fire trucks. Now the floors were padded and mini-fridges scattered the room, filled with raw meat and water. The chains that held them each full moon were hidden under latches in the floor. The garage door was rigged to stay permanently closed, and the door to the rest of the firehouse was latched using heavy weights on a lever.

The walls had obviously been patched up many times, but there were no obvious markings from claws, no blood smeared on the floor or walls. Too much blood was spilled each month from the werewolves trying to free themselves from their chains.

Sebastian, Cael and Alex waited at the far end of the room. Alex paced, with Sebastian glaring at him irritably, but Cael stood eerily still, his eyes following Heath and Raphael's entrance.

"Well, everyone's here." Heath shot Sebastian a pointed look.

Alex rubbed his hands together, his rings *clack*-ing against each other ominously. "Let's start with Jeremiah's involvement in human trafficking. Now *that's* someone I want to judiciously determine my fate. Don't you guys think so?"

Jeremiah's job wasn't only to report their wrongdoings to the Elders, it was also to report their progress in rehabilitating into valuable members of another werewolf pack. Without Jeremiah's word, none of them would ever be freed. Heath had been here even longer than Raphael, and they had been the only two in the *clan prohibitum* for fifty years before Alexandre's arrival, two hundred years before their relocation from France to New Orleans.

From what Raphael knew, no one had ever been freed from this clan. At least, not with Jeremiah as *lupus dux*.

"No, but our word means nothing," Sebastian said. "We can't do anything about Jeremiah."

Which was why Raphael and Heath's fates were sealed.

"We can still do something about the botos and human women they're hurting," Raphael said.

Alexandre looked at him in disbelief. "Even with all of us fully armed, with Jeremiah on their side there's no way we can beat them. Not to mention we'd have to kill humans in order to get to them."

Heath looked at Raphael, understanding dawning. "Jeremiah said the weres won't get involved unless one of our females is kidnapped," he said. "If that happened, this city would be crawling with free weres trying to get her back."

"No," Cael spat. He smoothed the rolled-up sleeves of his button-down. "We don't know what they'd do to her. I won't be responsible for another woman being hurt."

"I'm with him." Alexandre's mouth was drawn down, his eyes narrowed. "I don't see how putting one of *our* women in harm's way will help anything. Extend our sentences, probably—"

"Our sentences are never-ending!" Heath shouted, kicking a mini-fridge. It spun across the room, ripping the cord from its socket before slamming against the wall. "Don't you see? I've been here for almost *six hundred* years, and do you know what for? I challenged the alpha of my pack, but I didn't kill him. *Does that sound worthy of six hundred years to you?*"

No one spoke. As far as Raphael knew, none of them ever talked about what they'd done to merit the New Orleans clan. They were the only wolf pack here—others steered clear, thought them too dangerous for their young to be around.

Maybe they were wrong. Raphael might be the only one of them who still deserved to be here.

He'd known Heath's story for a few centuries. Heath was also the only person who knew he'd sentenced himself and why. *"You were brainwashed,"* had been Heath's response. *"If it hadn't been you, Hans would have found someone else to do the same thing. Only he may have convinced them to torture women and children."*

"You shouldn't be here, and neither should I."

Hans had tried to bring a woman or a child to Raphael more than a few times, arguing that they could also be converted to werewolves. After all, most witches were women. Raphael had so hated disappointing the man who'd treated him as a father would, praising him, criticizing him when necessary, feeding and clothing him. But he'd never considered doing as Hans asked. If only he'd looked beyond his seldom refusals, he would have seen that *everything* he'd been told to do was wrong. *So wrong.*

Raphael's only solace, his ray of light in a storm of guilt, was his refusal to harm, or even interrogate, women or children.

"We would tell this woman exactly what botos are, what they do," Raphael said. "She will know everything we know. I *don't* want her harmed—as soon as we're sure they have her, we'll alert her pack. They'll get her back within hours, and help us end the botos."

And I die knowing I helped, rather than harmed. The thought was supremely satisfying, but it wasn't enough.

Mary. If he died after having Mary, bringing her joy and saving those women, he would die happy. It was far more than what was due him, but he would have it all anyway. *I'll make Mary proud to have been with me.*

"No pack would just allow those *things* to continue," Alex muttered. "But would a woman put herself in that position?"

"We can't let her. There's no woman strong enough for this," Cael growled.

"Oh, there is." Sebastian ran a hand through his hair, making it stick up even more than normal. "I know the woman who'd *want* to do this. She could probably make the botos cry if she wanted," he said under his breath. He pointed a finger at Raphael, then Heath. "But if she is hurt in any way, I will take it out of *your* hides. And then I'll let her do the same."

"Agreed," Heath said.

Raphael nodded shortly. "Who is she?" he asked.

Sebastian cursed. "My twin sister, Sophia."

Cael turned to Sebastian, his face twisted into a grimace, his eyes slits. "You deserve whatever hell you'll find yourself in, my brother," he snarled. He roared, his claws coming free, before he stomped from the room.

"I wonder why he's been exiled," Alex said lightly.

"Can Sophia hold her own? Does she know self-defense?" Raphael asked.

Sebastian barked out a sardonic laugh. "She grew up with *me,* kicked my hairy ass half the time. Trust me, she's exactly who we'd want."

Heath clapped Sebastian on the shoulder. "Then it's settled. Contact her and let us know if she agrees to come."

As they left the garage, Alex caught Raphael's eye. "This sucks," he said.

Raphael considered his friend, Alex had always been the most even-tempered of the group, the one who'd tried to bring everyone together with humor. *He probably shouldn't be here.* "You have no idea," he said. Alex cocked his head in confusion, but Raphael strode past him, unwilling to waste a second he could be spending with Mary.

He found her in his room, sitting cross-legged on the end of his bed with a tattered paperback in her hands. When she saw him she smiled welcomingly, marking her place with a frayed bookmark. "How did—whatever that was—go?" she asked.

"Well," he said truthfully. They finally had a solution for the boto problem. Not that Raphael would allow the free pack to do all the work. He wanted to kill Richard himself.

"What's this?" He lifted the book, which had a pair of

headphones on the cover. "A music book? Do you write music?" He imagined Mary could do anything.

She laughed, shaking her head. "It involves music, but it's really about family and growing up, overcoming obstacles thrown into our lives." Rising, she placed the book in her drawer. "I've read it over and over again since Mom and Dad died. It helps." Despite her words, she didn't seem sad. Mary was *confident* as she stood before him, one hand on her hip as she assessed the man perching on her bed.

"If not music, then what?" Raphael asked curiously.

"I used to paint," Mary said wistfully. The corners of her lips tilted up. "I'll paint again, someday."

Someday would be soon, once Raphael bought her supplies. If it made her happy, she shouldn't have to wait.

Mary moved to stand in front of him. "Don't feel like you have to turn away," she said. It was her only warning before she took off her shirt, allowing the thin material to float to the floor. It took longer to peel the jeans from her shapely legs. In only a plain white bra and a pair of barely-there underwear covered in small strawberries, she climbed under the sheets of his bed. Her delicate hand patted the space next to her.

Raphael didn't need a second invitation. Too impatient even to take off his own clothes, he slid in beside her, molding her warm body against his. They fit together like pieces to a puzzle. *Mine.*

"You said I needed rest," she murmured, her body completely relaxed against his. She'd given him her complete trust, again. "Will you sing me to sleep?"

Raphael sang the Estonian lullaby as he held her, reveling in her forgiveness, healing and acceptance. She'd been through hell, and she wanted *Raphael* to sing to her. She trusted him to protect her while she slept. She was his, and he would give every part of himself to her. He felt light. This moment, knowing Mary was smiling without seeing her, knowing she would share her bed with him this night and all the others until his death, was the happiest of Raphael's life.

For the first time, he fell asleep with a woman in his arms. He would *never* willingly let this woman go.

* * * *

Mary woke to a warm body curled around her. It was the same feeling she'd had sitting in Raphael's lap—she was ridiculously comfortable, mattress commercial comfortable. If she could sell whatever it was about Raphael that caused her to relax, to finally rest her head, she would be an instant millionaire.

She squirmed in his arms, just to see what he'd do. Raphael grumbled under his breath in his sleep, the bands around her tightening protectively. She sighed, contented, deciding to give him this battle.

Yesterday, she'd been crushed by his words, but when he'd tracked her down, she could see his remorse. It physically weighed him down, as if it sat upon his shoulders. She didn't want to be the cause of such pain to anyone, and especially not Raphael. Besides, it was obvious there was something else at play, something that absolutely infuriated him. She had no idea what it was, but she hoped he would tell her.

They were running out of time. Mary didn't fully understand *why*, but she couldn't pretend to be an expert on werewolves and their rules. For all she knew, werewolf packs banned human-were relationships. Still, she wanted to know what angered him yesterday. He'd done so much for her, for Leila—she would help him through this, no matter what it was.

She turned around to watch him as he slept. It felt slightly creepy, but she couldn't help herself. The man who, out of all the werewolves in their pack, looked the most dangerous, with his rippling muscles and general darkness, literally and figuratively, was *cute* when he slept. His long, curling lashes fanned at the tops of his cheeks. Stubble shadowed his jaw. He wasn't tense or wary, but *peaceful.* She'd never seen him so at peace while awake. *Maybe I can change that.*

Raphael blinked his black eyes open, frowned at her, and pulled her tightly against his chest. "You're supposed to be resting, *ülikena,*" he mumbled.

She laughed. "I think I've rested as much as my body will let me."

His huge hands ran up her arms, resting on her shoulders. He opened his eyes fully. She felt like she could lose herself in their opaque depths. Maybe she already had.

As he awakened, his body became more and more rigid, tension showing around his mouth, tendons jumping at his neck.

"Let's see your injury," he said gruffly. Mary pulled down the sheets, again revealing her underwear-clad body, as well as the cut on her thigh that had completely healed, thanks to Aiyanna tending to it a second time. Her gris-gris didn't extend to aesthetics, however—there was a jagged, puckered scar where the cut had been. It was objectively hideous, but Mary didn't care too much. It no longer hurt her; she had nothing to complain about. She was grateful Aiyanna had extended the energy to finish healing her.

He looked at the mark, intensity flaring in his eyes.

"I know it looks ugly." She tried to cover it with her hand. "But now I can shower without hurting myself," she said lightly.

He only looked at her, his expression unreadable.

"I'm just glad to be healed," she continued.

Raphael shook his head, strands of black falling around his face. "There is *nothing* about you that isn't beautiful." Conviction laced his every word.

Mary smiled. "You really mean that." She wove her fingers through his hair and gently pulled her face to his. "I'm going to kiss you. I'm *not* asking if I can."

Her lips met his, and for a long moment, Raphael did nothing. Then he growled, his lips softening, mouth opening, his tongue seeking hers. She caressed his face as she nibbled his lip. Raphael groaned against her lips, his hands curling into fists at her waist.

She kissed him harder, grabbing his wrists and placing them on her breasts. "Yes," she whispered. "You can touch me whenever you like, however you like, for as long as you'll have me."

Raphael looked like he wanted to respond, his mouth opening and closing, but instead he pressed his face against one breast, and then another. "So soft," he said wondrously.

He kissed every inch of them, kneaded them gently. He hissed in displeasure when she leaned away from him. "I'm taking my bra off." She laughed.

Gazing at her breasts like they were precious, Raphael palmed them softly as if afraid she would cover them back up. His tenderness brought tears to her eyes. "Kiss me again," she implored.

He did, taking her mouth in a kiss so passionate, he couldn't possibly *want* to leave soon. She ran her hand up and down his T-shirt-covered chest and torso, finding herself sinking her fingers into the chiseled grooves of his abs. *This* was a body she wanted to explore in-depth.

Too soon he broke away, placing unnecessary distance between them. "There are things I have to do," he said raggedly, vaguely. Mary hoped it was as hard for him to stop as it was for her. She was nowhere near ready to be separated from his body. She positively *ached* for his touch.

Raphael stood. The hand he held out to her shook. She was glad. He helped her rise before he changed into a clean set of clothes. His erection stood proudly under his shorts until Raphael adjusted himself, shooting her a half-amused, half-accusing look that did nothing but feed the fire inside her. She barely kept her hands to herself as he strapped a covered machete to his back.

Raphael marched to the door and turned, cursing, before sweeping Mary to him and crushing her mouth against his. For a long moment they kissed, his tongue dancing with hers. When he pulled away, Mary so badly wanted to ask him what he was about to do, if she could help.

The question died on her lips when he brought the palm of her hand up for a kiss. "We will continue this later," he told her, his expression grave. It was a promise Mary prayed he would be able to keep.

Mary couldn't stop herself from saying, "Please be safe today ... in whatever you're doing."

For a moment, he looked as if he wanted to smile, his shoulders straightening. Instead, he kept his expression stern as he finally left the room, his "I will," drifting back toward her.

With Raphael gone, Mary decided to rinse the rest of the horrible dye from her hair, no matter how many washes it took. She needed a cold shower, anyway. Today she would make herself feel beautiful. She would buy herself a couple of new things, just like she used to, to boost her confidence. She could use some mascara and lip-gloss.

It wasn't for Raphael, but for her. He'd made it perfectly clear where he stood on how she looked, the truth of how he felt making her spirits soar. But after her time working for Richard, she needed to reevaluate her own image of herself. For too long she'd been afraid to feel beautiful.

Now, she needed to. She wanted to make the best of her time with Raphael, and she wouldn't allow herself to feel anything less than gorgeous with him. It was only fair, considering his incredible sex appeal. She *was* turning her life around. She wanted to be with a man for the first time since college. She knew she was taking a risk, being with this man for such a short time, *knowing* he would leave her.

The thing was, there was no real choice for Mary. She wanted Raphael however she could get him. *But will I ever want another man?*

At that particular moment, she didn't care.

Chapter 7

Jeremiah's phone rang, and most of his callers didn't react well when their calls went ignored. He didn't mind. They paid him so handsomely that he'd have daily phone sex with his "clients" if they so desired. Money was money, after all.

Jeremiah excused himself from his titillating conversation with Richard, the leader of the encantados who'd recently relocated to the largest mansion in Lakeview. As he waved away the two women assigned to him for the night, he laughed inwardly at the confusion in their eyes. The river shapeshifters really did a number on their women's minds. It was pathetic, really, how weak humans were. He was genuinely surprised there were still so many of them—by now, he would have expected them to be closer to their inevitable extinction.

On the third ring, he picked up. "Hey," he said, careful to keep his voice pleasant.

"Is it done?" the man demanded.

Jeremiah sighed. "The Elders are being difficult—" A dissatisfied grunt on the other end. "—but I'll make sure your problem is eliminated."

"You'd better."

The other man clicked off. Jeremiah stuffed his phone into his pocket and rejoined the party, more than one feminine hand slipping around his waist.

His plan was taking longer than he'd anticipated, but eventually he would get what he wanted, what his "client" so desperately needed. He was a *lupus dux*—his word was law.

* * * *

Sebastian ignored the constant buzzing of his flip phone, turning up the ring volume on his other phone, the latest souped-up smartphone. He peered out the large bay window of his office, hovering over the brewhouse below. His clan *technically* owned the brewery, as it would go to Cael in the case where something happened to Sebastian. They needed an income, and outside help would never be given to them.

Nothing seemed amiss—there were no fires, no unauthorized workers. Then why was his second-in-command, a witch named Harry, blowing up his work phone?

Finally, the call he'd been anticipating, dreading, came through. His shiny new phone glittered, the name *Sophia* gleaming. His twin, the only woman on this Earth who could make him come *this close* to committing murder, who knew all the right buttons to set him off. He'd rather die for her than put her in danger, and he knew she felt the same way for him. He'd seen for himself when he'd received his sentencing. The way she'd acted could have earned herself an extended trip to New Orleans. But the pack leaders had been lenient. *"She's a female, after all,"* they'd said.

Sebastian knew Sophia had never been more furious.

As she would be now, if he didn't pick up his damned phone. *Please say no.* He clicked the green bar.

"I'm coming, of course," Sophia said in greeting.

Sebastian felt as if a two-ton rock had been placed on his chest. "You don't have to," he said as calmly as he could. "*No one* could blame you if you don't want to do this. You'll be placing yourself in an extremely unpredictable, dangerous situation."

Sophia scoffed, as he'd known she would. His sister was the epitome of strength. Never in her life had she cowered before anything, even when she should have. But she'd never, ever lost a fight. Her will to live was even stronger than the fiery spark of unruliness within her.

Sebastian had known she would be thrown to the botos as soon as the idea was presented. She was, quite simply, the only woman for the job. Many, if not most, werewolf women were babied, raised to remain fragile and meek. Sophia had something else the other women didn't—she understood what it was for a man to force himself upon an unwilling partner. Her attacker hadn't been successful, but it was a night that had changed both his and his sister's lives forever. He'd held her as she cried, helped her bandage the wounds the man had given her. If she could prevent such actions toward other women, he knew she would without hesitation.

He was so proud of her, so *terrified* for her.

"Bastian, I won't be there long—our pack thinks I'm so weak and helpless, they'll get there within an hour of hearing I've been kidnapped." The last part was murmured bitterly, resentment coating her voice.

"It only takes a second for you to be seriously hurt," Sebastian reminded her. "Think on that."

Sophia took a deep breath, most likely telling herself to be patient with him. "It would be *wrong* for me to sit on my happy ass when I can do something to help these poor humans. You know that," she snapped. "Besides, I've never lost a fight."

"I know," Sebastian answered. She brought it up most times she spoke with him. She was right on both points, and at the moment he *hated* it.

"I'll be at the firehouse on the day after the last night of the full moon. I'm going to pretend I'm a human—I don't need them *knowing* I can light them up like matches."

Sophia's element was fire, just as Sebastian's had been before it was taken away from him. As always, the reminder of his loss stung like a slap to the face.

"I'm sorry, brother," Sophia said softly. *Brother* was an endearment she only used when she'd decided he deserved to be acknowledged as such.

"It's all right, Soph," Sebastian said. "Make me a promise?"

"Anything," she answered instantly.

"Find out what you can about the creatures who will take you. You may find something we don't know—I've told you everything we have. If for *any* reason you decide to back out, don't hesitate to. We'll ask no questions of it."

Sophia paused for a moment. "I promise," she said. "I love you, Sebastian."

"Love you too, sis."

"See you Saturday."

Sophia clicked off, and Sebastian gripped the phone so hard the screen cracked. He wanted to kill that *entire* organization, human guards and Jeremiah included. He would flip open his favorite Zippo and spread the fire into a sword, cutting through all of the evil until there was none left.

But there were rules he had to obey. It would be impossible for him to ever gain his freedom if he followed his base instincts like an animal.

Someone rapped on the door. Sebastian cursed, opened it to find Harry. The young mortal was angry, as evidenced by the fire engine red hair he'd tied in a loop at the base of his neck. "Why haven't you picked up the phone?" he barked, his hair changing to the color of blood.

"I've been busy with other matters."

Harry stormed past to point at the brewhouse beneath them. "Everything that has gone through our brew kettles today, and I mean *everything,* has been poisoned. Our taste testers are all sick, leaving me as guinea pig for the rest of the day. Who has beef with you, man?"

I'm so stupid. It was only a matter of time before Jeremiah told the botos about Full Moon Brewery. Hell, it wasn't as if they were subtle. There was a Cael's Pale Ale, for Pete's sake, something that brought endless amusement to Sebastian, and an equal amount of ire to Cael.

With the botos' mind control capabilities, they could have coerced any members of his staff to poison the beer, and none of his employees would be at fault. No humans could be allowed in the brewery until all of the botos were dead. *They will die, one way or another.*

Sebastian explained the situation to Harry. He trusted the witch; it had been Harry's idea to place a Smart Sober spell on each brew, ensuring no humans accidentally drove or did something else equally stupid while drunk. Sebastian's justification had been self-serving; he didn't want to be accused of killing humans. Harry, apparently, just liked humans and beer. Either way, Harry had become a vital part of Full Moon.

"We're going to be grossly understaffed." Harry frowned. His hair turned a light shade of orange, indicating he was nervous. He didn't like change. Sebastian had noted his hair turned that color every time he added or took away a particular brew, or changed a recipe.

"I'll pay you double if you help me straighten this out," Sebastian said. They had distributers to satisfy, and he wasn't about to let those botos cost him a dime.

It was either throw himself into work or obsess over what state he would find his sister in on Sunday. One, he could control. The other, he would have to trust Sophia's grit and luck, and their Canadian pack. They had betrayed him—would they betray Sophia? Would the botos end her perfect fighting record?

Sebastian closed his eyes and took a deep breath. "Who was poisoned?"

Harry rattled off a half dozen names, and Sebastian shook his head. He had work to do. He had beer to make, and a clan of unemployed werewolves to fund. They needed the money, because Sebastian was going to finally buy that fancy flamethrower he'd been lusting over.

* * * *

After Leila left for Tulane with Alex, Mary fetched her purse from the room she'd started to consider both hers and Raphael's. She needed to work a few things out with Leila, but before her morning classes was not that time. Resolving to speak to her sister later, she put her mind to the task at hand: shopping.

Mary didn't make it out the front door.

"Where are you going?" Cael folded his arms across his chest. The man may as well have come from thin air, he'd moved so silently.

"I want to go buy a few things," Mary said, disconcerted as always by his harsh disposition. He looked ready to kill. "Why, do you need anything?"

Cael shook his head, turned, and lifted a phone to his ear. "Hey, I need you to come over here." He paused. "Just hurry," he snapped before hanging up.

Unease wrapped around Mary. Who had he called? "I'll ... see you," she said awkwardly. She sprinted for the door, but Cael made it before her. He casually stretched his arms out, blocking her in.

"I called Aiyanna." He actually smiled. "I want her to go to the stores with you."

"Why?" It was daylight outside, and Mary hardly planned to go near the seedy parts of the city. She'd never felt unsafe at the mall before.

"Humor me this one time?" Cael asked.

The door swung back behind him, revealing a grinning Aiyanna. "He knows how much I like shopping." She reached around to squeeze him in tight hug.

For a split second, an expression of pure bliss crossed Cael's face. It quickly turned to disgust. He pushed Aiyanna away. She ignored him, linking her arms with Mary. "Bye, love," she called over her shoulder. Cael released an exasperated sigh. Aiyanna pulled Mary out the door.

Aiyanna and Cael have a strange relationship. Well, glass houses. You're falling for a man who's leaving soon. At least Cael and Aiyanna had time on their sides, even if Cael didn't seem to want it.

She steered Mary to a white, two-passenger convertible. "So where are we going?"

"The drugstore. I need to get some stronger shampoo." Mary lifted up her barely-brown hair. "And some makeup."

Aiyanna nodded. "Where else?"

Mary rattled off the name of a fairly inexpensive clothing store. If she bought a single pair of nice jeans and a cute top, it would be a successful trip.

Ten minutes later, Aiyanna pulled up to one of the most exclusive hair salons in the city. Embarrassment flooded Mary; she couldn't afford to walk into such a place, much less have anything done.

"I think a Rite Aid would be better—"

"Just shut up and come with me."

Mary grabbed Aiyanna's arm and pulled back until she stopped. "I can't *pay* for this," she managed.

Aiyanna put both her hands on Mary's shoulders and looked her straight in the eye. "Think of me as your panther godmother," she said. Her golden eyes softened. "I know your prince charming is going to turn into a pumpkin soon, and I know what it's like to want something that's impossible. I think it's holding on and laughing in the face of tragic odds, *that's* what creates hope. Let me help you."

She was right—hold on was exactly what Mary would do, for as long as she possibly could. She'd just gotten her first taste of Raphael, and she knew a matter of days wouldn't be enough. *Maybe Aiyanna knows something I don't.* "What do you know about werewolf packs? Do they normally prevent freed weres from dating humans?"

Aiyanna just looked at Mary, her eyes narrowing slightly. "That's between Raphael and you," she said. "I'm not touching that conversation."

A handsome man in a deep V-neck and sunglasses stood at the entrance of the salon, his arms crossed over his chest. He lifted a sculpted brow at them.

"Nik's getting impatient." Aiyanna rolled her eyes. "Trust me, he's too good for us to piss him off."

For the rest of the day, Mary lived the life she'd seen, but had never been able to touch. Aiyanna gave a gold credit card to Nik, who in turn left Mary's hair silky, shiny and its trademark Newman blonde. He dabbed a bit of makeup on her face before she bought it, too. Mary almost cried when he turned her chair around to face the mirror.

The emotions didn't come from feeling pretty. For the first time in years, she felt like *herself.* She didn't say anything to Aiyanna, who had tears in her eyes as well, but Mary thought she understood.

Mary liked who she'd been before her life had changed, but she didn't want to be that person, either. Too much had happened, too much changed her. Maybe there was room for both versions of herself: the sorority girl who loved to paint and flirt, and the cautious mother hen.

After today, she could add another identity to her list: *sexy.* In college, one drunken sexual mishap made her steer clear of future mistakes. She'd flirted and dated, but never tried to be overtly sexual. As she stood, blushing, next to a laughing Aiyanna in a lingerie store that sold everything from leather bustiers and whips to thongs made entirely from feathers, she decided she could be overtly sexual. She was twenty-five. It was about time she had a black lace bra and panty set.

It turned into black, red and white sets to go under an inordinate amount of clothes Mary bought at a few stores Aiyanna picked out. Sitting in front of a bakery, cups of gelato in hand, Mary felt more comfortable in her skin than ever. She couldn't wait to show Leila, who constantly called her drab. Most of all she wanted Raphael to see her, to hunger for her the way she hungered for him. Maybe this time, he wouldn't be able to pull away.

A short, stocky man stood across Magazine Street, watching her. Mary openly stared back at him until he turned his gaze elsewhere, ambling off toward the river. "Who was that?" Aiyanna asked. She was watching the man curiously.

"I have no idea." Mary shrugged. "Maybe he thought I'm someone he knows."

"Hmmm," Aiyanna said. She pointed at Mary with her spoon. "There's a guy you should watch out for, but if you tell any of the dogs I'll deny saying a word."

Mary nodded. "I won't mention it."

Aiyanna glanced around, as if afraid she'd be overheard. "His name is Jeremiah; he's basically their warden and jury, all in one.

He has dark curly hair down to his shoulders and cold eyes. That's all I'll say about him." She clapped her hands together. "Now, for our last stop."

Mary didn't think she could possibly buy anything more—there literally wasn't anything left to buy, or any room left in Aiyanna's trunk.

Aiyanna and Mary pulled up to a veterinary clinic with a beautiful mural of tropical animals covering an entire side of the building. The man from Magazine Street walked by, puzzling Mary, but she was more concerned with their reasoning for visiting a vet.

Aiyanna held up a hand to silence Mary's questions. She walked inside, Mary following warily through a few sets of doors, hesitating at a sign that read VETERINARY PERSONNEL ONLY. Aiyanna had already passed through. Mary did the same, finding the shapeshifter facing an older Native American man she assumed was the vet.

"Hey, Ofi," Aiyanna said casually, despite the doctor's nametag reading NEKA PREJEAN, DVM. "I need three dozen tranquilizers loaded into at least six or seven guns."

The man inclined his head and turned to rifle through the sterile-looking cabinets behind him. Mary gaped. Did he normally hand out tranquilizers like candy, or was Aiyanna a special client? Mary suspected it was the latter, and wondered what else her friend had come to the vet for over the years. Which brought her next question. *Why does she need thirty-six tranquilizers?*

When she asked Aiyanna, she responded without missing a beat. "Thirty are for Cael, just to screw with him. The others are just in case his buddies start to notice what I'm doing and try to intervene."

The vet chuckled.

Mary blinked. "Try again," she said.

When Dr. Prejean brought them the guns, Aiyanna surprised Mary by giving them to her. "You need to hide these in the house." Instead of using the card, she handed a wad of bills to the doctor. "Make sure no one but you knows where they are."

"Why?"

They left the clinic, Aiyanna twisting her mouth as if debating what to tell her. "I'm willing to bet my beautiful car," she said slowly, tapping the hood, "that humans will attack the firehouse in the next few days. When they do, take out these guns and give them to the werewolves. I'm not there quite as often as you are, which is why you're taking care of this."

Why would humans attack the firehouse, and why would the men need tranquilizer guns to defend themselves?

"Werewolves can't kill humans?" Mary asked.

Aiyanna rolled her eyes and shook her head. "Werewolves can kill whoever they want." There was a hint of anger in her voice. "*Exiled* werewolves can't kill humans. Something about restraint and punishment, blah blah."

Mary imagined Raphael didn't mind that rule. What reason would they have to kill humans, anyway? Even without all their powers, human men were no match for the men of their small pack. They shouldn't *have* to kill.

But if the werewolves were vastly outnumbered, or the men were armed ... they would be at a major disadvantage, one that could cost them their lives. They *needed* those tranquilizer guns. Which brought Mary back to her first question.

"Why would humans attack them?"

Aiyanna gave Mary a hard look. "What do you think your old boss is?"

Since waking up in Raphael's bed, Mary had tried her best not to think about Richard. His image in her mind brought humiliation and insecurities with it, but she shoved them away. *It's over. There's no reason to focus on that.* Richard couldn't be human; he had razor-sharp teeth when he wished, and his eyes turned an oily black. He'd thought he could control her. Was he the reason the firehouse would be attacked?

"Not human." A hard knot settled in Mary's stomach. "Tell me what he is, and why he wants to hurt our men."

As Aiyanna spoke, Mary's dread increased. *I've endangered all of us.* The tranquilizers would have to be enough to protect herself and the werewolves, but they weren't enough for Leila or Molly. Neither of them could be anywhere near the firehouse for a while.

There was no reason to place them in the line of fire.

Mind control. Mary shuddered. Botos were capable of so much evil, it was unimaginable. Those humans probably didn't want to hurt *anyone.* Regret whipped at Mary, sending her stinging reminders of every chance she could have taken to leave her old job sooner, every time it had been obvious, so obvious that there was nothing remotely good about Richard.

She'd royally miscalculated, but she could help fix things now. The first thing she had to do was have a discussion with both Wish and Leila. She wasn't a child, but she was Mary's charge until she finished college. Her parents would have wanted it so. Leila would leave with Molly and Wish until the firehouse was safe.

Mary would stay and help the werewolves. When it came down to it, they couldn't kill, but there was nothing to stop Mary. If she had to kill a boto or a controlled human in order to save Raphael, she would do it without hesitation.

Nothing could hurt that man, not so close to his hard-won freedom. She'd make sure of it.

* * * *

It had been a fruitless day.

Raphael, Alex and Heath watched the mansion on the lake for hours. They saw no glimpses of botos or Jeremiah: every single being that crossed the manicured lawn was human. Armed guards patrolled the perimeter, just as they had before. Raphael assumed they'd been told to forfeit their lives if need be in order to protect the botos. It chilled him.

Worse were the men who the guards allowed inside. Raphael didn't think about what they were doing there. If he did, he knew he would kill the humans for their crimes against those women.

They had learned what they already suspected—the humans were never allowed to leave. There were two guards Raphael watched in particular, and in a span of five hours neither spoke with anyone else or gave himself a break. They didn't eat or drink. The men simply watched, their eyes darting as if intruders would make a beeline straight for their throats. The botos had made them terrified for their very lives, that much was obvious.

It also made the men that much more lethal. A man would do almost anything to simply *live*.

Ultimately, amid Alex's complaints for food and Heath's inability to stand still for longer than a moment, they'd left after accomplishing nothing. *I can't do anything.* Raphael desperately wished there was something, *anything*, he could feasibly do.

Otherwise, why should he spend his days apart from Mary? Leaving her that morning had been nearly impossible, and he'd gained nothing for it.

He'd kissed a woman for the first time and loved it. He knew it was because of Mary. Only she had ever given him a taste of the life he'd always wanted, but known he would never have. Mary trusted him with her body, and she'd honored him with her permission to do whatever he wished. He would do what he wanted, he decided, so long as it pleased her.

Finally, he would mark her, maybe in multiple places.

Maybe he could lounge with her, learning this woman he'd claimed as his own for his last number of days. *I would die with a smile on my face.*

"Hey look, Aiyanna's here." Alex swung from the car onto the sidewalk. "I wonder how much she'll charge me to clean my room again."

"Just do your own damn laundry," Heath muttered, wiping off his already spotless dagger.

"I've *never* done laundry," Alex said, affronted.

Another squabble, and one much more likely to turn violent, was taking place just inside the firehouse's foyer. Aiyanna was waving her hands around as Cael stood eerily still beside the pole, easily accomplishing what Heath had struggled to do all day. Leila stood beside them, shifting awkwardly as if she didn't know whether or not she could leave without their noticing.

"*You* called *me*, remember?" Aiyanna shouted.

"I didn't ask you to take my credit card."

Raphael couldn't help but smile. Aiyanna drove Cael absolutely crazy on a near-daily basis. Cael thought she was the bane of his existence, but Raphael suspected she was the highlight.

Leila watched the exchange with rounded eyes. She tried to slink away, but Aiyanna shot her a warning glance, effectively freezing her in place.

"I'm sorry, I had no idea you'd *mind* so much!" Aiyanna exclaimed. "Don't you think it's okay to steal your boyfriend's credit card?"

Leila signed, *No,* shaking her head vehemently.

"See, she agrees with me!" Aiyanna said vehemently.

"I'm not your boyfriend," Cael barked.

"Sure you're not."

Raphael put himself between them, earning a growl from Cael. "Get a room," he told them. "Leila, come with me."

"I'm *not* with her," Cael roared from behind him. He thought he heard Aiyanna shove Cael before leaving, slamming the door behind her with a *bang.*

"I'm hungry; want anything?" Raphael asked Leila. She nodded eagerly, and he led her to the kitchen.

"Sandwiches okay with you?" He took out some brioche bread and a few meats and cheeses. Leila nodded again, signing *Chicken and Swiss, please.*

After they ate, Leila stopped Raphael from putting the bread away. *Peanut butter toast on brioche bread is Mary's favorite thing,* she signed. *You should make her some.*

Raphael did, putting it on one of their nicer—not cracked—plates.

"What else does Mary like?" he asked. He liked the idea of wooing her. It would be like the courtships he'd seen over the years. *That's exactly what I'll do.*

Leila scrunched up her nose, thinking. She looked a lot like Mary; they both had fair skin and long, straight hair, though the dye made Mary's hair significantly darker. She had blue eyes, while Mary's were the color of leaves in the spring. Their builds were similar, but Leila was covered in muscle, while Mary was far too thin. Still, Mary was more beautiful. She was a magnet he couldn't draw away from.

She was the smiling face of his absolution.

When Leila started signing, she signed fast, excitedly. *She loves things that are sweet and salty, like chocolate with popcorn, or fries dipped in milkshakes. Her favorite movie is* Legally Blonde, *because she's convinced Delta Nu was based on her college sorority. She loves romance novels and that po-boy shop in the Irish Channel that used to have a* South Park *pinball machine.*

Leila's smile turned sad. *Most of all, she likes to paint. She hasn't painted since our parents died, but I know she wants to every day. She used to be considered one of the best upcoming artists.*

"What did she paint with?" Raphael asked. He'd already planned to buy her all the supplies she needed begin painting again.

Oils, Leila signed.

Raphael nodded, recalling a nearby shop that sold paints and materials for art. Leila waved in front of his face. *Richard did something to her, but you're fixing it. Please, keep doing whatever you're doing.*

Pure happiness burst through Raphael, touching his every cell. He felt himself grinning from ear to ear. *I've brought Mary joy. I've helped her.*

He'd never made another person's life better, but that would change with Mary. He just had to make sure she never learned of his death. It would hurt her, and he couldn't allow that.

Mary swept into the room, her head held high, shoulders straight. Her hair was a trace more golden than her sister's almost-white hair, and her lips were redder than usual. She radiated confidence, something Raphael hadn't noticed before. His Mary was truly breathtaking.

When she saw him, she smiled brightly, sauntered up to him and surprised him, giving him a light, too-quick kiss on his mouth. On a reflex, he growled and pulled her back for another. She allowed it for a moment before breaking the kiss, jerking her head in Leila's direction.

Leila winked at him.

Mary took his hand. "I need to talk to Leila. Can I come find you in about an hour?" She leaned in, kissed his cheek and whispered, "You promised we'd pick up where we left off this morning."

Raphael straightened, nodded. "We will, *ülikena.*"

He thanked Leila and left the kitchen, hating the distance he put between them, but he had a few people he needed to speak to as well. He was surprised to find the man he was looking for in the living room, playing Alex's racing game. Sebastian glanced at Raphael and cursed, the split-second lapse causing his car to plummet off some sort of winding road in outer space.

"Do you have property with plenty of windows and light?" Raphael asked. Sebastian ran the brewery and used some of that money to invest in rental property all over the city. He even owned the building that housed one of the more popular bars on St. Charles Avenue and fed the renters a steady stream of Full Moon beer for a discount.

Basically, Sebastian made it so none of them ever had to worry about money. That included Aiyanna, whether she knew it or not, and now Mary and Leila.

"I do," Sebastian said. "It's only a few blocks from here. Want it?" Sebastian liked to make money, but he was equally as generous with it. It was one of the reasons Raphael liked him; if someone in the pack needed something, Sebastian always did the best he could to help, no questions asked—unless it was Alexandre asking. The last time he'd needed money, he'd tried to buy a strip club on Bourbon Street. After a few days he'd grown bored of the place, fired all the dancers and handed the deed back to Sebastian.

"I want it," Raphael said, "but not for me. Put it in Mary's name—it's going to be her art studio."

"She's an artist?" Sebastian asked. He had the same hungry look in his eye he'd had when he first thought to buy property. "I can hook her up with some big name galleries. I'll take a finder's fee, of course."

Raphael wondered what her paintings looked like, wished he would be able to see one. He knew with certainty they would depict how she saw the world, with relentless hope and unwavering love. Sebastian would be smart to invest in Mary, and Raphael told him so.

"I'll make sure she's taken care of," Sebastian said. "Heath already spoke to me about it. You don't need to worry about how she'll be ... after."

Raphael nodded, emotion nearly choking him. He didn't doubt his friend. He knew bone-deep that he could trust Sebastian, Alex, and Cael to watch over Mary and Leila. He was relieved Alex had taken such an interest in Leila, meaning he'd always look out for Mary as well. These men were his friends. They were convicts, but Raphael was starting to doubt the werewolf judicial system more with each hour that passed.

His friends rallied to save human women, risking their lives in doing so. They took care of each other and those they cared about, and had never once betrayed each other. None had committed any serious crimes since moving into the firehouse; they never set out to hurt another being.

None of them deserve exile. They've earned their powers back, earned their freedom back.

They probably would never get it, and Heath would die for his loyalty.

Doubting his ability to speak, Raphael clapped Sebastian on the shoulder and grabbed a controller. They raced a few times—Raphael lost all three games. He didn't understand how pressing a button on a piece of plastic could emulate driving a racecar. His car slid into a pit of lava. "Do you know what a Delta Nu is?" he asked.

"Oh, man." Sebastian grinned. "I think I know what you're talking about. Those things are so *girly,* but I can help you get one."

Raphael didn't care; he was going to court Mary. When they parted ways, she would have no doubt how he felt about her. She would know she was *his,* whether he could be with her or not.

Chapter 8

What's up? Leila signed.

She looked happy. A smile played at her mouth, and a secret glinted in her eye.

"First, tell me what's up with you," Mary said. One of her favorite scents wafted toward her; on the counter were two pieces of toast liberally spread with peanut butter. "Those had better be for me!" she exclaimed, grabbing the plate.

Raphael fixed it for you, Leila signed.

Mary sighed around a mouthful of toasted brioche. "This is why we like him," she said. "Your day?" she prodded.

Leila hopped on the counter and swung her feet, her toes habitually pointed. *One of my dance professors pulled me aside after class,* she signed. *Apparently Richard went to the arts counsel and asked them to rescind my scholarship.* Mary's heart sank, but Leila beamed. *They told him no—they think I'm the best dancer for the award, and they're renewing it for my senior year!*

Mary put down her toast and pulled Leila into a tight hug. "I'm so proud of you," she said. "Look how your hard work has paid off; dance companies are going to *beg* for you after you graduate."

Another weight had been lifted. Mary had expected Richard to try and take away Leila's scholarship, but she hadn't known what to expect of the counsel, the ones who had the real power. She wanted to kiss each and every one of them. *People can be good.* Things really were looking up.

Even so, Leila had to move from the house. Mary already spoke with Wish, who agreed to let Leila stay at his home right near Tulane's campus. He wouldn't let any harm come to Leila or Molly. Mary had had no idea he was a professor—still didn't understand *how* he taught, considering his undead status—but it was apparent he was very educated. *Maybe someday I'll finish my degree.* First, she had to get her sister somewhere safe.

"I need you to go live with Wish for a while," she said. "Please, trust me. The same people who hurt me before may attack here."

Leila slammed her palms on the counter, causing the cabinets to shake. *I can help,* she signed. *I'm not a child.*

No, she wasn't. Mary shook her head, putting her arm around her sister.

"You're a student, and your studies have to come first." She squeezed Leila's shoulder. "The firehouse is going to be a distraction for a few days, not to mention *dangerous.* The semester ends in a few weeks anyway. Finish strong."

You'll come by and let me know how everything's going, right?

"I'll keep you updated on everything," Mary promised. "As soon as you can, you'll be back here."

Leila nodded. *Thank you, Mary,* she signed, *for everything.*

Tears stung Mary's eyes. Everything they'd gone through had been worth it. She'd made mistakes but the fact was her goal was being met. Leila would be okay. *Better than okay. She's going to live her dreams.*

"Let me help you get your things together," Mary said. Leila nodded, wiped away her own tear. They left the kitchen together, arms linked.

* * * *

"You can come with us," Wish said seriously. Beside him, Molly clutched his hand like a life raft. She wore a shirt depicting the cover of *To Kill a Mockingbird.* Mary couldn't help but hug the man, startling him.

"I can't," she told him, "but I appreciate the offer." She raised a hand, blocking her mouth from Molly's view. "I think she knows who you are," she whispered.

Wish puffed up his chest proudly, a grin spreading across his face. He looked up when footsteps sounded down the hall, his expression turning wary. Cael followed Leila to the foyer, one of her bags in one hand, and a masculine-looking bag in the other.

He's coming to stay with us, Leila signed.

"Added protection." Cael set down his bag. "Don't worry, I'll come back here for the full moon."

He held up his hand for Molly, who slapped it in a high-five without taking her other hand from her father's grip. Cael smiled at her. For the first time, Mary thought he looked genuinely content. It seemed to be good enough for Wish, who relaxed slightly, floating upward an extra inch.

Mary watched as the motley crew filed out, Leila giving her one last wave over her shoulder.

A warm body pressed up against hers, strong arms wrapping protectively around her waist. "Why are they leaving?" he asked, his voice rumbling through her.

"I didn't think it would be safe for Molly or Leila." Mary leaned back against him, uncaring of her hair catching in the stubble on his chin. "Aiyanna told me the botos might attack here."

Raphael gently turned her to face him, sliding his large hand down to the small of her back. Mary reached up and untied his dark hair, watching it fall around his face.

"Why didn't you go with them?" Raphael asked.

Mary rubbed a hand over his collarbone, covered by the thin cotton of his shirt. "I wanted to help you," she said, meeting his gaze. "I can kill humans who threaten us."

"Aiyanna told you too much," Raphael grumbled. He scooped her up in his arms, making for his room.

"Where's Leila?" Alex called as they passed.

"She left for a few days," Mary answered. "Don't worry, Cael went with them."

Alexandre roared. Mary thought she heard him punch something. Raphael looked down at her, arching a brow. "That was a mistake," he said wryly. Mary elbowed him in the gut, earning a grunt from Raphael.

When they reached his room Mary shut the door behind them, flashing Raphael her most wicked grin.

He threw her on his bed with a smile of his own, following her down. She released a surprised gasp at his weight, and he quickly flipped them over so she was draped across him. His chest rose and fell rapidly; he was breathing hard, and the hand at his side clenched. She glanced up at him to see his eyes closed.

Raphael didn't resist when she peeled his black shirt up, obediently lifting his arms for her to take it off. She did, marveling at the vast expanse of his chest. His skin was deeply bronzed over the taut muscles that covered him. Yet somehow, he was the most wonderful cushion she would ever find. *He* was becoming her favorite place to rest her head. A few thin scars dotted his left side, over his ribs. She traced them with her fingers.

"What are these?"

Raphael watched her hungrily, giving Mary chills. "A few humans tried to mug me," he said. "They stabbed me three times. Aiyanna healed me."

Mary gasped, covering her marks with her hand. He'd been *stabbed.* "What did you do to them?"

Raphael lifted his shoulders in a shrug. "Nothing. They were just kids. Younger than Leila."

Mary wasn't surprised. It was too easy for some to fall into the wrong crowds here, especially teenagers. She'd been lucky, having been sheltered for so long. That Raphael was merciful toward them, hadn't thought to retaliate... She slid up his body until her face was level with his. Her hair fell on either side of them. "You're a good man, Raphael," she told him, her lips less than an inch from his. She leaned down to kiss him. *You're also* my *man.*

His hands cradled her face as they kissed. She felt his erection against her leg, yet his focus was on her face, her lips. She took his shoulders, pulling him even closer to her, and just held on.

Raphael's kiss was sweet and hungry, gentle but restrained. She tore her mouth away. He growled, his eyes narrowing at her. "Stop holding back," she said. "I want *you,* Raphael, not who you think you have to be."

She could sleep with him right now and never regret it. Raphael would never be one of her mistakes.

Raphael's eyes blazed with emotion, but he said nothing, flipping them over again, pinning her underneath him. He lifted himself onto his elbows, relieving her of his weight. He gently brushed her hair from her neck, kissing her from ear to collarbone.

Then he brought his knee up between her legs and bit her throat gently, kissing the mark she was sure he left. She'd never felt like this in her life. Her body was on fire, begging for more of his touch.

"*Mine,*" he growled, his hand drifting to her chest.

Mary was aching against her shirt. The fabric felt heavy against her; she wanted it *off,* wanted Raphael's hands on her skin. "Take it off," she gasped. Raphael swiftly lifted it over her head, unsnapped the front clasp of her bra. When he brought one of her breasts to his mouth, she inhaled sharply.

Her Raphael knew how to use his tongue.

She ran her hands up and down his hard back as he laved her breasts. When she pulled at the waistband of his shorts he stopped, leaving her feeling cold. She shot him a frown. He smiled in return, again revealing those devastating dimples.

Raphael took her hands in his and kissed her sweetly before rolling to his side. "Where I'm from," he said, placing a kiss to her wrist, "a man courts a woman before making her his. I'd like to court you." His smile turned wicked. "I promise, in time I will have you."

"Courting, huh?" Mary mused. In college, if a date included dinner the guy was considered old-fashioned. Most of her friends considered trysts in fraternity houses "dating," no courtship required.

Could this man be any sweeter?

"Sounds like fun," she said, running her fingers through his hair, "but I'm going to court *you* first."

"You are?" he asked, surprise coating his voice.

"Yes." She rose, putting on her shirt and bra. "Starting now." She raised her eyebrows at him. "*I* may prefer you without a shirt, but that may be frowned upon in public places."

Raphael finally pulled his shirt back on. Mary held out her hand to him; he took it with no hesitation.

"I see how you punish yourself, how you restrain yourself." She pulled him closer to her. "I can't convince you that you're wonderful, which you are." She put her hand to his chest. "But I can to show you how I treat the most kind-hearted man I know."

She kissed him, ignoring his bemused expression, and led him from the room. "I hope you're up for a walk."

Mary took him to Café du Monde, where they bought beignets to go. As always, she bought hot chocolate, despite the heat. She showed him her favorite spot to sit along the river, where she liked to watch boats and barges slowly pass.

"I can't believe you've never had a beignet before," she exclaimed. Growing up here, she'd rarely been allowed to venture downtown. Now that she was older the old coffee stand had become a treat she'd gifted herself whenever she could afford it.

Raphael grunted, the pile of powdered sugar atop the beignet he was biting into blowing into a cloud. The tough werewolf was unfortunately clad in black, which was now dotted with puffs of sugar. Mary couldn't help but laugh, so hard she was clutching her middle, rocking on the bench.

He blew the sugar at her, catching her in the face.

"Do you like it?" she asked, gasping for breath.

Raphael drew her in for a kiss. "Yes," he said, "but I like you better." He tasted sweet. She kissed away some sugar that landed by his ear.

She loved seeing him like this. He was *playful.* The man needed playfulness, she decided. There was no shadow over his features, no weight upon his shoulders. He was just a man on a date, absently patting his now-gray shirt.

As she watched him steal one of her beignets, she knew she would give him everything she had.

* * * *

Raphael held Mary tightly the next morning, luxuriating in the feel of her soft skin against his. Her lilac scent wrapped around him; her leg tangled with his. She'd woken him up by grabbing his hand and placing her face against it, her even breaths never changing rhythm.

She'd shocked him last night with her declaration to court *him.* She had no idea how well she succeeded; she showed him some of her favorite places in the city, and they'd instantly become his favorites too. They watched the river calmly move forward, unconcerned with botos or werewolves or the petty problems Raphael heard humans scream into their cell phones about. Mary made him *laugh*. Only for her did he feel light; only in her did he see hope for himself.

Raphael got out of the bed, careful not to wake her. He wouldn't interrupt her rest; although, she looked much better than she had a few days ago. Her eyes were no longer bruised, and her cheeks were filling out. She looked healthier, more alive. Simply watching her sleep made Raphael's body harden. He burned with desire only she could sate, but he held it back, closer to him.

He wanted to do right by her. She wasn't a woman to tup and forget about—there was nothing forgettable about Mary. So he lightly padded from the room, knowing he would have her only when he knew she wouldn't live to regret her actions. He wanted to earn her trust.

Raphael refused to mar the only good in his life.

She would be crazed with desire for him before he would take her. Every time she took another lover, she would remember Raphael.

The thought made his claws come out. Suddenly he wanted to kill all the men who would ever look at Mary with lust. *What can I offer her? Just these few days, nothing more.* He should want her to have lovers after him, to mother children who shared her glowing eyes.

There was something else he could do for her.

A few blocks uptown, Sebastian met him on a corner in front of an older building covered in windows. It was empty and a little dusty, but Raphael could already see paintings lining the walls, Mary sitting on a stool in the center of the room with paint smudged on her cheeks.

"There's a loft apartment above the studio." Sebastian handed him a set of keys with a Full Moon Brewery bottle opener attached. "Tell her she has her first commission. I need a design for the labels and boxes of a new line we're going to release in about six months."

Raphael took the keys. "Give her some time," he said. Living in the firehouse, realizing she's a banshee, losing Raphael—it would all be a great adjustment for her. Mary was strong enough to withstand it all. Sebastian nodded. "It's a good idea," Raphael told him sincerely. "Thank you."

"I'll have some art supplies delivered, get the place cleaned," Sebastian said, moving to the black Mercedes G-Wagon he probably loved *too* much.

"I want to get the supplies," Raphael said.

"Need a ride?"

Raphael took his friend up on the offer, and spent an hour choosing which paints to buy for Mary. He found colors that mimicked the color of her lips, her cheeks and her eyes. He looked for the colors of a bright, cloudless day. He was only satisfied when he'd purchased the best of the paints, canvases and brushes. The older woman who owned the store sneaked a few small bottles into the bag, claiming Mary would need them too.

He took his purchases back to the studio and set them in the corner so they wouldn't be stepped on. Light flooded the room. He smiled. It was perfect for Mary. Fitting another key to the door leading upstairs, he curiously explored the loft Sebastian mentioned.

Dust covered the kitchen counters and the small, covered couch that faced an old television. A spiral staircase led to a tiny bedroom and bathroom. Raphael loved the balcony encircled in wrought iron. It overlooked a park where he could see children running around their parents and pets exploring healthy, groomed foliage. *Mary will love this. She will be happy here.*

She would be perfectly content at the firehouse too, but Raphael wanted her to have a place all her own. She didn't realize it, but she needed someplace for herself.

He left the studio and walked back to the firehouse, where an unfamiliar human regarded him from across the street. Raphael shrugged, dismissing him as a threat. He hadn't seen the man guarding the botos' mansion yesterday. Those were the only humans he would concern himself with.

"Raphael!" Mary shouted, leaning from an open window upstairs. "Come inside, now!"

The human looked from Mary to Raphael, lifting the same semiautomatic gun the botos had given their guards. "Don't fight him," Mary cried, turning the human's attention to her. "Please trust me, and *get inside!*"

The human aimed his gun in her direction and shot several times. Fury almost overcame Raphael. Mary was gone from the window, but had she been hurt?

He cursed at the man, a bullet tearing through his shoulder as he sprinted to the door. The human's footsteps pounded behind him. Raphael turned and kicked him in the chest. He heard the crack of bone; still, it shouldn't *kill* him. The human flew backward, crumpling at the bottom of the stairs leading to the door.

Raphael slammed inside, bolting the door behind him. "Mary!" he exclaimed, crazed with worry. *If anything happened to her...*

She met him in the hallway, a plastic box in her hands. Blood rolled down her arm. Raphael roared. She ignored him, running forward to wrap her arms around his waist. "I'm fine," she said breathlessly. "It only grazed me; it barely hurts." She looked up at his shoulder and gasped. "You were hit!" She lifted his shirt off and wrapped it around the wound. Her expression was murderous.

Raphael shook his head. "We need to focus. How did you know he intended to hurt us?"

Mary tore her angry gaze from his arm. "I saw him twice when I was out yesterday. I thought it was a coincidence until I looked out the window earlier."

Raphael wrapped his good arm around her, steering her down the hall, away from the danger. "Is anyone else here?" He knew Cael and Sebastian weren't, but he hoped Heath and Alex were nearby in case more humans came.

"I don't know," Mary answered. She shoved the plastic box into his hands. "These are tranquilizer guns. Aiyanna bought them for you all yesterday."

"With Cael's credit card," Heath said dryly, having entered from the stairwell on near-silent feet. He rubbed his sleeved arm and yawned, as if he'd just woken up. "Did I hear gunshots?"

Mary nodded as footsteps sounded outside. Motioning for Mary and Heath to stay back, Raphael approached the door. He could smell humans, at least a dozen of them. They didn't say a word to one another, but their steps shuffled in unison, their hands shifting on something.

"They have a battering ram," he yelled seconds before it crashed into the door, cracking the wood down the middle. He opened the box and threw a gun to Heath, and one to Mary.

"I want you away from this," he murmured when he met Mary, shoving her behind him. "Where's Alexandre when we need him?" he growled at Heath.

"He's stalking her sister." Heath jerked his head at Mary, who sighed.

"I should have known he'd follow her," she said wearily. "But I'd rather her not be here for this."

The ram hit the door again, sending splinters flying across the foyer.

"Go downstairs and lock yourself in the room with the steel door," Raphael ordered. No humans would be able to break into their garage.

Mary didn't move. She was unapologetic, unwavering beside him. She held up her gun. "I stayed to help you, not to hide."

She didn't flinch when the ram finally went through the door, but he caught the tremor in her hands. The blood had leeched from her face. She was choosing to stand beside him, to protect him, risking her own life.

He wouldn't let them touch her.

"We've got to control this," Heath hissed. "It's too great a risk to let them inside the house."

"They're scared of us," Raphael said. The door fell down flat, light pouring in around the humans whose guns were still pointed down as their eyes adjusted to their surroundings. "They're going to shoot first—we're outnumbered." *Again.*

Heath released a round of tranquilizers, bringing down three humans. "We'll have to be quicker," he snarled.

A shot went off, tearing a hole in the wall. Another had Heath stumbling backward. Raphael spread his arms in front of Mary, dropping his gun. He couldn't—wouldn't—risk her being shot. He could recover; she would die.

She clapped her hands over his ears and screamed, and it was like nothing he'd ever heard before. The sound of her voice was so full of woe, it *willed* his heart to stop. Hers was the voice that whispered death was coming ... gleefully.

He felt blood ooze from his ears.

The humans writhed on the ground, their torsos arching, legs kicking. Blood poured from their eyes, ears and mouths. Raphael realized that Mary was taking care to aim her scream at the humans; it was barely affecting him or Heath, who stared at her with his mouth open.

Mary stopped, cleared her throat. "That's harder when there's more than a few people," she said, her voice husky. Raphael ignored the way her voice turned him on, adjusting himself surreptitiously.

This time when he told her to stay back, she did, clutching her unused gun to her side.

About half of the humans were sprawled in the foyer, pieces of wood scattered around them. Raphael took their guns while Heath shot them with tranquilizers. He shot a particularly large man twice.

Those who hadn't yet made it inside the house fared better. They gripped their heads or were trying to breathe, hands on their knees, but they weren't down. Raphael barreled into one of the men, bringing him and the man behind him to the ground. They were unconscious before Heath shot them.

Heath tranqued a man whose head was between his legs. He fell to his face, unconscious.

The last three humans were the largest of the group. They looked like they lifted weights—one of them even wore a shirt that said so. At the sight of Raphael and Heath, they seemed to shake off the pain Mary caused, horror dawning in their expressions. The man on the right recovered first. He shot at Raphael and missed, hitting the house. Brick flew everywhere, littering the sidewalk.

Raphael used the distraction to two-punch one human in the

stomach and the next in the face. The last pissed himself. *What did the botos do to these men?*

Heath hit all three of them with the tranquilizers, double-tapping each man. "What do we do with them?"

Raphael had no idea. They could use the garage to hold them, but it wasn't a permanent solution. They would need the room free of humans by tomorrow night, the first night of this month's full moon. Then, any humans who found themselves there would die a terrible death.

"I'll call Aiyanna." Mary clutched the doorway as if it were the only thing keeping her from crumpling to the floor.

Raphael rushed to put a supportive arm around her, and she sagged against him. His shoulder throbbed; he wished he could lift her.

"The tranquilizers were her idea," she continued. "I'm assuming she knows what to do with the humans now that they're down."

"You're right." Raphael kissed the pulse at her temple.

"Guard your wallets," Heath murmured.

Mary shot him a murderous look. Heath raised his hands in surrender. "Just don't scream at me, please," he said with a raised brow.

While Mary cracked a smile and dialed Aiyanna, Raphael and Heath went from human to human, checking for pulses. Each had one, however sluggish.

Mary hung up, resting her head and her hip against the wall. She was obviously tired, but she didn't complain. Her pallor hadn't left her, but her eyes glowed, as always. Raphael was in awe of her strength.

"Aiyanna said these men are going to jail, and to trust the cops who come by."

Soon three NOPD SUVs pulled up to the firehouse. Each was driven by a shapeshifter, but Raphael couldn't quite pinpoint which species. They didn't smell of panther like Aiyanna.

The tallest of the three, a man with a shaved head and tattoos that rose above the collar of his shirt, surveyed the unconscious humans with a frown. "They're controlled by botos?" he asked gravely.

"Yes," Raphael said. "I think they were commanded to fear us, fear breaking orders, or both."

The female officer played with the rim of her backward baseball cap. "That's typical," she said. "Their fear feeds the botos' powers, just like any other intense emotion."

"What're you doing at a scene like this, sweetheart?" the last officer asked Mary. He was walking toward her, one arm extended as if he intended to help her. His light hair was tied back in a queue, his straight teeth bared in a self-assured smile.

Raphael caught himself from leaping for the man. He couldn't stay with Mary for another week, how could he expect her refuse other men?

"I was just helping out my boyfriend here," Mary said lightly, pointing to Raphael.

He felt himself grin. He wanted to beat his chest, put her over his good shoulder and carry her to his bed. He might just, once these humans were squared away. Mary had publicly claimed him—there was no going back from that.

She shot him a sheepish, apologetic smile over the officer's head, as if he would be angry over what she said. He met her eyes, letting her see how much he wanted her. Finally color leapt back to her cheeks, followed by a broad smile.

"Mary's a banshee, you know," Heath said, watching Raphael and Mary knowingly. "She took out most of these guys."

"Nice!" the female officer fist-bumped Mary.

The shapeshifter who spoke to her widened his eyes, stepping back to put distance between them. *Good.*

The six of them loaded the humans into the SUVs, Heath and Raphael pretending to let Mary bear some of the weight. The slight female shapeshifter hefted one of the heavier humans over her shoulder; Mary watched, her own shoulders drooping. "I'll never be that strong," she murmured.

"You can take out many more enemies at one time than she can," Raphael whispered. He took her hand and kissed it. "You're strong, *ülikena.*"

Mary instantly squared her shoulders, lifted her chin. "I am, aren't I?" She smiled, pleased with herself.

Raphael was pleased with her too, and he intended to show her just how much. This might be their last night together, because of the upcoming full moon. He wanted to make the best of every moment they had.

Chapter 9

The men who attacked the firehouse were carted away to jail, apparently to await the death of the botos. *"For their minds to be their own again,"* the large, bald policeman said, *"that's what it would take."*

Raphael and the man had exchanged a look; it seemed they had an agreement. Aiyanna stopped by soon after to heal Raphael and Heath, the latter of whom was shot four times. Mary hadn't seen him flinch. Of course, Raphael made Aiyanna heal Mary's minor graze before letting her touch him.

Heath took the weakened Aiyanna home, leaving Mary and Raphael alone in the firehouse. Before the door closed behind the two, Raphael had Mary in his arms. He charged up the stairs, taking them two at a time.

"I'm in need of a shower," he said, looking down at her. "Would you like to join me?"

Mary didn't hesitate. "Yes!" She wanted to see water slide across his body—this time *without* clothes covering him up.

In his bathroom—she'd never gotten used to how large it was—they stripped off their clothes, throwing them to the tile floor. Mary hadn't realized how much blood covered them, both their own and from the poor humans.

Like Aiyanna, Mary had weakened herself. One glance in the mirror showed how frail she appeared. She looked thinner than she had earlier, and she couldn't stop trembling. *Worth it.*

If she hadn't acted when she did, she was sure Raphael and Heath would resemble Swiss cheese from all the bullets that would have hit them. Raphael dropped his gun to protect her. He hadn't considered how painful the result would be for him, and she was certain he wouldn't care.

She didn't want him to do that again, not for her or anyone else. When he was shot, it almost undid her. She'd been more scared than during her last night working for Richard. The bullet had gone straight through him, but still it pained her to see him hurt in any way. Nothing should ever wound Raphael. He was too kind, too *good,* for that sort of treatment.

Mary's thoughts ground to a stop when Raphael patted the space beside him on the shower's bench. Completely unclothed, she obeyed, laughing as Raphael lifted her from her place, putting her in his lap. He pressed the button for the steam; Mary sighed happily. She put her head against the hollow of his throat, only for him to lean down and bite her ear.

"Hey!" She stretched up to bite him on the nose. "Banshees can bite too."

He laughed, a deep, rumbling sound underneath the hiss of steam. Even as close as they were, his face became foggy. Sweat dripped off her, slickened his skin beneath her hands. She put her fingers through his damp hair and pulled his mouth to hers.

She slid atop him while they kissed, tongues battling, hands exploring. He gripped her ass, keeping her from sliding off his lap, groaning into her mouth. She kissed the small scar where he'd been shot, then up to his ear, where she nibbled for a moment. Raphael's rapt attention was on her breasts; both behaved as if they were in subzero temperatures.

Finally his hand crept lower, teasing the curves of her thighs. He broke their kiss, pulling back as if to ask her permission. She smiled in answer and ran her hand across his hard length, ignoring the whispered warning in the back of her mind. *He's too large for you. He can't possibly fit.*

Mary kissed him with more force, not taking her hands off him. Her encouragement worked; he touched her center, and she thought she would explode. She was *so* close. She ground against him desperately. "Please, Raphael," she murmured, her voice still raspy from her screams. He growled in approval against her mouth, finally making her see stars. Her body erupted and put itself back together from a single, well-placed finger.

Never in her life had Mary felt so good. "Thank you." She gave him a long kiss. She pressed the steam button, turning the function off. Now, she wanted him to see her.

She slid down his sweat-slicked body until she faced his impressive erection. "Mary—*ah!*" Raphael exclaimed when she took him into her mouth. She licked, sucked and stroked until he found his own release, this time growling her name, his hands gentle in her hair.

Smiling, Mary rose to face him. "I want to be with you," she said, taking a seat beside him.

She did. She wanted him to *really* be her boyfriend, someone who meant more. She knew, soul-deep, he was her *The One,* her soulmate. There would be no more wondering *what if*—Raphael was it for her. She would never want anyone else. Every time he kissed her, she found her future. When he touched her, she saw stars. "If there's any way we can be together once you're freed, I want to do it."

Raphael turned away, crushing her hope, breaking her heart. "Once I leave, we cannot have a future," he said, his voice broken.

Finally, he faced her, taking her hands in one of his. He gently palmed her cheek, preventing her from avoiding his gaze. In what had to be a trick of the light, his dark eyes shone from unshed tears. "If there was *anything* I could do to stay with you," he promised, his voice unwavering, "I would. I don't want to be anywhere else but with you, no matter the consequences."

He was so full of pain, grief etching itself into his features, Mary couldn't take it; she just kissed him, hoping the tears that freed themselves were mistaken for sweat. He didn't want to leave her. His words meant everything, even if they came far from fixing the situation. Soon he would be gone from her life, and she would miss him every minute of each day.

They silently showered, each bathing the other. They stole kisses at every opportunity, fleeting touches lingering on her skin, her fingers. Mary didn't bother to cover herself before climbing into his bed. She smiled tremulously, reaching her hand out for him. He took it and kissed her passionately.

She held on to Raphael as if he would be taken away any second. He held her just as closely, murmuring soothing words in her ear until she fell into sleep.

* * * *

"Where are you taking me?" Mary asked, tugging against his hand.

Raphael only smiled, shaking his head. "It's a surprise for you."

"I used to love surprises," Mary said softly. She caught up to his stride, hitting her shoulder against his. "Are we close?"

"Not much longer," he said. He caught her as she tripped over a place where the sidewalk cracked, rising above the rest of the cement. Soon they reached the corner studio. Raphael unlocked the door and held it open for Mary.

"It's yours." He held the keys out to her. "This building and everything in it."

Mary looked around, gasping, her eyes wide. The sun haloed around her, making her hair look like fire. She reverently ran her hands over her new brushes and held her paints to the light. "It's so beautiful," she whispered. "I can paint here?"

"You can do whatever you want here," Raphael said, "but I'd like for you to paint, if that would make you happy."

Mary laughed; it was bubbly, ecstatic and beautiful. She held out her paints, the paints Raphael had pained over choosing. "With these and this?" She spun around, grinning madly. "I'd be here all day, every day, with a paintbrush in my hand."

She barely had time to put down her gifts before Raphael lifted her up, luxuriating in the feel of her soft hair against his palms, memorizing the curve of her waist.

He put her down reluctantly. She looked up at him, lifting her hand to his face. "How can I ever repay you?" she whispered.

"Promise me you'll be happy, no matter what happens," Raphael said roughly. Lives changed, and not all changes were good, but he wanted her promise. He wanted her to always choose happiness. No matter what, she would have this place. Sebastian would make sure she never wanted for supplies. Now she could always do what she loved.

"I promise," she said softly. "It's going to be hard without you."

Raphael nodded. "I know," he told her, pressing her against him. "But you'll be busy. Sebastian already has a project for you."

"Oh yeah?" Mary asked.

"Do you know Full Moon beer?"

Mary nodded, and then slapped her palm against her forehead. "You're kidding!" she exclaimed. "You're not?" She shook her head as she laughed. "*Of course* it's you guys."

She fumbled with her keys for a moment, plucked at the Full Moon opener, and pulled up the key to the loft, her expression curious. "What does this key open?"

Raphael showed her to the loft, which had her speechless. Like downstairs, Sebastian had had the place cleaned. There wasn't a speck of dust, only gleaming counters and new appliances. Colorful pillows had been thrown onto the white denim couch. Mary ran up the spiral staircase, Raphael following close behind. "This place is incredible," she murmured, palming the soft-looking quilt that covered the bed.

"It's all yours."

Spotting a large box of condoms helpfully placed on the dresser, he pocketed one and put the rest in a drawer, turning in time for Mary to grab a fistful of his shirt. Having seen what he'd just palmed, a grin flirted with her mouth even as her bright eyes blazed.

"I would have loved you just for thinking of this," she said fiercely and released his shirt. "I can't believe you've done all this for me."

"You love me?" Raphael whispered. He should be horrified; the first time someone expressed genuine love for him, he would lose her soon after. Instead, he was relieved. He craved her love like addicts needed a fix. He hadn't thought of his crimes in days, his guilt lifted away by Mary's delicate hands. She'd given him one last chance at absolution, at peace.

He loved her too. There was nothing he wouldn't do for her, nothing she couldn't ask of him. He'd thought she was his, when in reality he had belonged to her since the moment their eyes met in Thump.

Mary nodded, her eyes never leaving his. "I love you, Raphael."

"You never asked why I was exiled here," he said. "Why?"

Mary frowned impatiently. "How many years ago did this 'crime' occur?" she asked, fisting her hands on her hips.

"About five hundred."

She threw her hands up with a huff. "That's why," she exclaimed. "You aren't the same person who committed that crime, whatever it was. I don't care what you did because you're a *good man*, and that's an understatement."

She pushed his chest until he was sitting on the bed. Mary leaned over him with a finger lightly poking his sternum. "You prevented my sister's kidnapping, saved my life, and then completely changed both of our lives. *And* I'm betting you've been targeting the botos, hoping to save the humans they're feeding from. You're a hero, Raphael. I wish there were more men like you, fur and all. The world needs you."

Raphael couldn't stop himself. He rose and tackled her onto the bed, ripping through her clothes with a claw. He may have paused, but Mary was fervently trying to take off his shirt and shorts, which he immediately shredded as well. He kissed her with everything he had, all the things he wished he could tell her.

She moaned, sinking her nails into his back. "More," she pleaded.

He kissed his way down her neck, to her breasts, covering every inch. Then he moved down past her navel and between her thighs, where he feasted. She tasted as sweet as he knew she would.

"*Raphael*," she gasped, gently tugging his hair. "*Yes.*"

He licked and nibbled, and when he pressed two fingers inside her, she came apart, panting his name. "Make love to me," she said, her eyes shining, her lips reddened from their kisses. Her hair was a white curtain behind her. "I don't want to waste any more time; I want all of you."

Raphael nodded. He sheathed himself with the condom from his pocket and leaned down to kiss her. "I love you," he said in her ear, and she guided him home.

As he moved inside her, Raphael knew everything about him had changed. He'd finally forgiven himself. He would fight for his life, for a life with Mary in it.

His strokes started slowly. At Mary's urging he quickened his pace, trying not to spill his seed too quickly. It was sweet torture, her mouth on his, her walls surrounding him, her hands everywhere. He told her what she meant to him, in English and Estonian. She murmured his name, clawing at the sheets as she found her second climax.

Raphael couldn't stop himself from following her. He shuddered from the force of his pleasure, from the intensity of how Mary made him feel. Mary made him *whole*, and he realized he never had been. She was truly his now, an integral part of him. He gently flipped them so she lay across his chest, holding her as closely as he could with one hand, the other running through her long hair.

Then her warm tears began to spill, running over his shoulders and onto the sheets. Terror seized Raphael; did she wish to undo what they'd just done? Was she disgusted by her mistake?

Mary sobbed, shaking from her grief, yet she gripped him tightly with both hands, pressing her face harder against him. "I don't understand..." he managed to say.

It took her a long time to gain enough control to speak. Raphael ran his fingers through her hair until there were no tangles, just as he'd done the night he'd found her hurt and bleeding. He gripped what little hope he had tightly, praying her tears didn't involve regret, that she still loved him.

"This is the last time I'm going to cry about you leaving," she said shakily, hiccups piercing her words. "I promise, I'll be better about this from now on."

Mary moved to wipe the tears from her eyes, but Raphael swatted her hands away, dabbing them himself. She smiled at him gratefully and pushed a few strands of hair away from her face. Raphael had never been so happy to be mistaken.

"With you," she said, her smile wobbly, "sex is just so beautiful."

Raphael pulled her to him until her legs wrapped around his waist. She rested her forehead on his shoulder, shaking her head, until he tilted her head back. "I wouldn't change a single thing," he said, kissing her. "Not one tear," he added, pressing a kiss to the corner of her eye.

She loved him; he now felt how much she cared for him, saw it in every tear she shed, felt it in her touch. Everything in his life led to this point, and damn if he hadn't done something right because it all led to Mary.

They had some time left. He would use every second he had, not only to enjoy her, but also to protect her. Soon he'd explain what would occur this night, the first night of the full moon. He'd have to make sure there were no distractions, and that Mary listened well, or the cost could be her life.

* * * *

For a few blissful hours, Mary lay in bed with Raphael. They talked, laughed, and held each other closely, each dreading the upcoming moment when they would be ripped apart.

After their lovemaking, Mary knew she would never be the same. Not only did she crave Raphael all the more, knowing what he could do with his mouth, remembering how he felt inside her, but she now felt physically altered as well.

Latent power surged through her, fizzing through her bloodstream, causing her to feel invincible. In that moment, she *was* invincible—she had Raphael's love filling her up, making her lighter than air. His reaction to their actions and confessions was tangible; he, too, was changed. The weight upon his shoulders had lifted away. She swore she detected a sliver of hope in his eyes—perhaps for them, despite the odds?

Mary wasn't giving up on them; no one would take Raphael

from her. The sheer *wrongness* of his leaving her, moving elsewhere to make a life for himself turned her stomach. Why punish the very person the weres intended to free? It made no sense.

"It's time I showed you something." Raphael pressed a kiss to each of her fingers. The solemn tone of his voice belied the sweet action.

Reluctantly they finally rose, hands entwined, and slowly made their way back to the firehouse. Raphael guided her to a set of steel doors covered in a large warning sign. BEWARE OF WOLVES. Raphael pulled the heavy door back, revealing the firehouse's garage. The great garage doors were also barred with steel. The place had obviously been hastily repainted many times in different spots, as the colors didn't quite match one another. Chains about ten feet long were spread out across the floor, each near a mini-fridge.

"This is where I'll be as soon as the sun goes down tonight," Raphael said. His back was to her. He lifted a great chain; one of its black, apparently bitten links was larger than Mary's fist. "These will keep us, and in case the impossible occurs and they don't, we won't be able to leave this room."

Raphael dropped the chain, which landed on the dirty floor with a heavy *thud*. He turned to Mary, his normally full lips thinned with worry. He wrapped her in a quick hug, almost as if he couldn't help himself from touching her, before he pulled back to grasp her shoulders. "You can't be near this room when the sun goes down, not until it rises fully," he said seriously. "No matter what happens, tell me you won't come here. We are *dangerous* in wolf form; it would take a single strike from one of us to kill you."

"I won't come here," Mary promised, despite her curiosity regarding their transition. She wanted to know what Raphael looked like in wolf form. She imagined he had a gorgeous coat of dark, soft fur and wickedly sharp teeth. She knew he wouldn't hurt her in his canine form as surely as she knew her sister secretly loved those dance movies she claimed she hated.

Still, she didn't argue with Raphael. If her absence gave him more peace in his transition, she would give it to him. It must be hard enough completely changing physical forms—she didn't wish to add to his pain.

"Where do you normally go?" she asked. She wanted to know which chain was his. Did he stay by the door or by the wall? Was he in the center of the room, nearer to the other wolves?

Raphael shook his head, his eyes narrowing. "I don't even want you thinking about us in here," he said sharply. "I'm not in control of myself," he said in a gentler tone. "Don't put yourself in danger. I couldn't bear it if something happened to you and I was powerless to stop it."

Mary found she couldn't lift one of the chains. She fingered a spot on the wall with more yellow in it than there should have been, picking a few bits of the paint off. Underneath there was a deep gouge, as if from a claw. Images of furious, restrained wolves filled her mind. *Listening to Raphael would probably be wise.*

"I'll be safely locked in our room." She reached out and rubbed the back of Raphael's neck. At her words he relaxed into her touch, a small smile forming. "I think I prefer sleeping with you." She walked to the door before pausing to add, "I guess tonight will tell, right?"

Raphael stalked after Mary, his predatory gaze never leaving her. He gripped her waist possessively and kissed her deeply until she moaned, softening against him. He leaned back, a satisfied smile spreading across his face. "You'd rather me sleep with you," he growled.

"Can't a girl play hard to get without you messing it up?" she grumbled, but she felt the corners of her mouth twitching. Raphael laughed, closing her out of the forbidden room. He seemed relieved, his grin never leaving his face until the rest of the clan, one at a time, found them where they'd camped out in the living room.

"It's about that time, bro," Alex said, taking a bite out of Mary's half-eaten peanut butter sandwich.

"Time to get locked up," a man who had to be Sebastian said. He looked slightly crazed, his dark red hair sticking up as if he'd been electrocuted. Out of all the men, Sebastian seemed to dread the night the most.

Four weres filed out, dragging their feet, but Raphael stayed behind. He looked at Mary, love filling his gaze, pouring from his touch as he tucked her hair behind her ear. He gave her a chaste, lingering kiss. "I love you," he said seriously, a hardness straining his expression.

"I–"

"Tell me in the morning. *Show* me by staying away from harm."

With those words, Raphael left her plagued with curiosity and encircled by sandwich crumbs. Mary made herself some hot chocolate and fetched her book. It would be a long night.

* * * *

The sun went down, and with the appearance of the full moon came chaos in the house. The men had definitely changed forms; howls tore through the night, agonized and feral. From Raphael's warnings, Mary expected as much. Hell, she'd expected *worse* from the werewolves as a collective.

Except one of them was in serious pain. Above the howls, one of the men was *screaming* as if he was being tortured. Mary set down her drink, marked her place in her book, and then slowly walked to the room she'd promised Raphael she would avoid at all costs.

She was compelled to the room—she knew that voice. Despite his transition, she knew it was Raphael who was hurt, who yelled so loud he had to be damaging *something*.

The air vibrated around Mary. It pulsed with her rapid heartbeat, reflecting her fear. *What's happening to Raphael?* Mary desperately hoped it was just another part of his transition, but since the others didn't seem to suffer the same way, she suspected it wasn't normal. The air around her buzzed, rubbing frantically against her skin.

She could have sworn she felt a slight push toward the steel door, hands pressing against her shoulder blades. Turning, she saw nothing.

What is going on with the air?

Raphael's howls became impossibly louder. Mary heard bones

cracking, limbs tearing. She wasn't sure if it was sympathetic pain, or if Raphael and she were connected by more than she knew, but for a few short moments she felt what caused his screams. The agony took her breath away; she was being ripped apart piece by piece, and then thrown back together.

Raphael was going through some sort of second transition, one the others seemed to be safe from, and it *hurt*. Any last pieces of her promise to stay away faded into dust.

She couldn't leave Raphael to suffer. She would find a way to ease his pain, even if all she could do was hold him. She knew she could help him, needed to be with him.

Before her, the great steel doors shielding her from the werewolves shook as if they were made from thin aluminum. She remembered Raphael's warnings from earlier. They were stronger than her, and they would do their best to hurt her.

That meant nothing to Mary; she couldn't leave him like this until the sun rose.

She put a shaking hand on the lever and pulled it down. With irritation, Mary discovered the doors were dead-bolted shut. *No!*

Raphael's howls fueled her fury, erasing her fear. *I have to get to Raphael.*

Mary pressed her hands flat across the thin crack between the doors. She heard a pounding against the steel and was surprised to look up and find marks from fists repeatedly hitting against the doors. Only, she hadn't been hitting them, and the fists were on *her* side of the construct.

That's not helping anything. Stop. The phantom fists stopped as if honoring her unspoken command, and a strain she hadn't realized she was feeling eased. Was she the origin of the fists? Had she been affecting the air?

In case she was, she imagined the dead bolts turning. Sweat dripped from her brow; she controlled *something,* for sure. The earlier mental strain returned to her tenfold. Humans were not meant to unlock these doors—the weight involved for releasing the bolts was far too much.

Finally, the doors released one last tremor with a *click,* and Mary was freed of the weights and locks. This time, the doors swung open easily. Her breath came in jagged pants as she faced a room full of feral wolves. Almost the size of small horses, each had a different coat, ranging from what looked to be blond to an inky black. Four sets of teeth were bared at her; the gray and white wolf on her left licked his chops.

At the other end of the room was the wolf that put all the others to shame. She never would have imagined Raphael looked this way, but she knew it was him. He had a coat of pure white. He simply stood silently, stock-still, watching her with piercing blue eyes. She almost thought he shook his head at her, as if to warn her away.

Warning or not, she moved forward, determined to make it to him.

Immediately, the weres on either side of her lunged. The sand-colored wolf to her right missed her by a few feet, his chain jerking him mid-leap. He fell to the floor with a pained canine whine, the heavy chain landing painfully across his haunches.

She was closer to the gray and white wolf, but she didn't move to the right, afraid it would put her in the blond's range. The gray wolf slashed at her with his claws, grazing her side. She stumbled forward, ignoring the blood flowing over her hand. Across the room, Raphael roared.

Now she faced a wolf with the same auburn hair as Sebastian and the bigger, solid black wolf. Both snarled at her, but Sebastian was violently fighting his restraints to gain access to her, drool flying as he jerked his head from side to side. She heard the floor crack, saw blood flinging from where the collar cut into his neck.

Mary took her chances with the black wolf, running as fast as she could past his territory. She tried not to look at him, but couldn't help a backward glance. He was right behind her. She screamed, trying to pick up her pace, but his paws slammed into her back, sending her flying toward Raphael. Ribs cracked, and Mary tasted blood in her mouth, but she knew the wolf had meant to help from the way his claws had been consciously lifted away from her, unlike the others'. He wasn't as feral the rest were, his movements more calculated rather than instinctually driven. *What makes him different?*

She landed hard on her knees, now in Raphael's space. One hand stemming the blood at her side, she held the other out in front of her. "It's me, love," she said slowly, rising to her feet. The great white wolf backed away from her, toward the wall.

"It's Mary," she said, hoping his lack of violence was a good sign. She walked around him to her right, keeping her distance. He would never forgive himself if he hurt her; she didn't want to cause him any more self-loathing than he'd already endured.

Without warning, a snarling Raphael leapt clear over her head, chains and all, coming nose to nose with Sebastian. She quickly moved out of the way of the falling chains.

Mary hadn't realized the other wolf crept so close. Raphael violently snapped his teeth at him before herding Mary toward the back wall with his furry body.

Raphael placed himself between her and all the other werewolves, allowing Mary to sit. She released a pained breath. Raphael whined low, nudging her side gently with his nose.

"S'okay," Mary mumbled, running her fingers through his thick white fur. It really was okay—now that she was here, he was no longer in pain. He merely looked up at her with expressive blue eyes, pushing his head under her hand.

When Sebastian ran for them again, catching himself painfully on his chains yet another time, Raphael gently moved his head away from her hand, lifted it, and roared at his friend.

With his hackles raised and his sharp teeth bared, Raphael was terrifying, even in comparison to the other wolves.

Sebastian bowed his head and shrank back into his own corner. Mary swore she saw shame in his expression.

Raphael settled back against her, wrapping his body around her protectively. Her blood created red blotches in his pristine fur, the macabre sight wrong on a creature who only touched her carefully, who used himself as a shield for her.

Mary laid her head on his neck, his fur prickling her cheek and ear. She had so many questions—how did she unlock the door? Why was Raphael the only truly controlled beast in the room? None of the other prisoners recognized her.

She lazily stroked the fur by his ears; Raphael grunted

approvingly, leaning into her touch. *Why did my presence take away his pain?* Just as she'd known it would.

Soon, Mary felt herself drifting into sleep. She noticed a gray spot the size of a dime on Raphael's right hip, stark against the pure white of his fur. *He's perfect as he is, spot and all,* was her last thought before unconsciousness took her.

Chapter 10

For the first time in five hundred years, Raphael was in control of his wolf form. He was still wolf, still had the same violent instincts, but his very human mind was able to reason through the violence. He knew fighting the chains was no use; there would be no getting out of them until the sun rose and he could simply lift the collar from his neck. The collar's width was almost too snug for the neck of a wolf his size, but it was large enough for him to raise it right over his head in human form. There was no latch to maneuver—he just had to wait.

Raphael considered the work that would have to be done to fix damage to the room; clawing the walls just wasn't worth it. He knew the other wolves were his friends, with Cael and Sebastian nearest him, and he noted which of his friends were more controlled, as well as who fought their bonds the most. Sebastian gave in the most to his wolf, while Cael had the closest to Raphael's temperament. Cael fought for control and lost, again and again.

What confused Raphael the most wasn't his retained humanity, but the pain that accompanied it. Something was very wrong with him—he'd already changed into his usual snow wolf form, but his body was still transitioning, only not outwardly, but *internally*. Something was shoving itself inside him, and there wasn't room for it. It burned him, drowned him, buried him alive, and wrenched him into a spinning tornado within his chains. He could hear himself screaming, even whimpering, and failed to muster any shame for his reaction.

He couldn't stop the brand from entering his blood, stabbing through his arteries, burning away his insides. *How am I still alive?* He wanted to pray for death, but a sound at the door stopped him. *Mary.* He could endure this for her.

In the back of his mind, he wondered how his delicate woman was turning the heavy locks, but his receding pain claimed his main focus.

When Mary entered the room, wonder and love bloomed within him, the burning disappearing as if afraid of her presence. His relief was closely followed by worry; there was no part of him that wanted to cause harm to the beautiful woman, but the others couldn't help themselves. To them, she was simply prey.

The moment Alexandre sliced into her side, he went to war with his canine nature. He wanted to fight his way free—*impossible*—and kill the man he *knew* was a friend. *Not his fault*, he repeated to himself, *he can't help it*. Still, he had to fight himself every time he saw red dripping over her shaking hand. Her whole body trembled from terror and blood loss, but she moved relatively quickly, choosing to go near Cael rather than Sebastian.

His Mary was smart. She could survive this, *would* survive it.

When she finally reached him, Cael having accidentally hurt her—he'd caught the were's apologetic whine—Raphael communicated no one was to make any further moves toward her. They were a pack, and while they might not recognize Mary, they knew when another pack member made a claim he was willing to defend.

He was the only one who could touch Mary. He made that clear when he curved his body, even his tail, around her. Rather than try to escape him in her fear, his brave female only petted him, rested against him.

When she fell asleep, Raphael took care not to move so he wouldn't wake her. With her this close, her lilac scent caressing him as much as her hand had, Raphael was utterly relaxed. He wasn't in his human body, but he had no complaints. Mary was with him, and she was safe. He would have this night with her after all, even if the circumstances were far from perfect.

Throughout the night, her bleeding slowed and finally stopped. A nudge of his muzzle revealed Mary was healing at a much faster rate than a typical mortal. She also shouldn't have been able to enter the garage in the first place. *What happened to her?* The sun was about to rise; he felt it on the horizon. *What happened to me?*

Blessedly, when the sun came up he shed his wolf form in a burst of light. The transformation's reversal was never as painful as the initial change. Naked, he took off his collar and gently lifted Mary from him.

His friends pulled on their clothes gingerly, each moving as if sore. Sebastian groaned nearby, clutching his head in his hands.

Cael, Heath and Alexandre were all staring at Mary, shock and concern on each of their faces.

"How did she—" Alexandre began.

"Is she hurt?" Cael interrupted, his voice tight.

Raphael yanked on a pair of shorts stashed in a latched compartment under the floor.

Using his back to protect Mary's privacy, he lifted her shirt to see deep, partially scabbed-over slashes in her side. In a few days, they would be healed completely. Her back sustained two dark purple bruises, her small bones still in the process of knitting themselves together.

He wanted to leap across the garage and rip Alexandre's throat from his body, but he knew the man wasn't at fault. Any other full moon, and Raphael would've reacted the same way toward a human female in his domain.

"Yes," Raphael said darkly, "but she's healing at a remarkably fast rate."

Cael released a held breath, his shoulders slumping. He ran a hand through his slicked-back hair; Raphael swore he saw him shudder.

"Uh, Raphael, how'd Mary get in here?" Alexandre asked uncertainly.

Heath moved around the doorway, stopping at the lever. "She

broke the damn thing." He held up the titanium rope. "Something you want to tell us about her?"

Sebastian whistled. "That bitch isn't just an artist, bro," he said, shaking his head.

Rage filled Raphael. *No one* spoke of Mary in that way.

Sebastian flew to the ceiling until he was pressed against it, his limbs spread. Sparks flew from the light fixture, growing until they formed flames that crept closer, closer...

"*Raphael*," Heath exclaimed. He was right next to Raphael, clapping him on the shoulder. "Let that idiot down."

Just before flames singed the tips of Sebastian's hair, Raphael willed him to the floor, unharmed. As if invisible hands carried him, it was done.

The fire quickly died without Raphael's attention, having nothing to catch on the steel ceiling. It was a precaution the previous tenants had installed, one Heath and Raphael had expanded to layers inside the walls and the floor in order to prevent a fire from reaching them while they were chained.

"How the hell did you do that?" Sebastian cried, patting himself. He looked impressed.

"I don't know," Raphael said truthfully. How *did* he do that?

Heath gestured to Mary. She looked so fragile in her slumber, her hands curled up against her chest, her hair shining around her. Her full lips were relaxed, her dark eyelashes unmoving against her cheeks.

"She's your mate," Heath said. "She's freed your elemental powers; to a certain extent, your abilities will be shared."

My mate. Raphael was stunned. He'd never paid much attention to the other weres when they spoke of mates. None of them were mated, so he hadn't thought to concern himself with the knowledge. How could someone like him, someone who had hurt so many, who'd torn entire families apart, deserve a woman who would be bonded to him for life, a woman who would become his family?

Of course she's my mate, he realized, looking down at her flawless visage. On some level, he'd always known. She truly was his, in every sense. She'd freed him, not only from having bound powers, but also from the pain and guilt that followed each night of every full moon. He'd never liked losing himself to the beast and much preferred keeping his rational thoughts, as well as the ability to keep her safely by his side.

Reality crashed down, smothering the joyous revelation. He would be executed soon, too soon after discovering his reason for breathing. What would that mean for Mary?

"Aren't mates' lives connected?" he asked brokenly, remembering snippets of overheard conversations that were over a hundred years old, but not enough to tell him the details he needed.

Cael nodded solemnly. Raphael's roar of anguish shook the room, causing the remaining lights to flicker.

"Hey!" Heath shouted, his own yell almost as loud as Raphael's. "I'll mess you up if you don't stop it," he growled severely, fury glinting in his green eyes. The lights grew brighter, unwavering. " *We don't have to die now.*" Heath enunciated every word. He looked as if he were refraining himself from shaking Raphael.

"What do you mean?" Hoped flared, dangerous and seductive.

"He means you've got elementals," Sebastian said, spreading his arms. "More than one, judging from your display of fire and air."

"It's enough to kill Jeremiah." Heath folded his arms. "He only has one element."

Cael said nothing, only watched Mary with a tortured expression. Alexandre laughed sardonically, nodding his head. "So you plan to kill the *respected* man who's been *trusted* to relay information about us to the Elders," he said sarcastically, pumping his fist in the air. "Great idea, men."

"It *is* a great idea," Sebastian said, his smile genuine. "When my old pack comes to rescue Sophia," the mention of his sister wiped the grin from his face, "they'll realize Jeremiah's been helping the botos hurt women, one of *our* women. They'll probably kill him, but if Raphael has to, there will be enough witnesses for Jeremiah's crimes that even the Elders won't fault Raphael."

Raphael lifted Mary, cradling her against his chest. She was his, and he would take care of her. That meant death wasn't an option.

When Jeremiah was dead, along with the botos, Raphael would

tell her everything. He would never hide anything from her again. Mary was his *mate*; he wasn't sure an immortal lifetime would be enough time with her, but it was a start.

Raphael looked around the room, meeting each of his friends' eyes. "I was put here so soon after I was bitten," he said slowly, awkwardly, "I never had elemental powers before. "Will you show me how me how to use them?"

Each of his packmates nodded, their determination mirroring Raphael's. In that moment Raphael knew not only he, but also every one of them, would become much more than just exiles. There was hope for them all, and for the first time in his life Raphael couldn't wait to see what was in store.

* * * *

Raphael tucked Mary into bed, pushing the heavy quilt so it covered just her legs. She always shoved it down during sleep, and he wanted her to stay comfortable. Her bandaged side was visible through the thin sheets; he ground his teeth, hoping the wound wouldn't cause her any further pain. He didn't expect her to wake for hours. The sun had just risen, and she wasn't accustomed to rising this early.

He left her a note telling her he'd be at a bar on Bourbon Street if she wished to meet him. Hating to leave her behind, he hoped he'd see her soon. Raphael didn't want to spend time apart from her. Rather, he wanted to lift her in the air and tell her they were mated, that they were connected by a bond so unbreakable their very lives were entwined.

Most of all, he was dying to tell her they might not have to be separated after all.

But he wouldn't just yet. There was so much he couldn't explain to her, and he abhorred it. His instincts rejected the idea of keeping his beautiful mate in the dark about anything, especially something so important, but there was no reason to tell her he was marked to be executed. Last night, Mary walked into a room full of feral werewolves for him. Raphael knew she'd fight Jeremiah for him, too, and he simply couldn't allow it.

Jeremiah would behead Mary without batting an eye, as he'd recently proven through his involvement with the botos. If he said anything to her about his probable sentence, she would surely be killed.

The mere thought cemented Jeremiah's own impending execution. Raphael brushed the pessimistic notion off, deciding he needed to focus on his elemental abilities. They were all that would stand in the way of death for Mary, Heath and himself, and he had a short amount time to learn before the full moon waned and all hell broke loose.

Heath drove Raphael and Cael to Pat O'Brien's, where Sebastian and Alexandre met them. Raphael had never been inside the bar, but after glimpsing the plastic leprechauns looming by front entrance, the large, empty courtyard was a surprise, as well as its fountains ringed in fire. Alexandre, who was wearing a plastic green hat, brought him a tall red drink. "You're going to need it, buddy," he said, handing it over.

"Why aren't there people here?" Raphael asked, ignoring the drink.

Sebastian, who'd just shaken hands with a retreating older man, said, "See those men in green? They're not only here to bring us drinks. They're keeping people out for the next few hours."

Cael threw his glass into the fire, shrugging at Alex's scandalized gasp.

"I would have drunk that!" Alex exclaimed, scowling.

Cael pointed to the flames, then looked at Raphael. "Can you affect it?"

Raphael willed the flames to spread toward Alex. They did, too quickly. Yelping, Alex had to jump back, spilling his own drink.

Cael only nodded, glancing at Sebastian, who shook his head. "We're going to have to work on that," he said. A hungry expression spread across his face. "Just so we're clear, finding a mate releases our powers?"

Heath held up a hand. Curling black designs crept up his fingers, surrounding an eerily inked eye. He tossed a shot of something electric green into his mouth and shook his head violently, his lips twisting in a grimace. "You get them back because they change with the mating," he said with a cough. "Both mates are more powerful because their powers are somewhat combined. It's helpful, considering if one dies, the other will too."

At that Raphael growled. He didn't mind his life being tied to hers, but the notion that anything could extinguish the bright ray of hope that was Mary didn't sit well with him.

Appearing satisfied with Raphael's answer, Sebastian gestured toward the rest of the courtyard. "I know you can control air—thanks for that, buddy—but what about water and earth?" he asked, wiggling his eyebrows.

Alex groaned, then stuffed his hands in a bed of planted flowers. "I miss my earth powers," he said wistfully, running the soil through his fingers. "They were just so damn *cool.*"

Immediately, everyone except Raphael and Cael started talking at once, each defending their elemental power.

"You must be high," Sebastian retorted, eyeing the fountain. "Fire is the most powerful element; everyone knows that."

Heath snorted. "Water beats fire." He mimicked dropping a microphone.

Alexandre argued with them, still lovingly holding the soil in his palm.

Raphael felt a stab of guilt. His packmates *missed* their powers. He hadn't realized how proud of them they'd been, or how much they meant to his friends' identities. He couldn't mourn for abilities he'd never had to begin with, and only now did he understand what a gift that was. He'd never had something that integral taken away from him.

He hated flaunting his gifts, but if he failed to kill Jeremiah, both Mary and Heath would die. He would use his powers and his clan's knowledge to protect Mary and the pack, hoping the other men would find their mates as well. Raphael would do everything in his power to help them, as they stood by him and Mary.

He didn't want them to find mates only so they could gain back their powers. To Raphael, the abilities were a means to an end, a way to keep his woman. His friends were good men—they deserved to find their own happiness, joy that made even the strongest elemental powers seem minute in comparison.

The men were still arguing while Cael watched silently. His friend met his eyes and nodded toward Alexandre and his ball of soil. Raphael imagined it rising from his hand, hovering eye-level with Alex. A solid, hovering mass, it rose up to Alex's chin before falling into pieces onto the concrete deck.

"That's not what you do with earth," Alex said, exasperated. He wiped his hands on his jeans and gestured for another drink, snapping his fingers impatiently. The waiter rolled his eyes, but turned to head for the bar. "With earth you can *grow* things, cause earthquakes. You just used air again. Grow me a flower," he challenged.

Raphael looked at the soil, concentrating on a flower taking root, growing up above the soil and into the light, and was rewarded with ... a miniature cactus. Alexandre roared with laughter, and even Cael cracked a smile.

"Good luck trying to impress Mary with that," Alexandre gasped, still laughing. Raphael scowled, jerking water from the fountain and into the air. It hovered above Alexandre while his laughter died down. Suddenly Cael was on his knees, laughing, his eyes fixed on the water above Alexandre's head.

Alex looked up and cursed. Raphael released his hold on the water, letting it all fall on Alexandre. Blond hair plastered to his head and neck, he spluttered, dumping out his now watered-down drink. "Screw you, guys." He smiled despite his words.

While Alexandre shook the water from his hair, Heath said pensively, "So you've got all four of the elements. I never would have guessed."

Sebastian nodded in agreement, stepping a few feet away from Alex, who was wringing out his shirt and flinging water everywhere. "I would've pegged you for an air type, not an *Omni*," Sebastian said.

"Someone who controls more than three elements," Heath supplied. He was more aware than anyone else of just how little exposure Raphael had to typical werewolves.

For the next few hours Raphael was inundated with information on all four elements. Cael warned him not to try and pick up anything heavier than a car for a few years, making Raphael wonder what exactly Cael had been throwing around before his exile. Cael had been the last to join the group, but he'd been in New Orleans long enough that he never had the chance to toss a car.

Sebastian told him fire couldn't be contained—Raphael could make it grow, but not lessen, and he could suggest its movements, but never completely control it. He had the opposite effect on water. He could change its form to solid or vapor and back, and keep it precisely as he wanted it. The problem was, Raphael couldn't throw it with force like Jeremiah. The icicles he threw at the brick wall barely cracked on impact, falling to the ground in defeat.

"Your adrenaline plays a part in it." Heath considered the large, heavy glass in his hand. Without warning, he threw it at Raphael's head. Raphael raised water from the fountain, forming an ice shield that shattered the glass inches before it reached his temple and cracked his skull.

Heath shrugged. "You're okay with defense," he said. "Air is still your greatest strength; you need to work on your water control."

"He can't grow for shit." Alexandre grinned. "I thought you were from Serbia, Raphe. I didn't realize you have cacti there."

Raphael didn't bother to correct the inebriated werewolf.

"He made a Venus flytrap-like thing once," Heath said helpfully.

"It was a Nepenthes," Alexandre corrected.

Raphael brought up about a bucket's worth of water, raising an eyebrow. He couldn't use it as a weapon yet, but he fully intended to douse Alexandre again. Mary's voice drifted toward him, claiming all of his attention; he evaporated the water.

"Let me in!" she exclaimed from the front entrance. She was irritated; this clearly wasn't the first time she'd asked.

"It's a private, er, party inside," one of the bouncers said. "Come back when we open tonight."

"My boyfriend's in there, and I want to see him!" she shouted.

Walking toward them, Raphael saw the man shake his head no. "Let her in," he said from behind him. His tone left no room for argument. He wouldn't keep Mary waiting any longer.

The men parted to let her pass, and Mary practically ran into his arms. A crease was still present on her cheek from sleep. She'd come straight to him, Raphael recognized proudly. After last night, she still *wanted* to see him. He released a breath he hadn't known he'd been holding.

Her familiar scent wrapped around him, grounding him. "Good morning, *ülikena*," he said against her soft hair.

"Hey," she whispered. She smiled up at him, wrenching his heart into her grasp. Mary looked over his shoulder, a puzzled furrow appearing on her brow. "Were you really throwing a party here?"

He was sure she was analyzing the broken glass littering the ground, the overturned tables and chairs, and the soil sprinkled everywhere from the fountain to the souvenir bar. Not to mention the table covered in the empty glasses from Alexandre and Sebastian's drinks.

It wasn't yet ten in the morning.

Raphael shook his head, aware of how strange the entire scenario looked. Ever-helpful, Alexandre saluted Mary with a hurricane—which Raphael had learned was the red drink—his plastic green hat sitting crooked on his head.

"There are things," *many things*, "I need to speak with you about," Raphael told her. He didn't release his grip around her, brushed a kiss along her hairline. "But not yet. Trust me?"

Mary's green gaze searched his face for a long moment. Raphael saw no indecision, only curiosity and hope. "When you can, you'll tell me everything?" She punctuated her question with a light squeeze to his shoulder.

"Of course," he answered. He wanted so badly to have that conversation with her, to tell her who she was to him, ask her if she would stay with him always. He wanted to see more of her favorite places, see what she would create from the supplies he'd brought her. He wanted to live, but he knew he would have to fight for it.

Hand in hand, they walked over to where the rest of the clan sat. All of his friends smiled at her, and Sebastian offered her a drink. As Mary settled between him and Cael, laughing at something

Alexandre said, Raphael couldn't help but think this was where she belonged—with him, with a *clan prohibitum* Raphael would make sure finally found justice.

* * * *

Wish wanted to send Mary flowers.

He flipped through the legal pad she'd written in, full of scribbled notes and absent-minded drawings intended to help him care for Molly. The pages would soon become frayed, he read through them so often.

Stopping on a page where Mary had drawn flames covering ornate curtains, he smiled at the pieces of burning fabric floating off into the air around an innocent-looking Molly. *DO NOT ALLOW HER NEAR OPEN FLAMES* was scrawled at the top of the page, along with a thought bubble coming from his daughter that read, *PYROMANIAC IN TRAINING.*

Along with Mary's warnings, she'd also gifted him lists of the foods categorized by *what she loves, what she'll tolerate,* and *don't even bother.* He tried to feed Molly something from the latter list once and quickly decided questioning Mary was unwise.

Her notes had become his guide to his currently napping daughter, who fully expected him to know her quirks and nuances. It was worth its weight in gold, as was the woman who'd written it. Molly asked for Mary every day, and for the last couple of days Wish had hated disappointing her, telling her Mary would be away for a few more days. He hoped it wouldn't be longer than that.

Molly asked for Natasha less often, surprising Wish. In fact, she'd only asked after her dead mother once, when a Barbie's head fell from its body. The sight had made Wish's blood boil, but he only told her that her mother was safe and living too far away for her to visit.

Natasha had been meticulous about everything in her life. For instance, she'd only seen Wish during certain hours of the night. She'd always placed her jewel-encrusted hairpins in that particular crisscrossing pattern she liked. Once she was pregnant, she had put herself on a meticulous diet suggested by her dietician, one specifically designed for an expecting woman living a high-stress lifestyle.

She'd never considered that Richard might be the father and had involved Wish in every way she could until his death.

Why hadn't she been involved in Molly's life? The only answer he could think of was maybe Natasha had been protecting the child, bringing her to Richard's attention as little as possible.

He thought of the way Molly lived with abandon, dancing to the classical music he played for her with childlike joy. *It worked, Natasha.*

His phone rang loudly from across the room, scattering his thoughts. He wanted to kick himself for leaving the device on; he prayed the sound hadn't woken Molly. Wish stalked across the open space that was his kitchen and living room and answered on the third ring.

"Do you need me to come in today?" Thérèse barked at him. She'd visited Molly the day before, quickly deeming his bungalow on Tchoupitoulas Street unfit for a child. Given a child had never before lived in the home, she was probably correct.

Apparently Molly liked to explore, which meant any cabinet that contained anything remotely dangerous for a four-year-old needed to be impossible for her to open.

Wish and his home were works in progress.

Wish suspected Thérèse would come whether he asked her to or not, and she'd also bring bubble wrap with her. "I think we're all right—"

"That's it, I'm coming over." Thérèse hung up. Etiquette was not the woman's forte.

His phone beeped, making him cringe and curse the technology. This time Mary texted him. *Is Leila all right?* She quickly added, *She told me she was fine, but I want to make sure.*

Wish responded that Leila was too immersed in studying for finals to be upset about much, which was true. He only hoped Molly would one day try as hard in school as Leila did.

Thanks! Mary answered. *Give Molly a hug for me.*

Wish told her to be safe, and set his phone aside.

After he graded six short essays for his Southern Fiction After 1850 class, which he'd successfully convinced Leila to sign up for next semester, she pushed through his door, bags full of books heavier than she was draping her arms. She was alone, a seldom occurrence considering Cael was currently living with them for added protection, and Alexandre followed her just about everywhere she went.

Wish helped her with her bags, slipping them from her elbows and shoulder and placing them on the counter. He didn't move from his spot behind his stack of papers.

He steepled his fingers, considering how to ask her the question that had been bothering him since the moment he'd met her. There really was no tactful way to put it, he decided, but he had to know. More importantly, he needed to convince her to talk to Mary.

"Leila, how long have you been dead?" he asked, his voice consciously devoid of judgment.

She froze, her eyes widening. She raised her hands as if to refute his statement, but Wish moved to hover in front of her before she did. Leila took a breath, looked him in the eye, and signed, *I've been dead for over three years.*

Chapter 11

I won't talk about it, Leila continued. Her blue gaze seemed determined, her mouth set.

Wish wasn't surprised. If she hadn't revealed her lack of mortality to Mary, there was no way she'd want to confide in him. He hoped she would, someday. He knew what it was to die only to continue in the same life, despite being irrevocably changed.

"I don't expect you to," Wish said.

How did you know? she asked, her gaze penetrating.

Wish sighed. He'd studied supernatural beings for twelve years; he knew when someone wasn't human *or* mortal, especially when they were trying to pass as both. "You don't breathe as often as a human," he began. Leila's hands pressed protectively against her throat. "But that wasn't what gave you away. Before you died, you were—"

"Leila!"

Alexandre bellowed her name from Wish's neatly groomed front yard. *Molly can sleep though* anything, *it seems.*

Seeing the weres tromping through his yard, Wish decided he might invent a paint that prevented their entrance if they ruined one of his flowerbeds. Molly liked his "ragin' Cajun red" ruellias and pastel dahlias.

His and Leila's conversation effectively put on hold, Wish

floated to meet them at the door with Leila just behind him. Alexandre's face broke into a smile when he caught sight of Leila.

Appearing bored, Cael brushed past his packmate to face Wish. "Where's Molly?" he asked.

"Sleeping, but I doubt that'll last for much longer."

Cael nodded and made a beeline for the refrigerator.

For a moment Wish watched a jovial Alexandre speak with Leila animatedly. She responded with just as much enthusiasm, smiling as she signed.

There were tomes of information Wish could give her to shed light on her condition, but seeing her flirt with Alexandre, her eyes twinkling as Natasha's had the night she'd seduced Wish, he understood that she just wasn't ready.

Someone had tried to cut her life short, and Leila simply wasn't letting them. For someone touched by death, she *lived.* She didn't even seem to mind being moved around like a ball in a pinball machine the last few days. Wish respected her, hoped she would be able to keep her outlook on life.

Soon Leila would have to face what she'd become, or the consequences would be deadly.

* * * *

"Sit *still!*"

Mary pointed her pencil at Raphael threateningly. He was unerringly brave, so strong it should scare her, and he absolutely could not sit for more than a moment.

She'd been trying to sketch him for the past ten minutes, and the poor man had squirmed and twitched for nine of them. He shot her an adorably apologetic look, and it was her undoing. She walked over to him, grabbed his hand and led him to her loft. It was so perfect; she still couldn't believe the place was hers. But then, it never would be hers.

It was *theirs*, both hers and Raphael's.

She pushed Raphael onto the couch and sat on his lap, straddling him so her knees pressed against his thighs. His hair was silky under her touch, his jawline shadowed with black stubble. His full lips were still frowning. Mary kissed him, sinking closer.

"I shouldn't have asked you to pose." She kissed his jaw. "It was unnecessary; I could never forget any detail of your face." She nipped his regally straight nose, the corner of his mouth. "*Or* your body, for that matter."

Mary could paint him right now with only a blank canvas and a few dark shades of paint; she wouldn't miss a single stroke.

She'd tried to alter the air around her as she had the night before, using paintbrushes as test subjects, but found the ability had left along with her frustration at being separated from Raphael. She didn't mind, so long as it came back should she ever need it.

Raphael took her face in his hands, joy lighting up his boundlessly opaque eyes. He kissed her eagerly, as if starving for her touch. He gently bit her lip, resting his forehead against hers.

"You broke your promise," he said, his words hoarse, reproachful.

Mary pursed her lips, but didn't break contact. "I don't regret it," she said. "I'll do it again if you stay in the garage tonight."

Raphael growled, pulling away. His frown was severe, his eyebrows black slashes over glinting onyx. "You could have *died*," he exclaimed, bringing her back to him. He rested his cheek against the top of her head; one of his hands drifted over her bandaged side, her bruised ribs. "You won't be able to get in tonight. Sebastian knows someone who can spell the doors to open only for werewolves."

Mary pushed against his chest angrily, but Raphael gripped her tightly. "You were hurting!" she cried. "I *couldn't* leave you that way. You wouldn't have left me like that."

"No, I wouldn't have." Raphael smiled. "That's why I won't be chained tonight."

Elated, Mary grinned, pressing kisses all over his face. She made a face at him. "Why didn't you start with that?" she asked.

Placing a hand against the back of her neck, he said, "Because you are everything to me, my *ülikena*. Your safety comes before anything else."

Tears pricked Mary's eyes. "What does *ülikena* mean?"

"Beauty," he said, wiping away one of her stray tears with his thumb. "Now that I've met you, the world is beautiful to me again."

She was crying now, touched by his love for her, horrified they would be forced to part. "I wish I were that poetic." She sniffled. There was no reason to mention her concerns, he'd do whatever he could to stay with her, just as she would.

Raphael's dimples made an appearance, making her heart lighten despite her sadness. "So we don't have to be separated tonight?" she asked.

Raphael shook his head, grinning. "We should stay at the firehouse, in case someone attacks again."

Mary cocked her head at him. "Does that mean *I* was protecting *you* when you all were chained?"

He nodded; her pride bloomed. "You were, but others would have stepped in as well, had you needed it," he said. Mary shivered. She hadn't known there was anyone else around last night.

They left the loft, stopping at a food truck on the way back to the firehouse. Mary learned her wolf didn't like hot sauce, his eyes almost popping out of his head when he took a bite of her po-boy. She bought him a carton milk to cut the spices and mercilessly teased him while he drank it.

Back in their room, Raphael's gaze became heated. Mary felt a blush creeping up her chest to reach her cheeks. Their clothes scattered the floor seconds later, and Raphael's hands were on her, her own hands reaching to touch every part of him.

They made love quickly, passionately. Mary couldn't hold back her screams as she fell apart again and again, Raphael learning what made her arch closer to him, what caused her to claw into the curves of his ass, pushing him deeper inside her.

After he joined her in ecstasy, panting and smiling, kissing every part of her he could reach, Mary put on a lacy camisole and linen shorts. She rested on Raphael's chest, delighting in the feel of his hot breath against her face

Almost an hour later he groaned in pain, twisting and rocking in her arms as his body shaped into something unnatural, yet wholly beautiful. Mary kissed the top of her white wolf's head, brushing a hand over his long back.

She fetched her book from her drawer and stretched her legs in front of her, Raphael resting his head in her lap. She read to him until they both fell asleep, a beast that could kill her in a millisecond tamed by something she could feel stretching between them, but couldn't understand.

* * * *

"The Elders have made their decision," Jeremiah said, his voice grave. It was a farce, delivered for the benefit of the man who'd joined him in order to witness the news being passed from *lupux dux* to the exiled.

The witness had Heath's green eyes and light brown hair, with a more pronounced jaw and a wider set of shoulders. Raphael's questions about their possible relation were answered a moment later, when Heath entered the room.

"Jeremiah." Heath nodded before he turned to the witness. "*Brother.*" He spat the last word as if it were disgusting to him.

The witness only inclined his head, his gaze on neither Raphael nor Heath, but somewhere above their shoulders.

"As I was telling Raphael," Jeremiah continued, spreading his hands. "I've come here to tell you of the Elders' decision, with Vale as my witness." He didn't pause for more than a breath. "You will both be executed this coming Sunday at first light. You have two full days to say your goodbyes and make any arrangements you might need. As always, you are not permitted to leave the city. If there is anything you may need from me, I will do everything in my power to help you."

"As will I," Vale said, reaching for his brother's shoulder. Sincerity burned in his green gaze, hurt flashing across his features when Heath stepped back, away from Vale's touch.

Raphael nodded to the two men, hoping he wouldn't have to kill Heath's brother. Raphael wouldn't allow the execution to come to pass, and he was sure Vale would be there for it. He only hoped the man loved his brother enough to listen to them before attacking. If not, Raphael would be forced to add another good man to his conscience. He wouldn't hesitate to kill him, though—Mary's life, and the possibility of having a life with her were worth another stain on his record, no matter how much he dreaded it.

He'd been spreading peanut butter onto toast for Mary when he received a text from Heath, telling him Jeremiah was waiting for them out front. For some reason Jeremiah had never contacted him directly, instead communicating though other members of the pack, usually Heath or Alex. Raphael had always wondered why, but never cared enough to ask. The truth was, he preferred Jeremiah leaving him alone.

Now he turned and left Jeremiah and Vale without a word. He had nothing to say to a man who hurt innocent, helpless humans, not without giving away the cards he kept carefully guarded. Revealing his new powers today would be a mistake. He still had time to further hone his skills, optimizing his chances to survive his fight with Jeremiah.

Heath walked beside him; he was almost silent, with only a murmured *"bastard,"* to give away the depth of his anger.

Inside the house, Raphael scanned the halls and living room for Mary as Heath shouted insults regarding Jeremiah and his brother. "He's an *asshole!*"

"He doesn't even do his *job*, how can Vale not see that? And my parents said *he* was the smart one!

"If not for you, they would really kill us. Un. Friggin'. *Believeable*," Heath continued, using his teeth to open a bottle of Full Moon Cael's Pale Ale.

The toast was gone from the counter. Raphael wondered if Mary had found it, or Alexandre or Sebastian had stolen it in his absence. Just in case, halfway listening to Heath continue to describe what he would do to Jeremiah if he could, and where he should shove the wisdom his brother lacked, Raphael slapped together more of his mate's favorite treat, intending to bring it to her.

He'd just received a death sentence, but he wasn't worried. He wasn't even *angry*, as Heath was. The news was no surprise—he'd known it would come, just as the full moon would come for one more night this month. Raphael had been given a way to find justice for both Jeremiah and his clan. Soon, the *lupus dux* would be exposed for the man he was: a predator even the cruelest of werewolves would reject.

His friends and he would have a fighting chance to regain their lives, to earn their freedom.

* * * *

Mary held up her finger, silently asking the man who looked strikingly like Heath to wait. He moved his head slightly, enough of a confirmation for her to fly down the stairs, grinding to a halt until she knew Raphael had passed through the front hall.

He wouldn't want her making demands of Jeremiah, the other man standing in front of the firehouse. She recognized him instantly from Aiyanna's description. Jeremiah was handsome, in the same way politicians were—his hair fell in tamed ringlets, his smooth blue button-down complementary to his bronzed skin.

According to Aiyanna, this man was Raphael's warden and jury.

Mary didn't have an option of whether or not to trust the werewolf. His was the only name she'd been given, the only person her limited knowledge indicated could help her keep Raphael for more than mere days. She would take her chances with Jeremiah. It was all she *could* do.

She burst from the doors into the bright afternoon sun, Jeremiah and the other man watching her expectantly, the former with a raised eyebrow.

He *did* have cold eyes. Like slivers of ice, they reflected no emotion, no trace of humanity. They were simply *cold*, puzzling Mary, making her wary of him.

A concerned expression drew the unfamiliar man's eyebrows together, making him appear softer despite his intimidating build. Jeremiah strode toward her with an air of confidence, his hand outstretched. "Jeremiah, *lupus dux* for this *clan prohibitum*, and this is Vale, one of our three head soldiers."

"Mary Newman," she said with a confidence she didn't feel. She shook his hand; it was as frigid as she'd expected it to be.

"I wanted to talk to you about Raphael," she began, purposefully meeting their inquiring gazes. "I'm ... attached to him. she said. If there is anything I can do so we can be together once he's been freed, I'd like to know."

Confusion had Vale angling his head, turning his lips down in a severe frown.

Jeremiah's expression didn't change. A breeze blew through them, whipping Mary's ponytail to the side, making her shiver despite the heat. "Would you do anything for him, even sacrifice your own life for his?" Jeremiah asked.

"Yes," Mary said instantly. There was no question—each day Raphael stood taller, laughed more. He'd even *played* this morning, chasing her around his room until she'd admitted his wolf was more handsome than the CGI wolves she'd seen in campy movies. She wouldn't allow his newfound happiness to be cut short, not after he'd spent so long punishing himself.

Jeremiah's gaze became penetrating, his mouth almost imperceptibly tilting up. "I will give you one chance to help Raphael," he said, his eyes glinting, "because I, too, am attached to the man—he was one of my first exiles. It would be nice to see him happy after all these years."

Hope soared within Mary. She had a chance to keep Raphael, to have a future with her werewolf. Maybe she'd been wrong in her judgments of Jeremiah. If he were so cold, he wouldn't be helping Mary and Raphael with nothing to gain for himself. *Raphael has another ally,* she thought happily.

"What do I have to do?" Mary asked. *Anything. Anything to stay with him.*

"Raphael is taking part in one of our most sacred ceremonies on Sunday," Jeremiah said with a benevolent smile. "If you take his place, you will never lose him."

Vale stared at him, his gaze questioning.

Mary didn't consider what the ceremony was, only the outcome. She didn't hesitate. "Of course I'll take his place," she rushed to say, aglow with the knowledge she'd so hoped to find.

Raphael would be free, pardoned of the crimes that had forced him here, for the actions he allowed to weigh him down for centuries. She didn't doubt his exile as sufficient punishment, but she knew Raphael punished himself far more than anyone else ever thought to.

He deserved happiness, and Mary was sure she could give that to him. She could help him build a new life untainted by his past, a life where his fellow weres viewed him as she did: as a compassionate, honorable man who would bleed without hesitation for the good of others. Never again would anyone, including Raphael himself, treat him like a criminal.

She thought she saw Vale shake his head.

Jeremiah summoned gritty, dirty water up from the street, using what Mary assumed was his elemental power. Again, she wondered what Raphael's was. Could he bring water up from the ground like Raphael?

The brown street water froze into an ugly, uneven blade that twisted toward Mary threateningly without touching her. She flinched; she didn't want it to come near her.

"Do you agree to be *thysía* for Raphael?" Jeremiah asked, his weapon quivering in the air.

Mary hesitated. She didn't know what *thysía* meant, but before she could mentally scroll through what little Greek and Latin roots she knew Jeremiah interrupted her thoughts, the point of his water dagger level with her nose.

"You said you would do anything for him," he accused, his eyes glinting.

She shook off her indecision; Jeremiah was right. "I agree to be *thysía,* so long as Raphael and I can be together as a result. *And,*" she added, a silent voice in the back of her mind making itself heard. *This is a blood pact. They're unbreakable.* "I will be *thysía* only if from that ceremony on out, Raphael and the rest of the *clan prohibitum* are treated in an objectively fair manner according to the laws your kind live by."

Ever since Raphael told her he'd been in exile for *five hundred years,* she'd had niggling doubts about the justification behind the decision. She would bet her left foot that less than half of that time would have sufficed, no matter what his crime had been. The rest of the werewolves she'd met didn't seem to be a danger to anyone, either. Alexandre looked out for Leila, and Cael volunteered to protect both Leila and Molly. He also put up with Aiyanna almost every day. Heath and Sebastian displayed no more of a threat. They'd never shown signs of violence, although, Sebastian and Alex showed signs of alcoholism.

Whatever she was agreeing to, she wanted to get the most out of it.

Jeremiah barked out a laugh, ducking his head. He shook his head, his long curls obscuring his face.

Vale's eyebrows drew together, creating a line down his forehead. The man glanced from Mary to Jeremiah and back, his jaw pulled tight. He looked as if there was somewhere he wanted to put her, but he couldn't decide *where.*

"So it shall be." Jeremiah said the words as the blade turned to him, cutting deeply into his palm.

It came for her next. She held her hand out, noting the lack of tremor in her fingers. The tip bit through her palm in one fast slice before falling back to the ground, once again liquid.

Jeremiah stuck his hand out. Mary shook it, combining their blood to seal their arrangement.

"Sunday, half an hour before sunup," Jeremiah said, turning to Vale. "We're finished here; now get me out of this godforsaken city."

Still frowning, Vale touched the other man's shoulder and the two disappeared. Mary looked around her. They really were gone, dissolved into the air. She inspected her bleeding palm, noting it would soon become infected.

She dialed Aiyanna, absently adding this instance to the list of things for which she and the werewolves owed the shapeshifter. *There will come a time, I'm sure, that we will be able to repay her.*

As Mary waited for Aiyanna to arrive, a sense of peace, of utter *rightness* came over her. She didn't know what it meant to be a *thysía* for someone, and she knew nothing of the ways of werewolves, but this arrangement would change everything.

She knew that just as she knew breaking the blood bond would kill her.

Electric thrill buzzed through her body, exciting every muscle, almost causing her straight hair to curl. *I can keep my Raphael.*

But at what cost? The voice of reason cut through her joy, but she shoved it back, opting for a moment of peace.

Besides, Raphael had saved her and Leila when he barely knew them. Now she could do something for him and those he considered friends.

Aiyanna pulled up, her convertible top down and her hair pulled into a severe, wind-proof knot. When Mary held her bleeding hand out toward the healer, her eyebrows lifted over the top of her large, round sunglasses. "What happened to your hand, girl?"

She got out of the car, immediately pulling Mary's hand into hers. Instantly, the stinging pain lessened, the skin of her palm weaving itself together until only a faint scar was left.

Smiling at her friend, Mary said, "I set something right."

My Prince Charming isn't going pumpkin on me after all.

Aiyanna's golden eyes narrowed knowingly. She pulled a wet wipe from her purse and dabbed away any traces of blood. "I hope you're sure about that, screamer."

* * * *

Jeremiah was back in New York City, his favorite residence. Its location was the reason he'd been given the only *clan prohibitum* in the eastern United States.

He expected it when Vale turned to him, his claws out and eyes blazing.

Jeremiah had seen a business opportunity and taken it, but Vale couldn't know that.

"She's an *innocent,*" Vale growled, shaking his lethal fist at Jeremiah. He knew Vale would kill him if provoked; the man's temper was legendary. Which was why it was so damn funny that Heath, the *reasonable* brother, had been exiled.

Heath was also the more powerful of the two, making it more ... beneficial for Jeremiah to oversee him, rather than his brother.

No one would pay ludicrous amounts to keep Vale out of their pack—he wasn't a threat to anyone. In fact, as a head soldier, he had close friends, powerful friends Jeremiah didn't want for enemies.

He couldn't kill Vale tonight, but he couldn't let the other were disrupt his plans, either.

He leaned against the polished door to his penthouse on the Upper East Side, choosing to appear unaffected by Vale's show of aggression.

"She chose." Jeremiah shrugged as if it were all out of his control. "*She* approached *us,* as I recall."

Red mottled Vale's face. "She didn't know, *still* doesn't know, that she's going to die for him now." He brought his claw in front of Jeremiah's face. "What if she could be his mate? That would automatically free him."

To punish a werewolf was to punish his or her mate, which was generally frowned upon. Mates were supposed to be treasured, *never* harmed, as many weres never found theirs. For Raphael to be mated with this woman would mean his freedom.

Jeremiah couldn't let that happen.

Five hundred years ago, he'd made a blood bond with Hans Ivar, a stone-cold alpha who'd had hundreds of humans killed, all without the Elders' knowledge. An alpha who couldn't control his pack, he became a member of the church and correctly blamed the crimes on werewolves, but pointed the finger at regular humans. Every couple of decades or so, Ivar would raise an orphaned human boy to trust him, to owe him so much he would do anything for the church he'd grown up in.

Raphael never stood a chance, the poor bastard.

When Raphael learned that all the interrogations, and the two executions in which he'd delivered the killing blows, were farces created to save face for a failing leader, he'd demanded the Elders to be taken far away and punished.

Worried his ill-kept secrets would be revealed, Hans paid Jeremiah enough he could have bought the Louisiana Purchase himself in exchange for a blood bond to ensure Raphael would stay in exile, his word worthless to the Elders and active pack members, until he died.

Jeremiah would contact the old ally, the terribly weak leader, and courteously inform him of Raphael's imminent death.

As for the girl, Mary, her head would be a wonderful gift for Richard Van Otterloo. The man was still livid over the death of Gaspar and wanted her blood for what she'd done. He was waiting for the right moment to seize the banshee, but Jeremiah had stepped in first.

He smelled a bonus check, maybe another wing added to his funhouse in Miami. Another dungeon-themed wing, perhaps.

Having been raised in abject poverty, his stomach never more than half-filled until after he'd been bitten in adulthood, Jeremiah appreciated the finer things in life. Now he liked to fill himself with expensive meats and wines. He preferred to have many plush options on which to lay his head each night, with just as many plush options to lie next to him.

It required many constant incomes and creative ways to gain them. So far the botos proved to be more lucrative than he'd initially anticipated, supplementing the yearly payments made by those who wanted to keep his other four exiles out of the way. With the financial stability they provided, the botos could be long-term partners.

Jeremiah was almost certain Raphael and Mary were mated, linking their lives. Their deaths would cement the relationship and fulfill his bond to Ivar, freeing him from the bond's death threat.

"If she were Raphael's mate," Jeremiah said carefully, "the Elders would have lifted his sentence. They haven't. There was never any question: Raphael must die."

Lies. The eight Elders had questioned him shrewdly, judiciously, and argued amongst each other for hours before deciding Raphael should be put to death. Arrogant in their age, they didn't suspect Jeremiah would dare lie to them, which would merit severe punishment. He'd been doing so for years, weaving tales about his criminals that shocked and disgusted. Some of the things he told them were acts he'd done. He liked to see their reactions, the frowns sinking into their lined faces.

They simply had better things to concern themselves with than to suspect a *lupus dux* with a spotless record.

"I still don't understand why she would have approached you at all if she weren't his mate," Vale said thoughtfully, unconvinced.

Time for Plan B. He needed to draw his attention away from Mary and Raphael, and toward Vale's own interests. He would tell Vale what he most wanted to hear, causing the powerful were to be in *his* debt. "A life is being taken," Jeremiah said, examining his lazily expanded claws, "I don't see why one the Elders didn't initially sanction has to be taken as well. I'll speak to them about today's events, and clear Mary to be *thysía,* as it hasn't been done in over two hundred years. Heath doesn't have to die this week," he finished gravely.

If Jeremiah cared to feel such emotions, he would have found Vale's expression to be heartbreaking. Tears swam in the man's eyes, an expression of unanticipated happiness crossing his features.

"Thanks, man," he said, thumping his hand on Jeremiah's shoulder. It *hurt;* the oaf didn't realize his own strength. "My pack— my *family* will never forget this. We owe you."

Jeremiah intended to receive his compensation too. The Elders didn't yet know Heath was to be executed, so this change was convenient for Jeremiah.

He simply wouldn't tell them about Mary; he had no doubt they would bring in a witch to break the blood bond.

"I'll see you Sunday," Vale murmured, swiping at his eyes.

The blubbering fool used his air ability to take himself back to Asheville, where he would sing Jeremiah's praises to his pack. *Life is sweet.*

What Vale didn't realize was, there would be a huge bonus for killing Heath, which Jeremiah fully intended to do ... eventually. Something heinous would be done by each of the remaining exiles. They were breaking down in their prison, going mad without their powers. They would *deserve* to die, and in turn Jeremiah would receive a massive parting check for each of them.

In time, all of their sentences would end in death.

The system in which Jeremiah worked was beautifully flawed, and he would expose those flaws for his own gain until the moment the risk outweighed the reward. The Elders were so blind, he would never be at risk for exposure. He'd been fooling them for twice as long as it had taken to convince them he was worthy of their trust.

In the end, Jeremiah had the protection of five very powerful, ruthless immortals, and now a pod of botos. He swung open the door to his apartment where a prostitute wearing only gold pasties greeted him, a hundred-dollar glass of cabernet in her hand.

He was untouchable.

⬚

Chapter 12

"There you are," Raphael exclaimed, a smile spreading across his face. Mary found him in the living room sitting with an irritated Heath, who stiffly nodded at her before trudging off, muttering under his breath.

A soft-looking navy T-shirt stretched across the expanse of Raphael's chest, his strong arms relaxed at his sides. Mary wanted that shirt off, those arms wrapped around *her*.

His expression was the most open she'd ever seen it. There were no shadows, nothing but trusting contentment, just from the sight of her.

Mary couldn't help it; she launched herself at Raphael, straddling him and kissing his chest, his throat, and then the palms of his hands.

"I'll give you your toast later," Raphael said, his voice muffled from her kisses. His deep laughter turned to hums of pleasure as pieces of clothing came off and lips pressed against bare skin. She took him into her mouth, warm and soft and utterly rigid, but he pulled away with a groan, reversing positions to lick her until she shook, shouting his name.

This time it was she who pulled *him* back up. She straddled his waist again, pressing herself onto him slowly, so slowly as he threw his head back. She could barely control herself as she rode him, losing that control when she shattered around him, his arms holding her tightly against his chest.

Soon he cried out his release, taking her over the edge again. Raphael kissed her temple when she slumped against him, exhausted from their lovemaking.

"Next time," he whispered to her, more than a little amusement touching his voice, "let's close the doors."

She gasped, realizing too late that the doors to the living room were wide open, exposing them to anyone passing by. "Did anybody see—"

"No," Raphael reassured her, rubbing his hand down her back. "If they had, I would have had to clean their eyes with sandpaper."

A giggle rose in her throat and escaped.

"I love you, Mary." Raphael ran his thumb along the lines of her smile, his eyes shining.

"And I love you." Mary kissed the underside of his chin. "There was talk of toast?" Raphael made her favorite treat better than she did.

He fed her by hand while Mary needled him about what foods he liked. She was surprised to learn of his affection for the beignets she'd introduced to him. They decided to grab a few before sundown, talking as they walked down South St. Peters. Tonight was the last night of the full moon.

Raphael filled her in on Sebastian's sister Sophia's role for tomorrow, worry filling his voice, the reality behind his unease causing Mary's stomach to sink. The woman had to be incredible or insane.

Beyond the concern for Sophia, who might be sacrificing herself for countless women, a part of her was screaming for attention, pleading that maybe, just maybe she'd made a grave mistake in being Raphael's *thysía*. She forced a smile to her face even as she wondered about the meaning of the strange word, and what it would mean for her on Sunday morning.

It's done. All she could do was enjoy the time she had with Raphael, and pray everything fell into place.

Mary wiped powdered sugar from Raphael's cheek, sipping hot

chocolate as a light breeze tickled her legs. Determination, relief and fear mingled within her. *Soon the botos will be gone, and there will be no threats toward Raphael.* Of that, she was certain.

They stayed as close to sundown as they could, preparing for the following day while they watched the barges float by.

* * * *

From Sebastian's description, Sophia was not who Raphael expected her to be.

He'd thought she would be tall and muscled; an Amazon warrior woman who'd never lost a fight.

Everyone agreed to meet at the brewery, which Sebastian said was Sophia's favorite place in the city. Raphael suspected she was proud of her brother, as the rest of his pack was. When she entered Sebastian's spacious office, doubt wrenched apart their plan for the night.

The woman they were sending into certain danger stood at least five or six inches shorter than Mary, her frame tiny. Her delicate face belonged on a doll, not a soldier going into battle. Indecision had Raphael exchanging a look with Heath, whose green eyes flashed toward Sebastian, his expression angry.

"You're letting *her* be taken by those sickos?" he exclaimed, disbelief coloring his voice. "Why don't you just kill her yourself?"

Sebastian flew at Heath, but Sophia was quicker. Her head didn't reach Heath's shoulders, yet her presence was every bit as large as his. Her gaze didn't waver as she looked up at him. "My brother couldn't stop me from doing this," she growled, her small claws coming out to aim at him. "So why don't you pull your misogyny out from your ass and focus on how we can help these humans."

She'd kept her elemental power to herself out of a kindness that belied her words. After that day at Pat O's Raphael had done the same thing, unwilling to see the sadness in his friends' expressions.

Beside Raphael, Mary grinned. "I think I'm going to like her," she said in voice so low the others wouldn't understand her.

Despite himself, Raphael's opinions of the sprite-sized were raised. Very few could stand toe-to-toe with Heath without backing down.

Alexandre, Raphael realized, was the only one who hadn't been surprised by Sophia. He must have met her before. "You'll nail their balls to the wall before they can touch you," Alex told her encouragingly. The way she still eyed Heath, Raphael didn't doubt she was capable of it.

Maybe she could walk away from her time among the botos with minimal scarring after all. Raphael, Heath, Sebastian and Alexandre would equip her as best they could given their limited knowledge of what went on inside the botos' houses. Cael still flat-out refused to be involved in the plan. As of that morning, he'd left more disgusted with them than ever after hearing Sophia would still be sent in.

A few minutes ago, Raphael might have conceded Cael was right. Now, he wasn't so sure.

They told Sophia everything they knew about the botos. They didn't believe the mind control would work on her, but they *knew* it was unsuccessful on banshees. They warned her she might be chained, and of the human guards who feared the results of disobedience more than anything else.

At that Sophia nodded knowingly. "They'll be dangerous," she said, pity filling her wide blue eyes. "I'll watch out for them."

The last piece of information they gave her sent Sophia into a round of cursing that sounded odd coming from her high, feminine voice. The woman uttered words even Raphael never spoke.

"*Jeremiah is in on this?*" Sophia shrieked, throwing her hands up. Steam wafted from her skin. Her auburn hair rose, as if alive. *Her element must be fire.*

An almost imperceptible gasp sounded beside him. Mary almost fell, her knees going out from underneath her. The color had leeched from her face, which was now as pale as her hair. Raphael lifted her into his arms, cradling her close. She was his top priority, and something was wrong.

"I'm fine, I'm fine," Mary said in a way that screamed *I'm not okay.* She refused to meet his eyes. Trembling, she still pushed at his chest, demanding to be put down. "I just locked my knees for too long," she said, but he wasn't convinced.

Raphael set her on her feet, keeping an arm wrapped around her waist. She didn't protest but leaned against him gratefully, ignoring his probing stare. Her attention was on Sophia's tantrum. He decided to address this with Mary later, instinct telling him his mate was in danger.

He wanted to lock her in his room until the storms passed, but he knew she'd never forgive him if he did. Raphael would have to be vigilant, watching out for her as well as his pack. It would be tough, but it was doable; it had to be. He'd been practicing his powers out of sight, gaining the strength he would need to kill Jeremiah. He only hoped adrenaline would help him control the ice he still couldn't use forcefully. Now it shattered against walls, slowly breaking into pieces.

On more than one occasion, he'd seen Jeremiah use ice to drill a hole through brick, likely just to show that he could. *I'll get there.*

"I *knew* he was a corrupt bastard. Working with the *human trafficking botos,* the *dickhead,*" Sophia shouted. "You never should have been sent here, Sebastian, and for *this long* ... this is just—" She broke into another string of cursing. Next to her, Alex blushed crimson.

Sebastian's hand on top of her head stopped her rant. The image caused them to look like the twins that they were. Their coloring was the same, their frowns similar where one side of their mouths drew down more than the other. The great difference between them was their height: Sebastian stood over a foot taller than her, his muscles prominent, while Sophia's were lean and subtle.

"Our pack will see what a piece of trash he is," Sebastian said soothingly. "They'll alert the Elders; changes will finally be made."

Mary let out a long breath, as if relieved. Had she met Jeremiah? *No, she couldn't have.*

"Oh, the Elders will know about this," Sophia promised, her eyes narrowed on her small face. Again, Raphael doubted their strategy. Sebastian would never recover if Sophia were hurt, much less killed.

But Sebastian was smart as well as strategic, characteristics he'd proven again and again while financing the pack. If he really thought the botos posed a great risk to Sophia, he never would have suggested her involvement. He knew better than anyone what his sister was capable of.

Soon Sophia was outfitted with enough weapons to outweigh her, including both a handgun and small tranquilizer gun supplied by Mary, but she simply stowed them away in various pockets and loops as if they were nothing. The group agreed to meet at Thump at ten that night, Heath silently frowning as they spoke, his arms crossed over his chest. His phone buzzed for the fourth time since Sophia's arrival, creating a square of light in his pants pocket.

"You going to get that, buddy?" Alex asked.

"No," Heath ground out.

Alex held up his hands in defeat. "Sorry I asked."

Raphael, Mary, Heath and Alex left the brewery, a solemn silence falling over them. Raphael knew they were all thinking the same thing: *What if she's not as tough as she seems to be?*

Heath was easily the most agitated of the group. He kicked a tree so hard bark went flying. Two blocks before they reached the firehouse, he jerked a one-way sign into a ninety-degree angle. Mary watched him with wide eyes, but she was the first to approach him. She touched him lightly on the back to gain his attention. He turned to snarl at her, his expression forcibly relaxing at Raphael's furious growl.

His friend seemed to have calmed down, but Raphael carefully watched every move he made as he interacted with his mate. It was unusual, but Heath was unstable.

"She will burn that place to the ground, like you and Raphael did to one of their houses," she threw affectionate, proud glance to Raphael, who'd told her about taking out the terrible place during their date last night, "before she'll let them so much as touch her, and I bet she can do it without harming a single human."

Heath shook his head. "Do you know how impossible that sounds? We're expecting too much of her."

Mary nodded. "I think she expects as much and more of herself," she said.

Alex walked backward to face them, his smile turning to a grimace and back as he tripped over a tree root in the cement. "She can do *damage*." He raised his eyebrows. "The woman is downright scary."

Heath snorted; Alex huffed impatiently. "Believe me or not, *asshat*, if anyone can hold their own long enough for backup to arrive, it's Sophia. And that's *if* she doesn't up and take them all out herself."

So Sebastian and Alex were in agreement. *Good.* The two weres who knew her best believed this would work. A small portion of his guilt receded, his concern turning to Mary. What had happened back at the brewery?

He asked her a few minutes later, back at the firehouse. Heath had made a beeline for the workout room, Alex following him to make sure he wouldn't break the treadmill he'd just replaced.

"I don't want to lose you," Mary whispered, her eyes filling up. She turned to look at the ceiling, trying to blink away her tears. Raphael wrapped her in his arms, wishing he could protect her even from the act of crying. He *hated* to see her cry.

A few minutes later, she met his gaze. "I don't want someone like Jeremiah to keep you from me," she said, salty trails marking her delicate features. Even sobbing, she was the most beautiful woman he'd ever seen. "I can't explain it, but I need you, Raphael." She hiccupped, shook her head. "I'm sorry, I know we agreed you would have to leave."

"No." Raphael's voice trembled from his own emotion. This was his mate; he couldn't have her thinking he wouldn't fight for her. He wouldn't leave her, no matter the circumstances. In that moment, he refused to believe anything could separate them.

It was why Jeremiah had to be eradicated.

He lifted her face to his and kissed her gently. "I'm not going anywhere," he promised. "No one, not even my *lupus dux* is going to stand between me and my woman." He kissed her again, harder. "I want to keep you too," he said. "I *will*."

Mary started crying again. Still hiccupping, she smiled. Their mouths met in the wettest kiss Raphael had ever experienced.

As he and Mary alternately pulled each other to his bedroom, Mary laughing and crying at the same time, Raphael absently wondered what Sophia meant to Heath. If anyone ever dared to place Mary in such a perilous situation—no matter what the circumstances—he would rip out their throats with his teeth.

* * * *

A content Molly in her arms, Mary watched Cael pace across Wish's open kitchen and living room, his heavy boots soundless against the polished hardwood. Almost an hour ago, Raphael and Heath had dropped her off before heading to Thump. Raphael flat-out refused to let her go with them, insisting it would throw the entire operation off should the botos or their henchmen try to kidnap her.

"I'd kill all of them," he'd told her earnestly.

She believed his harsh statement, the words wrapping around her like a blanket. She also knew he didn't want her to see Sophia being taken, as it would haunt her even more for witnessing and allowing it to happen. It would deeply disturb Raphael, no matter how necessary Sophia's kidnapping was.

"Go," Aiyanna said from her perch on the granite countertop, her legs swinging out, punctuating her command. "We don't need you here." She threw her car keys at Cael. A strange doll hung from them, an unnatural smile drawn on its face. Cael caught the keys without a glance in their direction, his eyes cast downward.

"I don't understand how they can do this to her," Cael said, his stride continuous.

"This is the only way they know how to end the botos' reign of terror," Mary said softly. "They could probably use your help." She didn't move from her spot in a soft armchair. Cael was on edge in a way that warned her away from him.

Molly didn't feel the same way. She scooted herself off Mary's lap, lifting her slight weight to stand. Mary thought she would make a beeline for Wish or Leila, who were poring over Leila's textbooks they'd spread across a coffee table, but Molly ran up to Cael, taking his hand and keeping speed with his pacing. She jogged for a moment, her dark curls bouncing, until Cael slowed.

Looking down at the little girl who clasped his hand, Cael asked, "You think I need to go help my pack, don't you?"

Molly nodded eagerly. "Go help!" she exclaimed.

Cael inclined his head to her. Heat seared his gaze as he looked at Aiyanna. "You're right," he said. Clutching her keys, he grabbed a salt shaker and walked out the door.

"I'm *always* right!" Aiyanna called after him. Molly waved.

Somewhat relieved Raphael would have more backup if something were to go awry, Mary turned to Aiyanna. "Now we wait," she murmured irritably. She didn't like being this powerless, unable to help Raphael.

"It won't be long," Aiyanna said self-assuredly.

"What?" Mary had expected them to be gone for hours.

Aiyanna held up her phone, touching a cheerfully colored application. "I can track where my car goes," she said with a sly smile. "Once they stay in one place for a while, we'll roll in and help."

"I think I can manage Molly and Leila," Wish said dryly. He'd warded the house against botos, using salt, which he'd found would greatly weaken them and stop humans under their control altogether. *"They're river dwellers,"* he'd explained to Raphael and Heath earlier that night. *"Their base form can't tolerate salt."*

Glad to be in a position where she could do *something*, Mary sat back and watched Aiyanna's car scuttle along a miniature map of New Orleans for a moment before taking out her own phone.

Unable to stem her curiosity, she used the spare time to Google search the term *thysía*. She'd hoped to go through Wish's books to find the answers she needed, but there were so many on his wall-to-wall bookshelves, she didn't know where to start without asking him. It was a conversation she didn't want to get into.

More search results popped up than she expected, but they were all in Greek. Before the translation downloaded, Aiyanna looked down at her phone curiously, and Mary quickly exited her browser before the shapeshifter saw what she was researching.

With a sigh, she conceded she would find what *thysía* meant soon enough. Never in her life had she feared a sunrise more.

* * * *

The music at Thump felt like a jackhammer against Raphael's sensitive ears. He couldn't understand how Sebastian and Alexander actually *liked* places like this. Like last time, Raphael didn't bother to dance. He stood, scanning the crowd for men drugging cocktails, or patrons scoping out the women a little too closely. Alexandre, Sebastian and Sophia were doing the same. Heath was preoccupied with keeping humans away from Sophia, something the female did not seem to appreciate.

"I'm a target, *remember?*" she jeered.

Heath ignored her, staring down another human who'd been moving closer to Sophia until he danced in another direction.

All of a sudden, Heath doubled over, breathing heavily. "*Son of a bitch,*" he moaned, grabbing himself protectively.

"I warned you," she said in a sing-song voice, her gaze constantly moving over the throng.

"There." Raphael jerked his head toward the back right corner of the room. Two men sat in a blacklit booth with two blonde women, the latter of whom were sipping pastel-colored drinks, their eyes drooping. The men watched the women stoically, as if waiting for them to pass out. They were obviously under the botos' control—their eyes were wide, the man on the right jumping when a dancing man accidentally slammed into their table.

The botos must have learned from Leon.

The others observed the group, each looking sickened. "You found them," Alex said morosely. He took a long pull of his amber drink.

Sebastian faced Sophia, who watched the booth in disgust, horror dawning on her expression. "You don't have to go through with this." Sebastian took her hands. "We can find another way."

All the men agreed, but Sophia shook her head. "Then what will happen to those women?" She pointed to the blondes. One of them was already passed out, her head falling onto the other woman's shoulder. "I'm going over there, I'm going to be taken to the botos, and you guys are going to make sure the cavalry comes as soon as they can."

She reached up and hugged Sebastian tight. "I love you, bro. I'll be all right."

His expression hard, Sebastian said, "I'm going to hold you to that. Love you too, sis."

With his nod, Sophia wound through the dancers until she was in front of the booth. The way she was dressed, in a shining red dress that barely covered what women *needed* to cover—something a few of the females here seemed to have forgotten—and heeled boots that didn't add enough to her height, Sophia looked like any other mid-twenties patron at Thump. At first glance, she may even be perceived as weaker than most due to her lack of height.

Raphael wondered how she could have hidden any weapons.

She appeared confident as she spoke with the men, waving daintily at one when he left to buy her a drink. It was only because he looked for it that Raphael saw Sophia's fear. She was breathing rapidly, fidgeting with the edge of the table while she flirted with the remaining henchman. She tried to speak with the two women, but neither responded. The one who clung desperately to consciousness only managed to blink at her slowly.

"He put something in her drink," Alex growled, his eyes on the man at the bar. Leaving an excessive tip on the counter, the stocky man made his way back to his colleague and Sophia, handing her the cup.

Raphael clenched his fists when she threw it back in a few long gulps, wiping her mouth with gusto.

"*No,*" Heath roared, surging toward Sophia. It took all three of them to hold him back, the din of the club having covered his cry.

"See that?" Sebastian forced Heath to look at Sophia while Raphael held his arms. "Look at her, man."

Sophia glanced up at the group, her eyebrows rising at Heath's position. She held up her phone slightly, saluting them.

"She's texting Vale and ten soldiers from our pack, telling them what's happening before her phone's taken away. They aren't going to waste any time to get her back. The cavalry *is* coming," Sebastian finished.

He and Sophia knew Vale, who was apparently famous among werewolves for his rare ability to transport himself and others long distances through the air. If the man could eliminate the hours it would otherwise take for Sophia's pack to travel from Nova Scotia, there was no questioning whether he should be involved.

Sophia should be captured for less than an hour—longer than any woman should ever be kidnapped, but a much shorter amount of time than Raphael had initially expected.

One of the men watched as she put her phone back in her small black purse. Sophia's eyes fluttered closed, then back open. She was feigning the effects of the drug; her breathing was just as quick and fearful as it had been minutes ago, but she obviously wasn't backing out.

Sophia's determination to save the kidnapped women had overcome her fear. She'd earned Raphael's respect, and he knew the rest of his pack felt the same way.

Heath's arms relaxed beneath his grip. "You good now?" Sebastian asked him. Heath nodded, his grimace murderous, but he made no move toward Sophia. He whirled around, drawing Raphael's gaze to Vale, who was approaching them.

"What the hell is going on?" Vale asked, his gaze sweeping the room. "The Halifax clan is taking up arms, and from Sophia's text I can see why—no wonder you haven't returned any of my calls," he finished, obviously disgruntled.

"We need you to take the soldiers from their pack here," Heath ground out, surprising Raphael. In five hundred years he hadn't spoken of his brother, and their exchange the day before didn't indicate any love lost between them. For him ask this of Vale, Heath was truly desperate to help Sophia.

An image of Mary appeared at the forefront of Raphael's mind. He understood the absolute *need* to protect his woman; although, he suspected Heath hadn't consciously realized that Sophia belonged to him.

Heath filled Vale in on the botos' actions in the city, neglecting to tell his brother of Jeremiah's involvement. No one brought it up. Unlike Sophia, Vale would likely have to see it to believe the *lupus dux* was capable of such things. As Heath spoke, Vale ground his molars together, his nostrils flaring. The air around them shifted, agitated.

Vale nodded jerkily, looking from Heath to Raphael. "I'll bring as many as are willing to come; we can't just leave those women." He followed their gazes to Sophia, who was now faking the drug's full effects. One of the men had her arm over his shoulder, helping her rise from the booth. "Where do you want me to bring them?"

Raphael told him the coordinates for the botos' mansion, where he was fairly certain the henchmen would take Sophia.

Vale blinked out of their vision and immediately came back, causing a few nearby dancers to do a double take. "I'm glad you're not being executed," he said sincerely, meeting Raphael and Heath's eyes. "I never supported it."

With that, he was gone.

Raphael and Heath exchanged a confused look. "I wasn't aware Jeremiah decided not to kill us," Heath said warily. "Were you?"

Raphael shook his head, his mind racing. *What did Jeremiah do?* Foreboding crawled underneath his skin. He didn't have time to focus on the possibilities behind Jeremiah's decision as Sophia and the two women were being taken from the club. Hardly any strange glances followed them, as if men taking unconscious women away were a regular occurrence.

Raphael *really* disliked Thump.

His pack followed the henchmen until they closed their captives into a black SUV, its tinted windows hiding Sophia from sight.

When the large sedan drove off, Heath roared again, throwing a punch into a nearby pickup truck. Its alarm went off, sending suspicious looks flying their way.

Lines of strain framing his mouth, Sebastian pulled out his own car keys. "Let's go make sure no one touches her."

A white convertible came to a screaming stop next to them. Cael was driving Aiyanna's car. "I can follow them in case they go somewhere new," he said. "Anyone want to get in?"

Heath moved toward the two-passenger car, but Sebastian stopped him with a feral look before giving him the keys to his G-

Wagon and getting into the convertible.

Sebastian and Cael sped off at a faster pace than the SUV, both men practically folded in half in order to fit inside the tiny car.

Ten minutes later, Heath swerved the Mercedes into a spot behind Aiyanna's car. Sophia had been taken to the mansion they'd watched days ago, when they were unable to touch the botos. Tonight would be different—tonight each one of the river creatures would die, freeing their human captives. It would be a warning to their remaining kin.

Stay out of New Orleans.

It was becoming the darkest part of the night. Heavy clouds blended in with the sky, blocking any stars and the waning moon from view. A harsh wind pressed against them, cool from the lake. For a Saturday night, the neighborhood was eerily quiet; there should have been a crawfish boil within the vicinity, with a band playing and beer flowing. Instead, Raphael could only hear the *whoosh* of cockroaches' wings as they flew from house to house scavenging.

A half block closer to their mark, Cael and Sebastian stood with five tough-looking weres, their black clothes bulging with weapons. As Raphael approached the group, Vale brought a sixth and disappeared.

"Salt?" one of them murmured doubtfully, throwing and catching a round case of it.

A man identical to him grabbed the salt from the air with a shrug. "Why not try it?" he said.

"It'll stop the human guards, and you don't want to kill them anyway—" Alex started. A were with black eyes and a silver mohawk cut him off. "*We* can kill as many human guards as we want," he sneered. Red patches appeared on Alex's cheeks. "We aren't criminals," the man continued. "Why should we trust any one of you?"

His words caused something in Raphael to snap. Technically, he *was* a criminal, as were the rest of his packmates, but they'd been punished enough. He would trust any of them at his back, and these newcomers were going to have to trust them as well, or the botos would win. *Jeremiah* would win, and those outcomes were unacceptable to him.

The man was thrown against a nearby fence, his hands and feet bound by growing vines. Heath helpfully flicked open his Zippo, giving Raphael a flame to work with. He pulled it into a ball, which started growing from his influence but continued on its own. He hovered it a few feet above the highest spike of the were's mohawk.

"You don't have a choice," Raphael snarled. Soon, the orb would envelop the man. "We have only told you the truth, and will continue to do so. But if you don't listen, and a *single* human is killed as a result, I will burn you alive."

The sphere expanded; now it was less than an inch away from its target, who ducked his head as far as he could, the back of his neck blistering from the heat. He looked up, meeting Raphael's eyes. "Tonight, we'll be equals," he said.

The other soldiers murmured their agreement.

Raphael brought water from the lake, dousing the fire. Drops fell onto the were while the vines unraveled themselves, freeing him. "I'm Tristan," he said, holding out his hand. Raphael took it and introduced himself and the rest of his pack, excluding Sebastian, who knew most of the soldiers by name.

"How did you do that? I thought your powers were bound," Tristan asked, respect lacing his voice.

Raphael glanced at Sebastian, who inclined his head, indicating Tristan was trustworthy. "I'm mated," he said.

Tristan nodded thoughtfully. Having just brought another soldier, Vale turned white, horror filling his expression. "You can't be," he rasped. "Jeremiah said—the Elders said..." He trailed off, violently shaking his head. "You should be freed," Vale whispered darkly.

"It's true," Theo, one of the twins, said decisively. "It's nonnegotiable too—our mates are not to be harmed. It went into place about a hundred years ago?" He aimed the last statement at his brother.

"Give or take a few years," the other twin, Eli, responded.

Vale drew a hand down his face, gripped the back of his neck, and disappeared. A minute later, he'd brought two female soldiers.

"Now that you're all here," Vale said, addressing the Halifax packmates, "I need you to listen to me. If you see Jeremiah, the *lupus dux* for the exile clan, do not trust him. Anything he tells you to do, run it by me first. I'm bringing the Elders here." His face was a mask of sorrow. "I've seen enough to know he has betrayed that which we hold most dear." Vale met Raphael's eyes. "Is Mary your mate?"

Raphael nodded shortly, violently subduing the urge to go for the other man's throat. How in the hell did Vale know about Mary?

Vale cursed. "I'm sorry," he said, his sadness genuine. "Jeremiah has made her your *thysía*." With those words, he disappeared. They meant nothing to Raphael—he'd never heard the term before.

"What did that mean?" he asked sharply. From everyone else's stricken expressions, he knew it was bad news.

Heath let released a breath. "It means she's being executed for us," he said.

Red coated Raphael's vision. When he yelled, it was guttural, unnatural. Ears bled around him.

"He's mated to a *banshee?*" someone muttered.

Raphael didn't wait for the others. Rage controlled him, coloring everything he saw. He marched for the mansion, pulling out his machete as he went.

⬚

Chapter 13

"They've stayed out in Lakeview for a while," Mary said, watching the unmoving dot that represented Aiyanna's car. It was parked in a nice neighborhood close to the one she'd grown up in. "That must be where they took Sophia."

Aiyanna murmured in agreement. "We're gone," she said to Wish and Leila, her voice soft enough not to wake Molly.

"Don't get yourselves killed," Wish said sternly, handing them a heavy bag of salt. Leila hugged Aiyanna, then Mary. *Go kick some ass,* she signed, smiling slightly. She narrowed her eyes at them. *And next time let me come with you.*

"If you don't have an exam," Mary promised, hugging her back.

They took Wish's Smart Car out by the lake, puzzling over the lack of movement in the area. It was early summer in the South; people should have been *out.* Aiyanna pursed her lips, turning another corner to see another dead street. "Don't people *live* here?" she asked.

Mary was just as dumbfounded. "It's one of the safest places to live," she murmured, disbelieving. "The botos must have gone to see their neighbors."

They parked by Aiyanna's car and an almost pristine G-Wagon Mary had seen near the firehouse, the only cars on the street. None of the streetlights worked, cloaking the block in darkness. It was so quiet Mary could hear the lake under the restrained voices belonging to a darkly-clad group. As a unit they stalked down a driveway, toward the home's backyard.

"I see Cael." Aiyanna's eyes glowed in the darkness. "Those are our wolves, with some add-ons."

"Raphael isn't with them, is he?" Mary thought out loud. She didn't sense his presence among the group, felt no tug toward any of its members.

"No," Aiyanna confirmed.

So cats can *see in the dark*. She wondered where Raphael was. Was he safe? Why had he left his pack?

Cael and a man Mary would have considered pretty if not for his silver mohawk spotted them at the same time. The man growled, freeing dangerously sharp claws that made Mary itch to run in another direction, but Cael knocked him back with a hard shove to his windpipe, leaving the man sputtering for air.

Mary could have sworn she heard him snarl, *"Don't ever threaten her."* Her thoughts were confirmed with one glance at Aiyanna, whose smile rivaled the Cheshire cat's.

"What are you doing here?" Heath demanded, leveling a frown at Mary.

"I only said I would stay away from Thump," she said truthfully. "Where's Raphael?"

A man standing next to an exact copy of himself jerked a thumb toward the lake. Mary started in that direction, stealth be damned. If Raphael was alone, she couldn't waste any time.

It was only he and Sophia against an unknown number of humans and botos—if backup didn't come for them, fast, Raphael, Sophia, and innocent humans would die.

Someone cursed behind her. "Cover her," Heath commanded. The others' footsteps quickening to keep her pace, Mary went in the direction the twin had pointed out. Two backyards and an alley later, she stood before a gaudy mansion guarded by human men holding large guns. An intricate fountain where two dolphins spat color-changing water from their crossed mouths loomed behind the guards.

The stained glass front door gaped open.

Mary ran toward it, belatedly noticing a guard aiming his gun at her. Just as she was about to scream, at least temporarily incapacitating all the humans, he was taken to the ground by an unfamiliar werewolf. From what she could hear around her, the rest of the guards met the same fate. She focused on making it inside the house, relieved no guns were fired.

Fisting a handful of salt in her purse, she entered the massive foyer overshadowed by a glittering chandelier. The house was dimly-lit but impeccably furnished. From the Persian rugs to the dark-hued paintings on the wall, Mary had no doubt the same interior designer behind Richard's house was responsible for this one too. The light reflected by the chandelier bounced along the walls. Someone was moving around upstairs.

Raphael.

Mary jogged up the curving grand staircase, wondering how such a heavily guarded house could seem so devoid of life. A glance over her shoulder revealed Cael and Aiyanna close behind.

At the top of the stairs, she noticed a human hiding behind a bookcase, his gun, equipped by a bulbous silencer, readied to shoot when she passed by. She stopped, waited for him to lean out to see why her footsteps halted, and threw a handful of salt into his face, bringing him to his knees, shaking and whimpering with fear.

Mary's heart went out to him, but Raphael was the center of her concern, closely followed by the brave Sophia. If anything had happened to her in the short time she'd been here, Raphael and the rest of his clan would never be able to forgive themselves.

Light poured out from the cracks in the doorways that lined a long corridor. A man slammed one of the doors open and stumbled into the hall, his black eyes furious. *Not human. Boto.* She'd seen him at least two of Richard's dinner parties, but doubted he would remember her. He wasn't one of the men who'd escaped with Richard the last night she'd worked for the horrible creature.

When he saw Mary and Aiyanna his anger lessened, only to come back in full force as soon as he realized Cael was with them. He held out his hands. For the second time that week, Mary felt as if something was close to her, *trying* to touch her, but a barrier blocked the contact.

"You did *not* just try to screw with my head!" It was the only warning Aiyanna gave before she went wompus on the man, slamming her paws into his chest and throwing him to the ground. One deep slash at his throat, and he was dead.

Still a panther, Aiyanna carefully wiped her claws on his shirt before changing back to her human form. She spat on the boto as she stepped over his body. As soon as she looked away, Cael smiled. Mary shook her head, stopping in front of the doorway the boto came from. No one was in the room, but its walls were covered in monitors. The boto Aiyanna killed had been watching the rest of the house. The other botos, humans and werewolves were depicted in low-quality black and white.

Some monitors displayed empty rooms. Others showed a human woman or two lying docile in chains. Two of them caught Mary's interest: one where Raphael was holding two men's heads and stalking menacingly toward another—*Richard!* In a different area of the mansion, one with better lighting, a seemingly unharmed Sophia spoke with Jeremiah, who gestured wildly.

Apparently, the rest of Raphael's pack and those who came to help them hadn't struggled with the human guards. In every monitor where Mary saw them, the only moving beings were weres.

"I'm going after Raphael." Mary pointed to the monitor labeled *BASEMENT.* She indicated to Sophia's screen. "You two should go check on her; I don't trust Jeremiah not to hurt her."

Cael's eyes darkened. "I don't either," he murmured, nudging Aiyanna's shoulder with his own. "Come with me." Aiyanna raised an eyebrow at Mary before following him from the room, leaving Mary alone.

She more carefully analyzed the rooms depicted, trying to better learn the layout of the house. Once she was more confident in her ability to find Raphael without getting lost in the monstrosity, she took the staircase back to the foyer, finding another narrower staircase leading to the basement.

Eerie blue light reflected onto the walls, similar to that of a lit pool at night. Soon Mary saw why. The floors were made of glass, water flowing underneath it. Each room she passed had narrow walkways made from the glass, with the vast majority of the space uncovered, the water spilling over the glass, licking the walls.

Thinking of the women she'd seen in chains, Mary threw handfuls of salt into the water as she passed by.

She could see Raphael beyond a set of open double doors at the end of the short hall. The blue light caused him to look as if he was covered in royal purple ink, but she knew it was blood. He'd let go of the heads; his fists were clenched, blood dripping from them, his legs apart and slightly bent. He was a hairsbreadth away from making a lethal strike, but restrained himself.

Why?

Even she wouldn't hesitate to kill Richard. From the lives it would save, there was no moral dilemma in her mind.

Quiet footsteps sounded behind her. She turned to see a tan elderly man with a shock of messy white hair approaching. The strength in his gait belied his age; considering him weak would be a mistake. She flicked salt at him, but he only smiled, covered his mouth with his index finger and used it to point at Raphael. Judging he wasn't a threat but unwilling to give him her back, Mary waited for him to stand beside her.

"Let's watch," he said without looking at her, his bright blue gaze on Raphael. His voice was surprisingly strong. "We may not need to intervene."

"Are you a werewolf?" she asked, eyeing him closely. Elderly or not, she wouldn't let him intervene if it meant harming Raphael.

He grinned. "Oh yes, I'm a werewolf," he answered, his lip continuing to curl up as if it were the most amusing question he'd ever heard. "You must be the banshee."

Mary nodded. *I guess "the banshee" is better than "screamer,"* she mused.

"You're mortal?"

"Yes," Mary answered. When were banshees *immortal?*

"Good," the man said decisively. He gave her a satisfied nod before turning to Raphael again.

Silently, they moved into the doorway. Raphael's stance hadn't changed. His back to them, he flexed his hands before clenching them again, allowing Mary to see that much of the blood on his hands was his own, caused by his claws digging into his palms.

She didn't move from her place. She didn't want to distract him, but desperately wished to help. Across the room Richard was pressed into a wall, held by invisible hands. *Like those that let me into the firehouse garage.* Raphael had Richard at his mercy. The heads of the other two men who'd been there the night Gaspar had stabbed her lay forgotten on the glass floor.

"Tell me where the rest of the women are," Raphael said, his voice lower, deadlier than Mary had ever heard it.

"If I did that you would kill me." Blood dripped from Richard's smiling mouth.

"You'll die either way," Raphael snarled. "It will be quicker and less painful if you tell me where we can find them."

"If you keep threatening me, they will all die of starvation." Somehow, Richard had given himself the upper hand.

Richard had put Raphael in an impossible position. Mary wanted to kill him with her bare hands, because she knew Raphael wouldn't touch him if it meant the death of innocent women.

Raphael slowly lowered Richard to the ground. The boto's hands moved behind his back until his wrists touched. Recognizing the disturbed air, Mary realized the ability she had came from Raphael. *He* was the one with real power, and her amazing man was using it to help the defenseless. Pride rushed through her.

"What do you want?" Raphael snapped.

"Freedom," Richard said simply. Despite his bound hands, his expression was utterly smug with the knowledge that Raphael would give him exactly that.

For the sake of the women, Mary didn't doubt he would.

The elderly man cleared his throat, murmuring, "I believe now is the time for us to butt in," so only Mary could hear. In a few long strides he stood before a bemused Raphael, holding out his hand. "Nathaniel," he said briskly, "and I know who you are, as well as who your lady is." He gestured to Mary, who'd been too dumbfounded to move.

She took her place at Raphael's side, pressing a kiss to his cheek. She took his hand as gently as she could.

He barely seemed to register her presence.

"I believe a blood oath is needed here," Nathaniel said, producing a knife. He gave Richard a hard look, one Mary was glad she hadn't received from him. No, she wouldn't be underestimating that were.

"You will both be bound by your oath. To break it will mean death." Nathaniel handed the knife to Raphael.

"If I allow you to live and go free, in exchange you will tell me exactly where *anyone* you have taken or influenced is being kept." Raphael's statement included potentially dangerous men and any nonhumans the botos may have kidnaped. A pleased gleam entered Nathaniel's eyes.

Raphael simply looked more furious than Mary had ever seen him. Tendons and veins stood against his skin. His muscles bulged; his jaw was a rigid line highlighting bared teeth. Not even the water's reflection drifting over his dark skin tempered his lethal appearance.

"I agree to those terms, so long as you don't touch me." Richard spat blood on the floor, his smile red. He looked like an entirely different man from Mary's old boss; the seams of his tailored suit were torn and frayed, his carefully combed hair a matted mess. Mary took a second look—his hair was matted away from a *hole* in his head. Richard had a blowhole only a shade or two darker than his black hair.

How did I not notice that?

Botos were dolphins—parasitic, shapeshifting, freshwater *dolphins.*

"Agreed." Raphael's response was so guttural, Mary could barely understand him. He slashed his hand and handed the knife to Richard, who did the same. They shook on the agreement briefly, their blood mingling just long enough for the oath to hold.

Raphael drew away first, his disgust toward Richard apparent.

Richard quickly rattled off four addresses. Two of them were on streets named for birds, indicating the houses were within blocks of where they currently stood. The other two were somewhat nearby, one in Tremé and the other in Mid-City.

It was over; everyone the botos had harmed would be safe now.

Richard lunged at Raphael, the dagger back in his hand. Before it could hit its mark a shield of ice formed between them. The knife lodged in the ice, useless. Raphael was shaking, he wanted to hurt the boto so badly. But he kept his hands to himself, allowing the ice and the blade to fall to the ground, still intact.

Mary didn't think. She ran at Richard, palming as much salt as she could. She brought it over his head, pushing it into his blowhole before Richard could realize what she was doing, Molly, Wish and even Natasha's faces forming at the forefront of her mind. He started choking, his face turning bluer than the water as he gripped his neck and clawed at his throat. "*Bitch*," he managed, sinking to his knees.

She punched him as hard as she could, feeling bones both in her fingers and his face breaking beneath the force of her hand. She smiled through the pain, turning to Raphael in time to see the shield melt. Nathaniel slowly reached over to take the blade off the floor. It lifted from his hand and embedded itself in Richard's heart, its speed akin to a bullet.

"Now he should be well and truly dead." Nathaniel wiped his hands on his neatly pressed khaki pants. "Let's go see how everyone else is doing." He ambled off, his hair appearing different shades of blue as he went.

A glance at Raphael revealed he was still shaking. Richard, dead and bleeding before them, had done nothing to improve his temperament.

"Raphael, sweetheart," Mary said, moving toward him. "You did it," she murmured. She ran her hands up his chest, cupped his face. "*You* saved all these people."

His glare was pure, sharp onyx. "But I didn't save you, did I? You, who should be protected above all others." When he lifted his hands, water rose from the pool, flowing around the glass walkways and into the air. There was no water left beneath them, only the stone bottom of the pool, its embedded lights glowing yellow. The water crystalized above their heads, some pieces of ice rounded, others tipped in wicked points. All were aimed at the fragile glass structures Mary and Raphael stood upon.

"Let's go." She pulled Raphael into the hall. They were in the stairwell when the ice fell, its clattering sounds mixed with that of breaking glass and separating stone.

"I don't need saving," Mary said, placing Raphael's hands on her waist. "See? I'm fine, completely whole."

He lifted her face up to his. "The deal you made with Jeremiah," he said through gritted teeth. "Tell me everything."

She did, leaving out no details. When she'd finished, she said, "I just didn't want to lose you. I love you, so much."

His expression unreadable, Raphael pulled her into his arms, wrapping her in a tight embrace. He shook and Mary could feel wetness falling into her hair, on her shoulders. "Mary," he said roughly, fisting a hand in her hair. "My *ülikena,* my mate."

That was what they were—Raphael was her mate. The sound of it felt *right,* and it caused something to click into place inside her.

But there was nothing right about Raphael sobbing over her. Mary clutched him firmly, trying to make sense of his words and actions, all of which pointed to one thing.

Now she knew, without question, how big of a mistake she'd made in approaching Jeremiah.

*

Upstairs, voices assailed Raphael.

Keeping Mary's good hand firmly in his, he followed the voices to the mansion's kitchen. An unharmed Sophia was putting ice in bags and handing them to bruised human guards, some of whom were sobbing uncontrollably. All of them had haunted expressions; they'd seen more than any person ever should, all while having no control over their own bodies.

"They're going to need counseling," Mary said sympathetically.

Raphael murmured in agreement. Keeping one hand in Raphael's, Mary rushed over to Sophia, taking him with her. "They didn't hurt you, did they?" Mary asked, looking her over. Sophia shook her head angrily. "They chained the others and me, then left us. It wasn't long until Sebastian found me."

Relief brightened Mary's expression, mirroring what Raphael

felt. Judging from the human men's freedom, all of the botos were dead. Their plan had worked; he almost couldn't believe it.

But nothing can be done for Mary. The thought made him bitter.

He tightened his grip on her hand until she yelped, sending him a surprised look. Raphael quickly apologized, kissing her hand.

Members of Sophia's pack were bandaging the humans' wounds and those of their own. Cael sat on the floor with a bottle of salve in his hand, Aiyanna asleep on a chaise behind him. *She must have overused her healing abilities.*

Cael was putting the salve in any woman's hand that was thrust at him. They rubbed it on the angry rings around their wrists and ankles, tears in their eyes.

Raphael and Mary sank to the floor, leaving the cushioned seats for those more injured, physically or psychologically.

Nathaniel, one of the Elders Raphael had stood before five hundred years ago, one of the six who had decided he deserved to die, was nowhere to be found.

Where are Sebastian and Alexandre? He wanted to tell them and Sophia's packmates about the other houses. He'd done enough for the night—now he wanted to stay as close as he could by his mate before she was killed.

Before he would die with her.

"Where's Jeremiah?" Mary aimed the question at Cael as she accepted an ice pack from Sophia for her swollen hand. Raphael held it in place for her, the ice numbing the stinging cuts on his palms.

"By the time we reached Sophia, Sebastian was already there and Jeremiah was gone." Cael's frown deepened as he spoke.

"He was telling me no one would believe me if I spoke of his involvement with the botos," Sophia said. She handed a wet cloth and some bandages to Raphael. "He even threatened me, told me I could be exiled for spreading lies about a *lupus dux.*"

"What did you see?" Mary placed the ice pack on a nearby table and went to work on Raphael's hands. "Don't do this to yourself again," she whispered to him irritably, gently cleaning his cuts. He didn't have the heart to tell her he wouldn't be able to.

"See for yourself." Sophia pulled out her phone and scrolled through her photo gallery, showing them picture after picture—most of which were blurry and hastily taken—of Jeremiah talking to Richard with a drink in his hand. "They didn't think to take my phone away," Sophia continued with a scoff. None of the pictures were damning until she reached a photo depicting a smiling Jeremiah standing a few feet away from a woman in chains.

Obviously, he was not attempting to help her.

Mary gasped. Satisfaction coiled around Raphael's broken heart.

"There's no coming back from that," Cael said. "Especially given another were had been taken, and he did nothing about it."

"He didn't even recognize me until someone came storming in and tearing things up," Sophia muttered.

All eyes went to Raphael. He said nothing, only wrapped his arm firmly around Mary's shoulders, breathing in lilacs. She sighed against him, and he could tell her eyes were drifting closed.

It had been a long night, and morning was fast approaching.

Quiet footsteps sounded from outside the kitchen. Cael and Sophia both stood, their expressions turning respectful. *The Elder.*

Nathaniel stood over where Raphael and Mary sat. He crouched down level with Raphael, a surprising move. Behind him, Raphael could see Sophia's eyes widen. He didn't loosen his grip on Mary, meeting the Elder's gaze with a scowl.

"She must go through with her agreement." There was no mistaking the seriousness in Nathaniel's tone. He raised his white eyebrows, pursing his thin lips. "It will be the hardest thing you've ever had to do, but you must *let her go.*" The man rose, looked down at him again. "Or you'll lose her."

"I lose her either way," Raphael whispered. If she fulfilled her duty as *thysía,* she would die. If she broke her blood oath, she would die. The man made no sense.

Raphael wanted to trash the mansion until it fell into a quivering heap of sawdust and stone, but he couldn't without harming those inside it who so desperately needed to heal.

The air stopped vibrating around him, satisfied with his decision to refrain from destruction. The way he saw it, what Mary did was her own decision. He wouldn't tell her what the Elder said—if she wanted to die in his arms, hidden from Jeremiah, Raphael wouldn't stop her.

She didn't deserve the violent execution of the weres.

◻

Chapter 14

"Wake up."

Mary smiled at Raphael's soft voice in her ear. "Just a few more minutes?" she whined.

She was *tired*.

"No, sweet." Hands on her face, running down her arms. "Sunup is in less than forty-five minutes."

That jolted Mary awake. She was to be *thysía* soon, something Raphael had wept over. Trying not to think about what that meant, what a man capable of helping Richard hurt women would do to her, she rose, stretching her arms and back. Fear curdled in her belly, but she ignored it. She'd made a promise for Raphael, and she intended to keep it.

No matter what happened to her, if she helped Raphael and his pack she would consider the move a triumph.

"Where is everyone?" She saw a still-sleeping Aiyanna with Cael watching over her, but the humans and Sophia had left. The house was quiet. It seemed even larger now, and even more grotesque in design. Now she noticed chains hidden behind a couch, hooked into the hardwood floor. On a wet bar, next to the whiskey, was a jar of the same herbs Richard's men had fed her.

She hoped the mansion's next owner would gut the place.

"Sophia and her packmates went to the other houses to free the women there," Raphael said, "but the humans beat them to it. Once they were free of their compulsions, the guards set every captive free and contacted the police." A slight smile curved Raphael's lips.

His words, his smile, brought what felt like light through Mary. Of course they set the women free. Mary didn't have to imagine their shock and horror—she'd seen it on the guards' faces when she'd first come up from the basement. That the men had worked together, helping others and calling the proper authorities, gave her hope that they would all move on from the terror they'd lived through.

In time, they'll be all right. She imagined the reunions happening at that very moment.

"It's about that time!"

Glass shattered as a back door was swung open so hard its window broke. Jeremiah had come for her.

"You don't have to go with him," Raphael murmured in her ear. "No matter what you do, you're not a coward."

Mary squeezed his hand, although she disagreed. "I'm going with him," she said definitively. She looked up at him, into his pained eyes. "Whatever happens, I love you. I don't regret trying to keep you."

But maybe I should have thought through how to go about it.

When Raphael kissed her, she felt gut-wrenching agony throbbing within him, intertwined with his love for her. She whispered how she didn't want to live without him, that he was her hero.

"I love you, my *ülikena*. Forever and always." Raphael never stopped combing her hair with his fingers, smoothing the strands over and over again.

"As sentimental as this is," Jeremiah said from the kitchen, "it really is time. Everyone's gathered outside."

He appeared frazzled, the complete opposite of what Mary had seen two days ago. His hair was a frizzed mess, as if he'd been running his hands through it, separating the tight curls. His shirt had splotches of brown stains in its wrinkles.

This time, Jeremiah held a real knife in his hand. Mary wanted to go near it as much as she'd wanted the street water shank to touch her. Hands tightly linked, Mary and Raphael followed Jeremiah to the backyard, leaving Cael's gentle attempts to wake Aiyanna behind them.

Beyond the broken door was pandemonium.

Shoulder to shoulder, Heath and Vale yelled at an unfamiliar older man, advancing toward him until they almost backed him into the kidney-shaped pool. Both hers and Raphael's names were brought into the argument.

Under an ornate cabana, Sophia stomped away from another elderly man, angrily swiping tears from her eyes. Sebastian, Alexandre and the twins were arguing with Nathaniel. Three other strangers, two women and one a man, all with graying or white hair, were in a deep discussion away from the younger weres.

What drew Mary's attention the most was the mohawked man sitting with his back against the ten-foot high brick wall that surrounded the yard. Using a small dagger, he cut grass away from the soil in precise squares, throwing the pieces in the direction of a middle-aged blond man wearing a priest's collar. The man stepped away before the dirt could hit him, eyeing the mohawked were in distaste.

"Here is the *thysía*," Jeremiah shouted suddenly, taking her wrist in his hand and jerking her toward him and the pool, away from Raphael.

Raphael roared, the sound a cross between a wolf's howl, a man's yell, and a banshee's scream. Blood dripped from Jeremiah's eyes and nose.

"Do you want her to break her oath?" Jeremiah snarled, using his shirtsleeve to wipe away the blood.

Raphael stopped moving toward her, but dark promise was clear in his expression. Mary would be surprised if Jeremiah lived out the day.

"Mary Newman," Jeremiah began, holding up Mary's broken hand, "is taking the place of Raphael Saar and Heath Frazier. She will be executed this third day of May in punishment for their crimes, the killing of humans."

As the reason for Raphael's tears crashed into Mary, she turned around to see him running for her. She met his gaze and yelled, tapping into her banshee powers so Jeremiah would *hurt* and everyone else would hear.

"They killed no humans."

She'd barely spoken the words before Jeremiah's arm reached out, slicing the blade across her throat. She gasped for air, only to choke on her own blood.

Raphael reached her before she hit the ground.

She felt herself dying as she fought for breath, but she couldn't bring herself to be angry. *I'm in Raphael's arms; he deserves nothing but love from me.* The world drifted away.

*

Mary died in his arms. His Mary, his *mate,* hadn't flinched at the announcement for her execution. Instead, she'd called Jeremiah a liar, the truth ringing in her voice like a warning bell.

The elders were stalking toward Jeremiah, but Raphael didn't care. He was about to die—wasn't he?

Across the pool, Heath watched him strangely. Cael pulled out his phone and called someone, looking perplexed.

Raphael rocked Mary's small, bleeding form against him, fully believing he was dying. Surely no one could outlive this pain. All hope for a future, all of his will to live had been slashed with Jeremiah's blade.

He had no idea how long he held Mary, his tears soaking her beautiful hair. He only looked up from her frail form when a body thudded onto the stone slabs a few feet away, forcefully enough for Raphael to hear the crack of a skull.

Jeremiah was dead, his sightless eyes appearing almost surprised.

Any other day, Raphael would have been merely curious. Today, he was *furious.*

He gently set Mary on the ground, taking off his shirt to put under her head. Her blood had poured into the grooves between the stones, turning into a cloud of red in the pool. He roared, punching a hole in the stone.

"Who *dared* take my revenge away from me," he growled, his words still tinged with ear-piercing banshee wail. "He was *mine* to kill."

Whoever killed Jeremiah gave him a mercy the man hadn't deserved. For extinguishing the bright light that was Mary, he should have had a slow and painful death, not a sudden one.

Standing among the six Elders, Vale actually smiled, galling Raphael. "Your mate did." He nodded at Mary.

Obviously, Vale was insane.

"They had a blood oath, and she kept her part of it. Jeremiah didn't," Vale exclaimed. "He promised that if she would be your *thysía*, he would treat you and your *clan prohibitum* fairly in terms of our laws."

Nathaniel stepped forward, his eyes on Mary. "The first thing Jeremiah said to us was a reassurance that you *have* killed humans. His death proved you didn't."

"Meaning everything he's told us over the years, regarding *all* of you, may have been lies," one of the Elder women added, her eyes narrowed.

The Elders kept speaking, but Raphael stopped listening. Something else piqued his attention, a slight sound so soft, he barely heard it under the cacophony surrounding him: a feminine cough, followed by a gasp for air.

He was back to Mary, pulling her to him so he was between her and those around them, before she took her next breath.

And she did. He wiped away still-wet blood on her throat to find the slash had healed, leaving a trace of a thin line behind. Feeling for her pulse, he found it thumping strongly against his fingers.

"*Mary,*" he murmured, almost unwilling to believe what he saw and felt. It seemed almost too good to be true; they were both *alive*. He needed her to open her eyes, to speak to him.

Raphael needed to know she was really back with him.

"Please, *ülikena*. Wake up for me." He brushed hair, some of the strands stained red, from her face. He kissed her hand, her eyes and her lips. "Please come back to me."

Slowly, green eyes opened to meet his. Obviously weakened, Mary lifted her hands to cradle his face. "I *knew*," she said hoarsely, her full red lips turning up into a smile, "nothing could keep us apart."

He kissed her with as much love and passion as he could, telling her without words how furious he'd been—still was—and how deliriously happy he was for her to be whole and alive.

He didn't need to hear her apology. It was in the tears in her eyes when she said, "No more secrets from each other. I'll *always* fight for you, but next time I'll tell you before I do anything rash."

Raphael growled, gripping her tighter. *She won't get the chance to fight for me,* he promised himself, noting he should find a way to lock her in her loft. He had no doubt she would find a way out. She was smart and stubborn, his mate, and he knew he would worry for her safety in the future.

But as he held her slender form, her heartbeat gaining more strength with every second that passed, he couldn't think of a single thing he'd change about her.

Before he could tell Mary, Cael squatted beside them. He didn't reach out to touch Mary's neck, but Raphael could tell he wanted to. He nodded in approval; he didn't want anyone else touching her, not until she regained all of her strength.

"You won't have to fight for Raphael anymore." Cael crossed his legs like a child, as if he sat that way every day. He turned to Raphael. "Did you hear a word of the Elders' decisions?"

Raphael shot him a dry look and shook his head.

Cael barked out a laugh. "They want to make you the new *lupus dux* for our clan."

"No." In their eyes he was a criminal, not the leader the *lupus dux* was meant to be.

"Cael's not lying." Nathaniel loomed over him, extending Raphael a hand. "Go on," he pressed. "Mary can stand."

His warning coming back to Raphael, he obeyed, helping Mary to stand beside him. She squeezed his hand, wordlessly reassuring him.

"You knew she wouldn't die."

"Oh, she really died," the Elder said ruefully, cutting a glance at Mary's throat. "But once a powerful banshee dies as a mortal, he or she will be brought back immortal."

Nathaniel smiled. "You're a lot harder to kill now, Mary."

"What do you mean?" she asked, looking down at herself. Raphael understood her confusion. There had been no transformation; Mary looked no different than she did before Jeremiah killed her, except for the blood that marred her creamy skin.

"You can only die by beheading," Nathaniel said bluntly.

Mary sucked in a breath, instinctively wrapping her hands around her neck. Raphael snarled at the Elder. "*She's had enough for this day,*" he growled so low, only the other man and Cael could hear him.

Nathaniel only chuckled good-naturedly, as if Raphael wasn't alarmingly close to punching him so hard he'd forget the night and morning's events. At the moment, Raphael cared nothing for his position; it was his respect for the man's age that protected him.

"Wish said the same thing," Cael chimed in, holding up his phone. "He said he'd explain it all to you, Mary."

She nodded gratefully, but her tug at Raphael's hand and the heat in her gaze when she looked at him said she wanted the same thing: to go somewhere they could be blessedly *alone.*

They'd just found reprieve from death. Raphael wanted to whisk her off to their loft where, after some much-needed lovemaking, they could begin building a life together. He could feel how impatient Mary was to talk to him, to touch him with no outside eyes and ears nearby.

"I think it's a great idea to make Raphael the *lupus dux,*" Mary said cheerfully, pride lacing her voice.

Again, Raphael rejected the notion. He shook his head; just to *consider* him for the position was ludicrous.

"You're free now," Nathaniel said, not unkindly. "You and your mate have earned your freedom—you're no longer bound to New Orleans. If you wish, you can go back to Estonia and join a pack there. I see how loyal you are to these men, but I've also witnessed the strength of your morals. If you choose to be their *lupus dux,* you won't set them free until they're safe to live in packs again, to interact with our youngest and weakest without risk."

Raphael listened to Nathaniel, but the mention of his homeland had him swinging Mary behind him so quickly she couldn't protest. He scanned the crowd and after a moment, found who he was looking for on the other side of the pool, by the garden along the high wall. "Keep her here," he said to Cael and Nathaniel.

"Where are you going?" Mary called out behind him.

He didn't answer, feeling the elements collecting around him. Ice and heat caressed his skin at the same time as wind blew through him, strengthening him, the earth cracking the stone slabs beneath his feet.

"Lighter," he told Heath in a low voice as he passed his former packmate.

Hans Ivar stood away from the rest of the group, so still he had surely gone unnoticed. He'd aged little since Raphael had seen him last; he still appeared to be in his fifties, with no gray frosting his short blond hair.

As Raphael expected, Ivar held a loaded gun at his side. Even in the medieval ages, the man had had a knack for obtaining the latest weapons. This gun was no different: a silencer screwed onto the tip, he fully expected the machine could blow him to pieces.

The second Ivar realized Raphael was watching him, stalking him like a predator, he shot his gun, stark fear in his blue eyes.

No one would have heard had Ivar not hit a fountain, sending marble and water splashing.

Raphael could feel both his packmates and Sophia's coming up behind him, ready to fight. He held up a hand. "He's mine," he said. He wanted to be the one to stop this man, this monster that had ruined lives and fractured families.

Today, he would end Ivar and pray those he'd hurt so many years ago would rest in peace. Raphael would never forget what he'd done to become a criminal, but he would no longer allow it to color his life.

With the death of Hans Ivar, Raphael would finally start anew.

He focused on the ground under Ivar; vines rose from the small patch of grass he was standing in, ripping the gun from his hands and rooting him to stand where he was. "You know what you did to those people," Raphael said to the were he'd once considered his father.

Using the flame from Heath's Zippo, Raphael spread the fire into a sphere that would encompass Ivar. He gently guided it in the older man's direction, but as if it had a sentient mind of its own, the flame engulfed him in seconds.

Agonized screams tore through the morning air, the spreading flames only adding to the quickly rising temperature. Raphael turned and walked away, ignoring the questions thrown at him until he reached Mary, who looked from him to the flames with wide eyes.

Raphael let the vines pull the man into the pool, putting out the fire before it rose above the confines of the wall. Ice grew in spider webs across the blue surface, locking Ivar underneath.

"You're going to explain that, right?" Mary asked, gesturing to the iced-over pool. "I'm sure you had a good reason, but you just *barbequed* someone. Maybe drowned him, too."

He told her everything, aware that everyone else heard his words. He told her how Ivar's church had raised him, expecting him to follow their demands. He told them exactly which orders he'd followed and those he hadn't, as well as the names of the men he'd executed.

Raphael told her his greatest mistakes, baring his charred soul for her to see.

When he was finished, Mary pulled him into a tight embrace, tears falling down her face. "You don't deserve what you've put yourself through," she said into his ear. "You were raised to be brainwashed, and even then you fought back. *He* was the monster to blame." She pointed to the indistinguishable dark mass under the ice.

"Are you sure about him?" a female Elder whispered to Nathaniel, watching Raphael as if he were a viper poised to strike. "He can't burn one of our oldest alphas."

"Oh, yes I am," Nathaniel answered, seeming pleased, "and I believe he just did." He turned to Raphael. "Now you can be the alpha of Hans' pack in Tallinn, if you wish."

Raphael shook his head. "I want to be the *lupus dux* for my pack here." This was his home, these were his people.

Nathaniel nodded. "If you live here with them, that would make you their alpha too."

Raphael turned to face his packmates. "Would you all be happy with this?" he asked, genuinely unsure of whether they would *want* an alpha.

In answer, all four of them stood in front of Raphael, inclining their heads so far they bared the backs of their necks, a were symbol for loyalty and trust.

That quickly, Raphael had gained his freedom and become the alpha of his pack. He met Heath's eyes. "I'm evaluating you first," he said solemnly. "You've been here the longest, and I have a feeling it's been *too* long."

Hope flared in his friend's eyes. Heath smiled. "I'll be on my best behavior," he said with only a hint of sarcasm. "Just find a mate," Sebastian said on a cough. Alexandre burst into laughter.

Nathaniel lifted an eyebrow, but he said nothing.

"I hate to be *that* person, but can we go home?" Mary's voice was weak; she had been leaning more and more heavily against Raphael as they stood.

More than a few weres gratefully groaned their agreement.

On the street in front of the mansion people were standing outside their homes, bewildered expressions on their faces. Despite the early hour, children ran or rode bicycles down the street. Many of the adults were still in pajamas, simply lifting their faces to the sun.

At sight of them, Mary stumbled, her enormous smile never leaving her face. "You did that," she said, her eyes on a baby fiercely guarded by an English bulldog, her parents holding each other a meter away.

Raphael picked her up in his arms. "We did this," he said, simply breathing her in. He flat-out refused to put her down, even when they reached the car.

He never wanted to let her go.

Sebastian stopped his G-Wagon in front of their loft. Still holding Mary, Raphael stepped out of the car and nodded goodbye to his packmates. When he opened the door to the studio, rays of morning sunshine spilled in, drenching him and Mary. It was a new day in a new life, and he would spend every second of it that he could with the woman in his arms.

"Let me down."

Raphael complied, steadying Mary where she stood. She put her hands on his shoulders and jumped up, straddling his waist, pressing her legs to his back. He felt himself hardening as she adjusted her long legs. "Better." She sighed, smiling. She kissed him soundly, clutching him with one hand and caressing the nape of his neck with the other. "You can take me upstairs now," she said after another kiss.

Laughing, Raphael obeyed.

"Are you going to shower with me?" she asked, stripping off her ruined clothes and throwing them in the trash. Her eyes were sparkling, her breasts tipped in tight points. Ripping his clothes off as quickly as he could, he followed her under the spray of warm water, anchoring his hand on the curve of her hip.

"You're going to change all your friends' lives, you know." Mary looked up at him from lathering a rag with soap. She handed it to him, and he took over rubbing the blood and dirt from her fair skin.

Raphael had a feeling she was right. "I only hope it's for the better," he said, running his free hand over the dimples right above her pert bottom.

She took the rag away from him, pinning him with a look so full of fierce love it took his breath away. "In time, in the correct way, you're going to set them all free."

With no words that could express how he felt about the woman he lived for, he bent his head to claim her mouth in a deep kiss, the forgotten rag slapping into the shower floor. Becoming a good leader would take time, as would finding his packmates their freedom. Because of Mary, he had the time, the patience, and the will to do it all. This brave, gentle, beautiful woman had given him everything.

Raphael would make her proud.

Epilogue

Three months later.

Waves licked Mary's shins, the sun beaming brightly enough for her to feel it on her bare shoulders. She stood on the second sandbar in Pass Christian, Mississippi, watching Raphael swim even farther out into the gulf. His movements were graceful and rapid as he cut through the water, reveling in his immortality.

Something about the beach brought forth pure joy in Raphael, something Mary hadn't anticipated. As soon as he laid eyes on the water, she knew they would be coming back, and often. Luckily, when she mentioned the stilted house her parents used to own and had lovingly painted lime green was on the market, Sebastian bought it.

Mary had been shocked by the purchase; Leila cried.

In the few months since the botos had been eliminated from New Orleans, Mary and Raphael moved into the loft above the studio where Mary now painted every day. Her current project was for Sebastian and Full Moon Brewery. Considering his generosity, she made sure her designs would knock his socks off.

Raphael constructed an office in the corner of her studio for his *lupus dux* duties, his desk already piled high with rules and regulations the Elders had sent him. When she'd asked how many rules he'd broken by killing Hans Ivar, he shot her a wry look and said, *"At least fifty."*

Mary was confident he regretted nothing.

Leila had wanted to live with Wish until after her finals were finished, allowing her to be closer to Tulane's campus—although Mary suspected he helped her study considering her final grades, which were even more fantastic than usual. As soon as her tests had passed, Leila shocked Mary by asking if she could move into a house a few blocks away from Wish's. Her roommates were all speech-language pathology majors who knew sign language, but the real reason Mary was thrilled for her sister was because they invited her out, including her in everything they did.

Now Leila was lying on a towel ashore, her hair pulled up so she could get an even tan. Mary had long ago accepted that tanning wasn't in their genetic makeup, but apparently Leila still had hope. Molly and Wish were building sandcastles while Thérèse followed them around with Molly's floppy pink hat and sunblock.

A particularly vicious wave almost pushed Mary over, but the warm air around her pulled her up, steadying her until the water calmed. Even one hundred yards away, Raphael was watching out for her. It was one of the things she loved most about him: before anything else, he was a protector. Not only for her, but also for Leila, his pack, Wish and Molly.

The truth was, Raphael would help anyone he could. He was already implementing a program for his pack to play after school sports with at-risk high school students. They claimed to go along with it because it would make the Elders look upon them more favorably, possibly reducing their sentences, but Mary knew they enjoyed their time with the boys, many of whom had been pressured to join gangs.

Heath and Alexandre had taken care of that particular issue, and had broken no rules in the process.

Raphael swam in a line straight for her, his powerful biceps rising above the waves, making Mary weak in the knees. Every day she loved him more, *needed* him more. Never once, even when they fought, did she doubt what he was to her: her mate, which she was convinced was short for *soulmate.*

She touched the amethyst on her left ring finger, feeling so full of happiness she could burst.

A minute later, he rose from the water, pushing his long dark hair from his face. As always, he reached his hand out for her. She wove her fingers through his while he slipped the thumb of his other hand under the bikini string at her hip. "You're so beautiful," he murmured before he kissed her.

She knew the truth: *he* was the beautiful one, inside and out.

A few long minutes later—hands still linked—they waded to the shore.

"It's about time!" Wish called. "The sun's about to go down. Want to head across the street with us?"

Across the road from the beach was a small independent bookstore and coffee shop Wish adored. If he had his way, he'd have been there all day, poring over books about Cajun French and the Native American tribes that used to inhabit the area.

"We'll head over after we watch the sunset," Mary answered, receiving a sweet smile from Raphael.

They took the towel Leila abandoned, Raphael pulling Mary's back to his front. As the sun dipped lower and lower, coloring the horizon shades of pink and orange so brilliant she could only dream to capture them in paint, Mary realized why this sunset meant so much to her.

When the sun rises, Raphael will still be right here with me.

The End

About the Author

Samantha Stone is a twenty-something graduate student studying speech-language pathology in Alabama. She's proficient in French and Signing Exact English, and considers New Orleans the home of her heart. Most days you can find her doing speech-related research, chasing her creatures around New Orleans (in her head), or curled up with a good book. She drinks hot chocolate year-round.

CPSIA information can be obtained at www.ICGtesting.com
Printed in the USA
LVOW07s2006130916

504435LV00010B/1041/P